WITH ONE LONG STRIDE
HE INTERCEPTED HER
BEFORE SHE FINISHED . . .

. . . and pulled her into an embrace. The first kiss was careful and sweet. The next one less so.

Excitement spun through her and she was glad when their embrace tightened and their passion brought more kisses, dozens of them, shared and separate, while they released some of the madness descending. Somehow, while still holding her and kissing her, he shed his shirt. The sensation of his warmth, of his skin under her hands and lips fascinated her so much she had to press kisses on his chest, just to experience it again. While she did he kissed her neck and brought one hand to caress her breast.

One note of reality plucked in her. One instant of hesitation followed. He must have sensed it. He moved his hand away. Furious with herself, she moved his hand back where it had been and kissed him hard.

His slow smile formed against her lips.

Also by Madeline Hunter

The Most Dangerous Duke in London

A Devil of a Duke

Never Deny a Duke

Heiress for Hire

MADELINE HUNTER

ZEBRA BOOKS
KENSINGTON PUBLISHING CORP.
www.kensingtonbooks.com

ZEBRA BOOKS are published by

Kensington Publishing Corp.
119 West 40th Street
New York, NY 10018

All Kensington titles, imprints, and distributed lines are available at special quantity discounts for bulk purchases for sales promotion, premiums, fund-raising, educational, or institutional use.

Special book excerpts or customized printings can also be created to fit specific needs. For details, write or phone the office of the Kensington Sales Manager: Attn.: Sales Department. Kensington Publishing Corp., 119 West 40th Street, New York, NY 10018. Phone: 1-800-221-2647.

Zebra and the Z logo Reg. U.S. Pat. & TM Off.

First Printing: May 2020
ISBN-13: 978-1-4201-4997-5
ISBN-10: 1-4201-4997-0

ISBN-13: 978-1-4201-4998-2 (eBook)
ISBN-10: 1-4201-4998-9 (eBook)

10 9 8 7 6 5 4 3 2 1

Printed in the United States of America

This book is dedicated to my sons
Thomas and Joseph

Chapter One

Did you kill him?

The voice spoke in his head vaguely, as if traveling through distance and fog. Not as the voice of his conscience, the way he so often heard the question. A different voice now. A female one.

I doubt it. Help me here.

He looks dead to me.

I promise that he isn't dead. Now, take this and hold it while I . . .

A bit clearer now. Closer. So close it made his head bang with pain. Each word created a hammer blow. The more words, the more blows, and the closer they sounded.

I should call Jeremy to come here.

We do not need Jeremy. See?

Bam. Bam.

Bad enough already, without that.

We are not the ones at fault here. Hold the lamp closer, so I can make sure it is safe. Wait, give the lamp to me . . . This is no ordinary thief, from the looks of him.

What are you doing with that?

Bam, bam, bam.

Bringing him around so I can find out who he is and why he is here.

Bam—

The fog disappeared, washed away by an onslaught of liquid that forced him back to full consciousness. He tipped his tongue out to lick some drips on his lips. Not water. Wine.

He did not open his eyes right away. He spent a few moments accommodating the pain screaming on his scalp. His legs felt strange and his arms hurt. He tried to move both and could not. He realized they were both tied behind him, and together, bowing his body. Someone had trussed him like a sheep, only backward.

He opened his eyes to see the end of a pistol mere inches from his head. His gaze traveled up the arm that held it, until he looked into the furious dark eyes of a very handsome dark-haired woman. She held the pistol like she knew how to use it. Her bright gaze said she hoped he gave her a good reason to.

Hell. Tonight was not progressing at all the way he had planned.

"He looks to be coming to," Beth said. She raised the bed warmer as if to give another blow.

"Put it down. He is tied and I have my pistol."

"He looks big. The ropes may not hold him. He may overpower you. I should be ready just in case."

"He will not attack me." He had indeed come to. His long lashes moved. After a moment he strained against the bonds. Minerva waited for him to accommodate his situation.

His garments appeared very high quality. Blood now

stained a cravat once pristine and crisp. His face might be called handsome if not for the strong bones that made the angles more severe than now fashionable. Something about him made her inner sense send out warnings that prickled her spine. He appeared to be a wealthy gentleman and . . . official. Whatever his reason for entering this house, it had not been to steal a few shillings.

Various reactions assaulted her while she trained her pistol on his harshly handsome face. Fear. Vulnerability. She experienced a surge of the unsettled spirit that had plagued her for over a year once, and that she thought she had banished forever.

Finally those lashes rose. Sapphire eyes focused on her pistol, then his gaze moved up until he looked right into her eyes. He again strained at the ties that bound him.

"Minerva Hepplewhite, I presume? My name is Chase Radnor. I apologize for the lack of a proper introduction."

Beth sucked in her breath. "Odd for a thief to be so particular about etiquette and such."

Except he was not a thief, was he?

"You can untie me," Radnor said. "I never take chances with pistols, and I am not a danger in any case."

"You are an intruder. I intend to leave you like that while I swear down information against you," Minerva said.

"If you do it will come to naught and will only delay my mission. Now, untie me. I have something important to tell you that will explain why I am here."

She hated how that provoked her curiosity, and also her trepidation. He might tell her that the investigation into Algernon's death had been revived. Then again, he might reveal that at long last the poacher involved in that accident had been found. Or he might tell her that he had come to take her to gaol.

She collected herself. It was foolish to build monsters out of this stranger's presence. There had been nothing to indicate he knew about her former identity and life.

"Explain yourself first." She leveled the pistol firmly. "I am not inclined to trust a housebreaker."

He gave one furious tug on the ties behind his back. He narrowed his eyes. "I have come to inform you of something that benefits you significantly."

"What is that?"

"You have inherited some money. A large amount of it."

Chase did not like when carefully laid plans failed. Now he grimaced while the servant called Beth dabbed at his scalp to clean the wound of blood.

A good deal of blood. He knew from his time in the army that scalp wounds were notorious for bleeding, no matter how minor.

Not that his felt all that minor. The hammer still banged.

He was sitting on a stool while the stout woman did her nursing. Fifteen feet away Minerva Hepplewhite waited patiently, watching. *Lounging*, damn it. The pistol now lay on a table next to where she relaxed on a divan.

She appeared composed. At ease. Minerva Hepplewhite had a level of self-possession that unaccountably irritated him.

"Explain yourself," she said. "If you had information to give me, why didn't you show up on my doorstep and present your card?"

That was hard to explain without putting her on her

guard. "I wanted proof you were Minerva Hepplewhite. I did not want to risk speaking to the wrong woman."

She frowned over that.

The hands on his scalp lifted, then returned and pressed against his head. He almost cursed the woman, even though he knew she only applied a poultice.

The woman Beth stepped back, taking the scent of cheap rose water with her. "Done. Shouldn't bleed much now. You will want your valet to wash your hair carefully for a spell. If he soaks your shirt in salt water, it should help get the blood out." She gestured to his coats. "Not much help for those stains, though."

The two women exchanged looks. Beth left the library and closed the door behind her.

"How did you find me?" Minerva Hepplewhite asked.

"It is my profession to find people."

"Ah, you are a runner. Is this not an odd assignment? I thought it was your profession to find paramours of married individuals, then tell their spouses about their misdeeds."

He did that too. It was the least interesting work, and an assignment he did not seek. Yet it came to him too often, since so many spouses committed so many misdeeds.

"I am not a runner. I am a gentleman who on occasion conducts discreet inquiries."

"If the fine distinction gives you comfort that you are not a servant, hold to it."

He stood. His scalp gave a few good hammer blows in response, but they were not quite as bad as they had been.

"Tell me about this inheritance," she said.

She wore an undressing gown. It sported a good deal of frothy lace around her neck and at its hem, but it had seen better days. Shapeless but soft, it revealed her form while she sat there with it billowing over the divan's faded rose toile cushion.

"A fortune was left to a woman named Minerva Hepplewhite, currently resident of London, by the late Duke of Hollinburgh."

He took satisfaction in how her eyes widened. Then she laughed. "How absurd. This must be a joke. Why would the Duke of Hollinburgh leave me a fortune?"

He shrugged. "Believe me, that is my burning question as well. You must be . . . a good friend? A retainer? . . . A lover?"

Her frown dissolved and a broad smile took its place.

"A lover?" She swept her hand—an exceedingly lovely hand, he noticed—gesturing at the chamber. "Do I look like I have enjoyed the favor of a duke? Did you see a footman in the entryway? A fine carriage in the yard?"

Like that undressing gown, only serviceable furniture populated the library, and none of it was new. This certainly supported what she was saying, for this modest house on Rupert Street would hardly satisfy a duke's mistress . . . at least, so it seemed.

Still smiling, she caught his gaze with her own. She had a talent for captivating one's attention with that compelling focus. She appeared to invite him to look into her soul, to learn whether she spoke the truth or not. To discover—everything. He was not immune to the lure. She was a damned attractive woman. Distinctive. Unusual. Her disconcerting self-confidence made her interesting.

"Mr. Radnor, not only was I not this duke's lover or mistress, but I never even met him."

And with those words, Chase's current assignment suddenly became much more difficult.

* * *

A fortune. A duke. Minerva tried to absorb the astonishing revelation.

"There must be some error," she murmured.

Radnor shook his head. "'Minerva Hepplewhite' is not a common name. I found you by putting a notice in *The Times*. One of your neighbors came forward and pointed me to you."

She stood and paced while she accommodated the shock. She all but forgot Radnor stood by the fireplace until she turned to retrace her steps and saw him there. Tall. Dark. Formidable. A strict posture. Perhaps he had been in the military. His somewhat craggy features would look good in uniform and giving commands on the field. His blue eyes alternated between deep pools and icy barriers.

He exuded power and authority. He was the kind of man that tempted a woman to depend on him for protection and care. And, perhaps, much more. Oh, yes, Mr. Radnor's presence contained that kind of power too. She experienced an urge to believe anything he said merely to obtain his good favor.

"How much is this inheritance?"

"There is a direct legacy of ten thousand."

She gasped, her eyes wide, then turned away as she absorbed her shock.

"There is also a partnership in an enterprise in which the duke had invested," he said to her back. "That holds the promise of much, much more."

For the very first time in her life she worried she would swoon. To learn such a thing, and in such a bizarre manner—

That sobered her. Her mind cleared and her thoughts lined up the events of this night. She turned and eyed him. "Who are you? Why were you the one sent to find me?"

He crooked his elbow on the edge of the mantel and relaxed into a pose of aristocratic nonchalance. "The duke was my uncle. His heir, my cousin, asked me to help the solicitor find the unfamiliar legatees so the estate can be disbursed in a timely way."

His cousin was the new duke. That made him the grandson of a previous one. She tried to picture him at a society ball, but instead kept seeing him in a Roman centurion's uniform. From the evidence revealed by his snug trousers, he had the legs to look good in one.

"How did the duke die?"

He did not respond right away, which only heightened her interest.

"His country manor house has a parapet at the roofline behind which one can walk. He often went there at night to take some air. Unfortunately, one night he . . . fell."

The slight hesitation and the subtle shift in tone sent a shiver up her spine. She conquered the alarm and held her composure. "An accident, then."

"Most likely."

"You are not sure?"

"It will probably be investigated. Dukes have their privileges, even in death."

She advanced on him until she stood only five feet away. She gazed right into his eyes. "I think you believe it was no accident. You believe he was pushed." She stepped closer yet. "Perhaps you believe that I was the one who pushed him."

The ice with which he met her gaze melted and for an instant she saw enough in his eyes to know she was correct.

"Not at all," he lied. "Now, to claim this inheritance, you will need to present yourself to the solicitor who is serving as executor of the estate." He reached into his frockcoat and removed a card. "Here is his name and the location of his chambers."

He made it sound so simple. Only it wasn't. This legacy would complicate everything, and reopen a perilous door.

She took the card.

"I will show myself out."

As he walked toward the door, she stared down at the solicitor's card.

"Oh, there is one other thing," he said, turning back. "The solicitor may ask you about your history, to ensure you are the right woman. The will referred to you as Minerva Hepplewhite, previously known as Margaret Finley of Dorset, widow of Algernon Finley."

Then he was gone, leaving her utterly stunned.

She would have sworn that no one in London knew about her history, except Beth and Beth's son Jeremy. *No one*.

Yet apparently this duke—the Duke of Hollinburgh—knew exactly who she was.

Now that she thought about it, she was sure Mr. Radnor had not entered her home to make sure he had her identity correct, as he had claimed. There were better ways to do that. He had done so because he had suspicions about her.

Perhaps because he already knew about the murder accusation she had run from back in Dorset.

The next morning, Chase left his apartment and walked across St. James's Square. He approached a warren of buildings on the western edge of Whitehall.

Robert Peel had written, asking him to meet at nine o'clock. No one else was about yet. Chase wondered if that had been the plan, or if as an industrialist's son the home secretary always started the day at this hour.

Had the request come from the last home secretary, Chase would have declined. He did not like Sidmouth, or approve of how he had used the power of the office. There had been too many poorly supervised agents making too much trouble throughout the land for his taste. Peel, however, had proven adept at finding other ways to hold down unrest, and had already shepherded a reform of the criminal laws through Parliament.

A good man, from the evidence so far. His father had accumulated tremendous wealth in his textile factories and other ventures, and the son had been raised and educated to have a place in government and society. The next Pitt the Younger, it was said. Home secretary already, and a protégé of Wellington's, eventually he would probably be a prime minister, and inherit not only that wealth but also the title of baronet his father had received.

As he turned into the Treasury passage and walked beneath its stone vaults, he spied a figure at the end. Of middling height and size, the man had fashionably cropped hair and a face with regular features except for a prominent aquiline nose. Peel was meeting him halfway, and wore his greatcoat. It seemed they would not talk in the office. Chase decided the early hour had been to avoid witnesses after all.

After greeting him, Peel eyed the poultice on his head. "I trust the other fellow fared worse."

No, the woman who did this is both unharmed and unrepentant. He had considered Minerva Hepplewhite long into the night, wrestling with the way she both annoyed him and . . . fascinated him. If he was correct about his uncle's death, however, she remained the most likely culprit. Not only her sudden good fortune said as much, but also the very self-possession that impressed him. She was not one to be underestimated.

"It is a small wound—it looks worse than it is."

"Walk with me," Peel said.

They fell into step together and began slowly retracing Chase's path.

"It is my hope that you can solve a conundrum for me," Peel said. "It has to do with your uncle's death."

Peel had been among the many at the funeral. As had Peel's father, with whom the late duke had some business dealings.

"Had things progressed as they usually do, if his heir received everything, everyone would say what a shame he fell, and that would be that," Peel said. "That will of his has got tongues wagging, I'm afraid. So much money, and yet so little to the family."

"That is common knowledge already, is it?"

"Your aunts and a few cousins have not been quiet about their disappointment."

"It was his personal fortune, to bequeath as he chose."

"Of course. Of course. And yet, so many angry relatives. Ambiguous circumstances. Mystery legatees. It begs explanation."

The mystery legatees certainly did. Three names. Three women. No one in the family had ever heard of any of them, and Chase had only tracked down one in the past week. In the fury that greeted the reading of the will, a variety of characterizations of these women had been cast down by family members, none of them flattering.

What were these women to Uncle Frederick? Minerva claimed she was not a mistress; perhaps the others weren't either. They may have never met the duke, just as she said she had not. They could be dead, for all anyone knew. Some relatives rather counted on that.

Would Uncle Frederick be so eccentric, so perverse, as to give a sizeable portion of his personal estate to three women he had nothing to do with? Chase did not reject the notion out of hand, but if that had happened, how had his uncle come up with these particular women?

"If you say it all begs explanation, I am not going to disagree with you."

"It is not I who says so. My inclination is to leave it all be. The king, however, says so. The prime minister agrees. Other ministers and several other dukes have called on me. My own father, heaven preserve us—I have been getting many earfuls all week. 'No way in hell he fell.' That sort of thing."

They continued their slow stroll out onto the street.

"I assume you went up there and took a look at that walkway and parapet. What is your view of things?"

No way in hell he fell. "I have not investigated sufficiently to have a view. I assumed if anyone pursued the matter, it would be your office."

"Ah, yes. Yet to do so would only feed the storm. It would be very public. Everyone would know that suspicions existed. It would be a scandal for your whole family, no matter what was learned. Hence the conundrum."

"Surely you have someone who can be discreet."

"It is sure to get out if we launch an official inquiry. Nor are the best agents at my disposal known for being delicate. The insult to your family will be sharp. The destruction of their privacy unthinkable." Peel stopped walking and faced him. "You have experience in such things, I believe. From your time in the army, and now in society. You are a man to contact if one needs discreet inquiries, I've been told."

"If you are suggesting that I conduct this investigation for you, let me point out that I am hardly disinterested."

"I am counting on your being most interested. He was like a father to you. You were a favored nephew. I'm sure you want to know what happened. In fact, I assume you intended to conduct an inquiry of your own, no matter what we did."

Hell, yes, he planned to find out what happened. That was different from acting as an agent of the Home Office, however. "My position will compromise whatever report I give."

"You mean that if the information points to someone close to you, or to a conclusion that casts aspersions on your uncle's good name, you will be tempted to turn a blind eye, or handle it the way gentlemen often do." Peel vaguely smiled. "Well, yes."

Did you kill him? That knowing smile made the question echo quietly in his head.

"However, your integrity in the matter will never be questioned," Peel continued. "You are known as a man of character even if your methods are at times unconventional."

Peel had been talking to people, that was clear. He probably had received more information than Chase wanted to think about. "No matter what I find, there will be those who will think the worst."

"Let us not worry about all the *those*. My only concern is with very specific people who want this laid to rest. You would not be in our employ, of course. You would not be one of our agents. Your report would be to me alone, and would be private. I in turn can then respond to those specific people, privately."

"What if action less private is required? We are talking about a possible murder." Using the word bluntly sounded stark within all this polite chatting.

Peel gave him a quick, deep scrutiny. "If you conclude justice requires formal and official action, it will have to be taken." They began walking back to the passage.

"Can I start my day knowing this has been settled?"

Peel asked. "I would like to send a few notes indicating an unofficial inquiry is underway."

Chase weighed the offer. Peel had shifted the conundrum onto him. Yet he had fully intended to use his skills to determine just what had happened up on that roof. If he accepted this private mission, at least there would not be some Home Office agent getting in his way. On the other hand, even in an unofficial capacity, his option to turn that blind eye would be seriously compromised. Finding the truth would become a matter of duty, not just one of personal curiosity.

Perhaps that would be for the best.

"You can write your notes to the king and prime minister. I will do the inquiry and see it through to wherever it ends."

Chapter Two

Two mornings after hitting Chase Radnor on the head, Minerva poured coffee into three cups sitting on the worn wooden table in the kitchen. Beth spooned porridge into bowls, then laid down a loaf of bread along with butter and some cheese. Jeremy, ever polite in his table manners, waited for both of them to sit with him beneath the ceiling beams in the warm chamber. Then he ate with the appetite of the young man he was.

Minerva still saw the boy Jeremy had recently been when she looked at him. She at times had to remind herself that he was one and twenty now.

She broke some bread and spooned at her own porridge and watched him devour the cheese. He was probably still growing. She remembered when he was a lanky blond youth of fifteen. Now he was a lanky blond man, filling out but still thin by nature. His hair hung long because he said his mother always made him look like a serf when she cut it.

He finally slowed down enough to talk. "You should have called me, that's all I'm saying."

He picked up a conversation from yesterday, when he had learned about Mr. Radnor's unusual appearance.

"If you hadn't moved into the old carriage house, you'd of already been here," Beth muttered.

"Not that again, Mum."

"I'm just saying that with you out back we could be butchered in our sleep and you wouldn't even know."

"At least he would not be butchered too," Minerva said. "We did just fine on our own, Jeremy. He didn't know what hit him until he came to. Now, I want to talk about the legacy."

Jeremy grinned. "I do too. That's a lot of money. I was dreaming of a fine pair and a carriage most of last night."

"I'm glad you were dreaming. I didn't sleep the last two nights at all. I've been too shocked," Beth said. "Ten thousand is a fortune. And there's more you said. Even a hundred would be riches I'd never dare pray for. You'll be wealthier than some fine ladies."

"We'll *all* be rich," Minerva said. "I am still as stunned as you are. It is too astonishing. All the more so since I never met this duke. I'm sure of it."

"You must of at some time and just don't remember," Jeremy said.

"I'd remember meeting a *duke*."

"Maybe he is one of those peculiar sorts who likes to do odd things like give money to strangers," Jeremy said. "You were just lucky."

"I have no explanation except that. Yet he knew about me, so it wasn't entirely random."

"Knew too much, to my mind," Beth muttered.

Minerva chose to ignore that. "Someday we will learn how this happened, but I intend to take advantage of the miracle it is. While you dreamed of horses, Jeremy, I was thinking of how we could use some of that money. I have some plans I want to tell you both about."

"You intend to visit that solicitor and claim it then?" Beth said. "I'm not saying it isn't tempting. I've done some dreaming too the last day. I could use some new pots, for one thing, and a few new caps. But it seems dangerous to me. What if—" She jabbed her spoon into her porridge. "Five years you've been safe here. Five years no one knew about your marriage, or about—the rest of it. Now, this could be opening up a door we'd closed and bolted." She gave Minerva a sharp glance.

Minerva considered Beth her best friend, so she took that glance seriously. Beth had worked for half wages as a servant in Algernon's home, in order to be allowed to have her young son with her. She had become a mother to the young bride Algernon brought home too. Long before Minerva had found a way to escape that house, these two had become her true family.

"Beth, rejecting the legacy will not change the truth that my past is now tied to my new name. Both names were used in that will."

"Stop trying to spoil the fun, Mum. Minerva is going to be rich." Jeremy held up his arms and shook his hands while he laughed. "*Rich! RICH!*"

"You better tell him the rest, Minerva, before he calls me a crazy old woman for worrying so much."

"The rest? What are you talking about?"

"Jeremy," Minerva said. "Yesterday when I told you about Radnor's visit, I left out a few small details."

"How small?"

"Not small at all," Beth said. "Big. Huge."

"Why not let me decide which it is." Jeremy had now turned serious.

"The circumstances of the duke's death were peculiar enough to encourage inquiries."

"You said he fell off a roof. An accident."

"That is the most likely way it happened."

"You mean maybe it wasn't an accident?" His face tightened. "You should have told me right off. This explains why Radnor snuck in and why he was in your study. He was looking for something."

"I can't be certain, but my inner sense says so. If there was a question about how the duke died, it would be natural to wonder about *me*. I am unknown to the family and I am benefiting from his death. Under those circumstances, it should be expected that Mr. Radnor would be curious. If I were in his place, I would be too."

"How reasonable you make it sound," Beth said. "It's like you're making excuses for the rogue."

Maybe she was. If so, it probably had to do with dreaming about Chase Radnor last night. She blamed her parched femininity for that. Naughty dreams had plagued her for several months now, ones in which her late husband, Algernon, mercifully did not put in an appearance. Rather, men who caught her eye did, even if she only glimpsed them. Passing footmen. Handsome shopkeepers. Gentlemen who walked by on the street. They would invade her head until she woke hot and frustrated.

She had assumed that after her experiences with Algernon she would never again have any interest in such things. Apparently, human nature will have its way eventually, even with such as she. Despite the restlessness of those dreams, she welcomed the indication that a dead part of her might be rejuvenating, even if only while she slept.

Last night, with Mr. Radnor, things had progressed further than normal. She still had not purged the dream's images from her head. In particular she kept seeing his naked legs. Her dream had blessed him with very fine ones indeed.

"Now do you see why I am worried?" Beth said to Jeremy.

Minerva could see Jeremy working it out in his head, and imagined every step his logic took. Her own thinking had followed that same path, after all.

If the duke had been pushed off that roof walk, someone did the pushing. If Radnor or a magistrate started looking for the culprit, those who benefited from the death would be investigated. If deep inquiries were made about Minerva Hepplewhite, someone would learn that when she was Margaret Finley she had been suspected of murdering her husband. Not only would she become an important suspect in the duke's death, but also Algernon's death might get another look.

"I say we leave London," Jeremy said. "It will be hell to give up a fortune, but it will be safer for you this way."

Not only for her, she knew. For her family too. For Beth and Jeremy.

She reached out both arms, and took Jeremy's and Beth's hands in hers, gripping them tightly. "Where would we go? How would we live? We have managed thus far here because I had some jewels to sell, but they are gone now." It had been a blessing that in the early days of their marriage Algernon had given her his mother's jewels, and that his creditors could not claim them after his death.

"I'll find work," Jeremy said.

"I can too," Beth added.

"No," Minerva said. "We are not packing our trunks and disappearing into the night. I promise you, if it ever looks like any of us are in danger, then we will leave England. Hopefully, I will have received some of the funds from this legacy by then, so we will not be doing it with only the clothes on our backs." She squeezed their hands. "I swear that I will not be swayed by any fortune to remain, if I believe any of us are at risk. But I'll not run until I have good reason to, and I intend to do what I can to ensure we never have to take that step."

Beth's brow puckered. "Ensure how?"

Minerva released their hands and stood. "Come with me and I will show you."

They went above and entered the little study on the street level, the one where Minerva had hit Radnor with a warming pan. Jeremy and Beth kept exchanging perplexed looks.

Minerva went behind the writing desk and opened a drawer. She slid out a large sheet of paper. Yesterday, while she laid her plans, she had worked out the wording now on it, and the layout of the cartouche surrounding them.

She raised it up with a ceremonial flourish.

Beth's eyes widened. Jeremy smiled.

"Hepplewhite's Office of Discreet Inquiries," Jeremy read. "It's a good name. Memorable."

"Do you think to actually do this?" Beth asked. "We've talked about it, but not seriously. It was just a dream we played with."

"It was never only a dream to me. I have been planning it for over a year," Minerva said. "We are good at inquiries. Very good. It is my one true talent. We proved that with Algernon. We just did that good turn for Mrs. Drable and even I was impressed by our skill in uncovering the identity of that thief. We delayed starting this service in a formal way because there are costs, but now I will have the money to pay them. This legacy will enable us to do this up proper, with calling cards and correct wardrobes and transportation when we need it."

"Not likely you'll leave that solicitor's chambers with ten thousand in your reticule," Beth said. "Could still be a long while before we can start."

"We will use credit at the shops, based on my expectations. That is commonplace enough."

"It is easy work, the way I see it," Jeremy said with a big smile.

His mother frowned at him. "It isn't a game."

"It is if you've a knack for it."

He did have a knack for it. They all did. They had practiced during a time when having a knack meant the difference between life and death. A person learns fast then.

"I have it all thought out," Minerva said. "I will bring this and have a tasteful sign made to put by our door. A small brass one. Then I'll order cards for all of us. I'm going to call on Mrs. Drable and ask her to recommend us to others who might have need of our services. However, we already have our first client."

"Who might that be?" Beth asked.

"Me."

"The door to the past has been opened, as you said, Beth. There is some risk to me now, I know. I spent the night after Radnor was here in panic, remembering how it felt to live with a noose hanging over one's life." Even now, as she spoke of it, the chill of dread wanted to conquer her once more. "However, I have decided I am not going to hide my whole life. I will meet the risk with action, not running away. Not fear."

They had moved to the library. Beth and Jeremy sat on the divan. She stood near the fireplace.

"Brave words, for whatever they mean," Beth said.

"They mean that the best way to get rid of the risk is to prove I had nothing to do with the duke's death. And the best way to do that is to prove that someone else did it. However, I would make this inquiry even if the legacy held no danger to me. This duke was a great benefactor to me. If someone pushed him off that roof, I want to know who. I also want to know why he chose to give me this money." She paced while she explained her thinking and decision. "Don't you want to know all of that too?"

"Of course," Beth said.

"Then, as of today, Hepplewhite's Office of Discreet Inquiries is a real enterprise, and finding those answers is our first endeavor. As to establishing ourselves—we will need to find others to help us. On occasion as we get started, but hopefully on regular wages soon. We will require a young woman, for example. Younger than me. More a girl. They can be very useful to inquiries."

"A fellow who can look like a gentleman would be helpful too," Jeremy said. "When we were setting things up to catch Mr. Finley the way we did, the lack of such a man caused some delays."

Minerva nodded her agreement. "You will have to wait on the carriage and a pair until I have money in hand, Jeremy. Until then we will use hired coaches. And new garments need to be ordered soon." She eyed Jeremy's long hair. "A visit to a hairdresser for you, as well. Soon. Although not for your first assignment."

"Do you plan to stay in this house, or let a better one?" Beth asked. "Not that I'm complaining, but my chamber is drafty."

"For now we will stay here." Minerva glanced around

the library's shabby furnishings. "The study is presentable at least, and that will do for now. Eventually, however . . ." She pictured a fine townhome on a better street, one with space for a servant or two.

"Before you spend every shilling of that ten thousand, maybe we should decide how we are going to learn about the duke's death," Beth said.

"I have considered that too. Such deaths normally are caused by family members. That is why the authorities looked to me when Algernon was shot."

"Hard to get near the family of a duke. Not as if you can call with one of those new cards and announce you want to conduct an inquiry."

"No, but one can glean much from a short distance." She paced again, while her mind traversed the path she had laid already. "Jeremy, you have your first assignment. Learn where this duke lived, and try to loiter around the stables among the grooms. Learn what you can."

"I'll offer my services for spots of work if they have it. Most stables need extra at times, and the ones near here will give me references if I need them."

And with that, Hepplewhite's Office of Discreet Inquiries launched its first investigation.

Three days after meeting with Peel, Chase dismounted outside Whiteford House while a groom took the horse's reins.

"You are new here," he said, watching how the young man handled the animal.

"I started two days ago, sir." Tall and blond, the fellow flushed from the attention. "I'll brush him down if you like."

"I won't be here long enough." It impressed him that

the offer had been made. His cousin Nicholas had hired well, it seemed. There must be a host of new servants, now that the old retainers had taken their legacies as pensions.

Chase approached the door of Whiteford House. One of the oldest houses on Park Lane, it nestled amidst trees at the northern end of the street. Built as a country villa when this area was still mostly rural, and the nearby western section of Oxford Street was still called Tyburn, it sported extensive gardens. The last duke had bought the property on a whim, mostly to keep a rival from tearing it down and developing the land.

He looked up the old façade, said to have been designed by Inigo Jones. It bore the stamp of classicism that the architect had imported to England, and showed similarities to the Banqueting House in its exterior decoration. The interior had not fared as well. The last duke had a strong eccentric streak, and it manifested itself as soon as Chase walked in the reception hall.

No classical restraint here, at least not in the furnishings. The accumulation of a lifetime cluttered the walls and corners. Exotic skins and weapons mixed with gilded metal. Jewel-toned upholstery contrasted with pastel walls. He wondered what Nicholas planned to do with all of this now that he had inherited the property.

Since Nicholas was now a duke, Chase had to suffer the formalities of having his card taken away, then being escorted up to the duke's apartment. A mere month ago, in Nicholas's last home, there would have been no footman to do the duties, or even many chambers to traverse. The eldest son of the last duke's eldest brother, Nicholas's fortunes had existed only in expectations until recently. As it happened, those expectations had not been realized quite like Nicholas had anticipated.

Chase found his cousin in the dressing room, lounging

on a fine chair set near a window that overlooked the park.
A ledger laid open on his lap and he frowned down at the
page he perused. Whatever he read occupied him enough
that he did not hear Chase enter.

Sons ran in the Radnor family, in the last generation as
well as this one. The result was the last duke had five
brothers, and those brothers in turn had six sons. Of all the
cousins, Chase and Nicholas had formed the strongest
friendship, one devoid of the bickering and arguments that
marked so many of the other relationships.

The only Radnor not to sire a son had been the last
duke. Uncle Frederick had never been one to conform.

"Bad news?" Chase asked.

Nicholas's dark eyes peered up. He smiled ruefully
while he closed the ledger and set it on the floor. "Terrible
news." He looked around the expansive dressing room,
with its mahogany wardrobes and raw silk drapes and
Chinese carpet. "Hell of a thing. By year's end, I'll be sell-
ing furniture to pay the bills. The rents barely bring in
enough to keep up the country houses."

"Perhaps a good land steward can change that."

"Not fast enough." Nicholas gestured to the ledger. "He
didn't enclose, of course. Nor did his father. A good-
hearted decision, but inefficient. Now I have to decide if
I will do it, and the displacement of families—" He
shrugged.

"His interests were not with the lands." Chase spoke
the obvious, but it was the root of the problem.

"The other investments are doing well. Fabulously. The
money pours in. Of course, he did not bequeath any of that
to me, did he?" He laughed. "Or you. Or any of us. He
was always a little strange, but his will was his most eccentric act yet. What a joke on all of us."

No one had laughed at the joke when the will was read.

Rather the opposite. An explosion of emotions greeted the bulk of it. Nicholas received the entailed lands, of course, and even one or two properties that were not entailed. But the duke's real wealth had been in all those investments he made. Land development, canals, shipping, factories—he had a Midas touch and had increased his personal wealth twentyfold before he died.

None of that, not one shilling, had been left to a relative.

Chase had expected nothing, so his disappointment had been muted. But other of the cousins had assumed a fat inheritance was coming. And the wives . . .

"Have you learned anything?" Nicholas asked. "I know it has been just over a week since the funeral, but what little will be left when the bequests are disbursed will be divided among us and I am not the only one who is anxious to know what amount will come to me."

"Some small progress has been made." Chase chose not to tell Nicholas about Peel recruiting him to make an unofficial inquiry into Uncle Frederick's death. Being in such an awkward situation was one thing. If the family knew, his position would be impossible.

"I have found one of them. Minerva Hepplewhite." He offered Nicholas less than half a loaf with the announcement. There were two other mystery legacies, and he had not begun to unravel them. He had hoped to make a quick report of success on all counts. He had predicted that Minerva would know about the other two bequests, and lead him to those people. He no longer believed she could do that.

"Was she his mistress?"

"I don't know. She says not."

"She's probably lying," Nicholas said. "To avoid gossip and such. Is she beautiful?"

Chase did not think Minerva Hepplewhite worried overmuch about gossip. "She is attractive."

"What a worthless word. That tells me nothing."

He pictured her sitting on the divan, that soft undressing gown billowing over her curves, while she captured his attention with her compelling gaze. "Very attractive. Is that better? Handsome more than pretty. Strikingly so. Whether she was his lover or not . . . Does it matter? The legacy is hers in any case. I can now move on to the next one."

Only not right away. That was the devil of it. In agreeing to look into the duke's death, he would be left with little time to track down these other legatees. He would need to go down to Melton Park in Sussex in order to examine closely where that fall had happened, and talk to the servants there. If he concluded the fall was not accidental, he would need to look into the people with whom Uncle had formed those business partnerships, and discover if anything was amiss.

It would take weeks, maybe months, to do a thorough inquiry.

Nicholas rose and walked to the window. He looked down at the park across the street. The recent replacement of the park's wall with an iron fence had improved the prospect. "I thought I would have heard from someone by now about how he died. The high chancellor, or the Home Office. Do you think they are being delicate, or ignorant? I can't be the only one who thinks that fall is suspicious."

"I expect that if there is an inquiry it will be very discreet. You may not ever be told it is taking place."

"I don't care for remaining in the dark. If an inquiry is taking place, I want to be kept informed. If no inquiry is taking place, I want to know why. Once matters are settled with the will, perhaps you will go down to Melton

Park to see what if anything can be learned there. If no one else thinks it a serious matter, I will do it myself. With your help, that is."

Chase said nothing to discourage his cousin's thinking. Nicholas's decision to act would be useful. He would not have to hide his inquiry from at least one member of the family. "I'll do that. I'll see what else I can find, if you want."

Nicholas emerged from his distraction. "How fortunate that my cousin is talented in such things. I would never trust a hired man for matters this delicate." He stretched his arms up, like a big cat expanding his spine. "I will go riding, and pretend my life is still carefree. Will you join me?"

"I have a client who grows impatient, and must finish the day as I began it."

"I hope this client is not going to divert you from my problem."

"You are the client."

They walked down together. "Aunt Agnes is insisting on a family meeting," Nicholas said. "She wants it held here. She said it is because I am head of the family, but I suspect it is so the costs of the meals are on me."

"I hope she doesn't expect dinners with eighteen courses."

"I'd like you here when they all descend. You can back me up when I explain it will probably be months before anyone sees anything. I don't think most of them comprehend how little is likely to be split up, and how small their portions will be."

"It is a simple matter of sums and subtractions. Have the solicitor attend, to explain it."

Nicholas sent word to the stables to prepare his horse

and to bring Chase's, then they walked out together. "You will attend?"

"I will come for the theater if nothing else." He would not have Nicholas face them alone, even though he could picture the exact moment when Nicholas, bombarded with complaints and a rising crescendo of accusations, dragged him into the thick of it.

None of them would believe that the simplest explanation was the only one. The duke had written that will that way because he wanted to.

His uncle had been a very unusual man. Mercurial in his emotions. Radical in his politics, not that he did much in that area. Generous at times, and miserly at others. Very smart, too. On a whim he had learned several foreign languages. Not German or Russian. Chinese and the tongue of indigenous Brazil.

The duke was not mad, but very much an original. He might well have given away fortunes to strangers, in which case finding those other two women would be nigh impossible.

Chase's horse came around the house, guided by that blond groom. He slipped the fellow a shilling before mounting. As he peered over the horse's back, something across the street caught his eye. He stopped, one boot in a stirrup, and watched.

A woman strolled along the fence that enclosed the park. Her bonnet's brim obscured her face and her garments appeared presentable but unremarkable. None of that garnered his attention. The edge of a memory did. He was almost sure that she had been there when he arrived, walking in the same direction.

"Sir?" The groom called for his attention.

"Keep him here. I will return shortly." With the groom

and Nicholas exchanging perplexed looks, Chase strode toward the street.

Minerva made it a point not to look at Whiteford House when she walked past it. While many probably did gawk at its façade, she did not want to draw attention to herself. There were only so many times one could pass a home before one did that, and she was well on her way to the limit.

On her way down the lane she had seen two men outside. One had looked to be Chase Radnor. All the more reason to remain inconspicuous. She wished she could take one good look, however. Perhaps the other man was the new duke. Jeremy, who had managed to be hired as a groom here, said the duke remained in the house most days, but that he often left around three o'clock. It was now quarter past three.

None other than Jeremy himself brought a horse around the house while she passed. From the corner of her eye she could see that attract both men's attention. She took the opportunity to turn her head and give the unknown man a good examination.

He stood as tall as Chase, and they shared other qualities such as dark hair. Her quick glance took in his boots and coats, which were of superior quality. The two of them had much in common.

She continued her walk with more purpose. After three to and fros, her time was up.

Warmth at her side. A presence hovering. The boots that fell into step with her arrived unexpectedly. She reared back and looked up. Chase Radnor was looking down at her.

She had not heard him approach. Normally she knew someone followed her as soon as they came within twenty-five feet.

"Out taking a turn?" he asked. "You are far afield from your home."

She stopped and faced him. That conveniently gave her an excellent view of the house over his shoulder. "I often come to Hyde Park, and today decided to admire the large homes on this lane."

"I would say you decided to do a close study, since you walked by at least twice. Four times, since I only saw you retracing your steps. Some would consider that suspicious activity. It is the sort of thing thieves do before they enter unannounced."

"You would know about sneaking into homes in ways I don't."

"Do you have a particular interest in Whiteford House, Mrs. Hepplewhite?"

She made a point of raising her chin and looking past him so she might appear vexed he delayed her. It also allowed her to watch that other man leave on his horse.

"Not at all, other than it being impressive." She returned her gaze to him. "And it is *Miss* Hepplewhite."

His blue eyes sparkled with humor, transforming his stern face into one much more alluring. Little stomach flutters almost distracted her from the house.

"You have chosen to style yourself as never married? What happens if you decide to wed again, and have to explain the truth?"

Her laughter burst out indelicately. "Oh, my." She caught her breath. "I think it is safe to say that I will never marry. You see, a friend I would trust with my life once confided that marriage was worse than prison." The details

of what such a prison could entail cleared her humor in a
snap, and dried her eyes just in time to see the duke ride
off his property.

She squinted, trying to observe details.

Radnor looked over his shoulder. "Ah. It is not the house
that interests you, but the family."

She tried an innocent expression. "I don't know what
you mean."

"That is my cousin." He stepped aside. "Look to your
heart's content."

Although annoyed, she did look. The horse came onto
the street and headed in their direction. She managed not
to stare, but still take him in. A handsome man, he resem-
bled Chase Radnor but had more regular features. The
strong bone structure made him appear dashing, not harsh.

The duke passed within ten feet of them, then all she
could see was his back. She gave up her examination to
find Radnor watching her intently.

"He appears a sober sort," she said.

"He is concerned about our uncle's death," he said. "He
thinks it may have been a murder." He bowed. "I must take
my leave. The groom who is holding my horse no doubt
has other duties."

"Do *you* think it was?" she asked when he had taken a
few steps away. "Murder, I mean."

He looked back at her. "I am almost certain of it."

Chapter Three

Minerva waited while Mrs. Drable considered the request presented to her.

Mrs. Drable fingered the white fichu at her dress's neckline, her slender fingers straying on occasion to the cameo pendant that dangled below her throat. Although at least fifty years in age, Mrs. Drable appeared younger, due in part to her soft complexion and her vivid red hair. A neighbor for whom Minerva had done a good turn, they had met today for a professional reason.

"There is one young woman," Mrs. Drable finally said. "I think she would do. She currently is without a situation, and I despair of finding her a new one. She is educated enough to write and read, and she has a decent hand. She has, however, no experience in what you describe."

"Where is she now? I will visit her if you arrange it." This young woman's experience or education were secondary to her spirit. Minerva required someone with a bit of adventure in her blood. Hepplewhite's Office of Discreet Inquiries would be no ordinary situation.

"She just started on a short hire. A week at most. The new Duke of Hollinburgh is hosting a family gathering and the housekeeper asked their usual service to supply extra servants just for that. They are woefully short of staff due to servants leaving with their pensions."

That explained why Jeremy had found work there so easily. He had only hoped to be taken on for occasional service, but had been offered daily work once they saw he knew the labor.

Mrs. Drable sighed. "Well, it is not the sort of thing we do, is it? Nor are there many decent servants available for such a brief duty. So the word went out to all of us. Elise was available and I sent her over. That is her name. Elise Turner."

By "us" Mrs. Drable meant those in the business of supplying servants to the better homes in London. Mrs. Drable owned one of the smaller, more discreet such offices. Minerva had come to know her as a neighbor and friend, but had stepped in when Mrs. Drable confided she needed help discerning who had pilfered money from her. The suspicion immediately fell on a housemaid recently hired, but Minerva had proven the culprit was instead Mrs. Drable's own nephew.

It had not been information well received, but Mrs. Drable was grateful to learn the truth. She had come close to accusing the wrong person, and claimed a debt to Minerva for sparing her that.

"She has no reference from her last employer. I need to tell you that. Hollinburgh's housekeeper only accepted her on my personal recommendation and because they are all but desperate."

"Why has she no reference?"

Mrs. Drable's expression turned sour. "Her last employer . . . the husband behaved badly. The poor girl was fending off the man almost every day. I had placed a cook in the household, and she came by to inform me. Tell her to leave, I said. Send her to me. She has lived here ever since while I try to find another situation. However . . ." She turned her hands up in a gesture of futility.

"Does she come here every evening after her duties at the house?"

"They are not demanding that this little itinerant army of help stay there, although they will allow it if necessary. She prefers to return here. If you visit at nine o'clock, she should be back."

Minerva stood. "I will return then. It was very good of you to take her in."

"It is a story too often told. A young woman leaves home and comes up to town and finds a situation in a good house, only to discover one of the men is no gentleman. I cannot tell you how often I have had to extricate some girl from the clutches of a lothario."

Minerva opened her reticule. "I am sure you have much to do, and I have another appointment. I will leave now. Before I do I want to give you some of my cards." She plucked out five of her newly printed calling cards. "I am going to offer my services to others as I did to you, only in a formal and professional way. If you learn of someone in need of me, I hope you will give them one of these."

Mrs. Drable eyed the card. "Normally men do this. A woman, however, will have appeal to other women. Some inquiries are rather delicate. I will give these out if I hear of anyone looking for your aid. You may use my name as a reference if you like."

"I appreciate that more than you can know."

She began to leave, but a sudden thought made her pause. She considered it quickly. It would be an outrageous thing for a woman of good birth to do, but also it would be an opportunity that the owner of Hepplewhite's Office of Discreet Inquiries would be foolish to lose.

No one notices servants. Her best chance of learning about this family was to enter the duke's household as one.

"I have one other request," she added on impulse. "I would like you to recommend another brief hire to Hollinburgh's housekeeper."

"Who might that be?"

"Me. I assure you that I am capable of housemaid duties."

Mrs. Drable frowned at her, then peered at the card. "I expect until this new enterprise gets on its legs you can use the coin, though it is a big step down for you. However, dabbling in service is not the same as becoming a servant forever, is it?"

"That is my thinking. If you will do this, I will be grateful. And I will return to meet Miss Turner this evening."

Minerva made her way back to the street, with her excitement building. It had been a good meeting, in more ways than she had anticipated. Not only might she have new clients with Mrs. Drable's help, but she also might have a new employee. Both notions gave her optimism about her plan. What really interested her, however, was the information that Hollinburgh was hosting a family gathering.

Jeremy now observed the house, but she had just found a way inside it for herself. That meant not watching from a distance, but from a few feet away.

That afternoon, Minerva presented herself at the chambers of Mr. Sanders, solicitor. She had changed into one of her best dresses, and worn her favorite bonnet, a blue one with crimson lining. Even so, her confidence wobbled as she entered the office the solicitor used with clients.

He seemed a kind man, mild mannered and given to

measured speech. Not too young, which reassured her he might know what he was about. Not too officious, which hopefully meant he would not be looking to cause her trouble.

After greeting her he proceeded to question her about her relationship with the duke. The lack of one did not dismay him at all.

"It is possible, of course, that an error has been made. If so, I am abjectly sorry." He flipped through the pages of the will. "Did you once live in Dorset, and were married to one Algernon Finley?"

"I was."

"Is there anyone who can support this?"

She told him about Beth and Jeremy. "They lived in my husband's house, so they knew me then."

"Do you have family in Dorset still?"

"My parents have been dead for many years. My relatives for the most part emigrated close to eight years ago. Nor did they live in Dorset, but in the county over."

"Any others who have known you under both names?"

"I don't think so. Although I visited London with my husband, I did not make friends or participate in society."

"I suppose a few more notices in the papers here will confirm there are no other Minerva Hepplewhites in London who once lived in Dorset under the name Finley. I think we can go forth on the presumption that you are indeed the woman in question." He jotted some notes. "I am curious. Is there a reason you changed your name?"

She had prepared for this. "My husband died with debts. More than his estate could pay. I chose to leave the area and change my name so creditors would not continue to hound me."

"Understandable."

He wrote again, then set his pen in its inkwell. "I can

imagine you were surprised to receive a legacy from a man you say you never met. Actually, it is more common than you think. In all likelihood it was your husband who had known the duke. His Grace, in making his will, felt some desire or obligation to leave the money to him. Since Algernon Finley was dead, it was left to his widow instead."

It sounded almost plausible. Only she found it hard to believe Algernon had met a duke and not told her about it, repeatedly. He was the kind of man who would hang a sign on his home announcing his connection to such a title.

"How did the duke know I now live in London?"

Mr. Sanders shrugged. "No doubt he conducted an inquiry. Not himself, of course. Now, I need to describe the details of this inheritance."

To her amazement, that was that. Mr. Sanders seemed not the least interested in her past, her present, or how the two had connected.

Sanders explained the inheritance. The part that captured her attention was when he spoke about possible challenges. "The will has been accepted by the courts as legal and binding. However, someone may still challenge the provisions the duke made to each beneficiary. If a person is named in the will, but does not think he received his due, he may be tempted to do that. If he can claim that he had good cause to think he would receive more due to being a dependent of the duke's largesse, he may make his case."

"Is that likely?"

"It is possible. I am confident none will be successful, however. No promises were made to the family members. None qualify as true dependents." He leaned forward. "I wrote the will, you see. I did so in a way to make such a claim most unlikely."

"Must I wait to see if anyone wants to challenge it?"

He shook his head. "As his executor, my role is to do as the duke requested and laid out in his will. Now, you received ten thousand, plus a partnership. The ten thousand was put into a trust almost a year prior to his death and cannot be taken. The partnership, however—it would be wise to let that lie for a while, and set aside any dividends or income it may pay. Six months at most." He smiled. "That is not long to wait before you indulge yourself. The trust has already paid once, so a few hundred or so already is at your disposal, or will be in a few weeks once arrangements are made with the bank."

"I think I can make do with that for now."

He chuckled. "Can you indeed? I expect most could."

He sent clerks to the scribners to pen documents for her to sign. After the preliminaries, Sanders advised Minerva on her new situation.

"I will contact you once the trust has been secured to your access. As for the partnership, the other partners will press to meet with you. Put them off for now. They may offer to purchase your share and you can use the time to decide if you prefer that. A partnership goes both ways when it comes to money. If it is profitable, it pays out. If the business requires funds, you pay in."

"I may well agree to sell. Do you know what a fair price would be?"

He pulled forward a portfolio, opened it, and flipped through some pages. "I am having valuations done of all his businesses, but at the last valuation of that one, your share was just over thirty thousand. It showed an income per annum of approximately fifteen hundred. It was one of the duke's smaller investments, but it was a good one."

She stopped breathing. Radnor had said the business

was worth far more than the direct legacy, but such a sum never entered her mind. Even the income astonished her.

Sanders set aside the portfolio. "Miss Hepplewhite, I would be remiss if I did not mention that with your new good fortune, there will be those who seek your company for less than admirable reasons. There will be friendships offered only because you can benefit the new friend. As an unmarried woman you will be the prey of fortune hunters too."

"You are saying that men will pursue me because of my money."

"I am afraid so. Should you ever consider marriage, I urge you to consult a solicitor who can explain the implications for you and your fortune, and perhaps advise you on the character of your intended."

"Thank you for your advice. I am quite sure that I will not be welcoming such attentions. However, if I ever do, I promise that an inquiry on the man will be done."

She left the chambers in a daze. As long as no one succeeded in challenging this will's provisions, she was now a wealthy woman. Even if she only received the income from the trust, she would never again have to worry about money. Rich, as Jeremy had said. Rich! RICH! She wanted to shout it to passersby.

The only thing dampening her giddiness was her awareness that Beth was right. A door long closed and bolted was now open again.

Chase returned to his apartment on Bury Street in the afternoon. He had spent several hours fencing with an old army friend who was now a member of the Horse Guards. The exercise had cleared his head, which he had counted on. He needed to do some clear thinking before he went out again this evening.

His manservant, Brigsby, had hot water waiting, and held large towels after Chase washed. Then he dressed for the second time this day. Finally cleansed and refreshed, he sat at a large writing table set in his bedchamber. Brigsby had already supplied it with a thick stack of good paper and a fresh ink and pen.

Chase opened a new portfolio and wrote *Hollinburgh's Death* on it. He always kept detailed notes on his inquiries. He had learned to do this in the army where such notes helped in writing the final report on any case being investigated. He also relied on written words to keep his thinking organized.

He took a sheet of paper and headed it *Facts*. He took another and wrote the heading *Paths to Pursue*. On a third he wrote *Inconsistencies*. On the next *Theories*. Finally, he pulled a clean page forward and penned *Suspects*. Not all inquiries required these pages. Some needed other, different ones. Part of starting an inquiry was considering the best way to organize the campaign, however.

Eventually most of the pages would be filled with lists of things to do and evidence amassed. With one review he could see if he had forgotten something. There had been inquiries where reading through his notes and pages had presented answers he had not yet seen.

He opened a letter and placed it in the portfolio. It had come from Sanders and included the list of the last duke's businesses and their partners. He found another list in a drawer of the bequests in the will and added that.

He spent a few minutes, jotting thoughts on the page regarding *Paths to Pursue*, and making a short list there of the most immediate actions needed. Finally, he flipped to the *Suspects* page.

He could fill this already if he listed every person with any motive at all. Instead, as was his habit, he would reserve it for those whom he believed might truly be strong possibilities.

He dipped his pen. He hesitated. Then he wrote. *Minerva Hepplewhite.*

Chapter Four

Chase looked out the library window and watched the carriages line up. Everyone stepping down wore their finest clothes. Even the children had been turned out suitably for a visit to a duke's home. Servants lowered trunks from the back and tops of the coaches, all full of yet more garments with which to bedazzle one another.

"Tell me this won't be hell." Nicholas stepped in beside him and gazed out. "Good heavens, that is Dolores. I haven't seen her in a year."

Dolores, a middle-aged, raven-haired woman of impressive height, was directing the servants working at her coach. Her voice could not be heard, but her mouth kept moving and her finger kept pointing and the servants kept grimacing.

"She would never let Agnes have all the fun," Chase said. The two women were sisters, the only female siblings among the men who populated their generation. Chase assumed that both had learned to be forceful in order to be seen or heard among six brothers.

"There is Kevin," Nicholas said. "I thought he was abroad."

"Not any longer, it appears."

Kevin strode up the drive, looking too much like a brooding poet with his refined features, deep-set eyes, and shock of dark hair. He acknowledged none of the cousins or aunts while he passed their carriages, nor did they call out to him. Chase assumed he had left his own carriage back in line and chose to walk rather than wait.

"There will be hell to pay with him," Nicholas muttered.

Kevin had not been in the country when Uncle Frederick died. He had not been present when the will was read. His resentment would be fresh. Worse, he had more cause than most to complain.

"The will was surprising in many ways," Nicholas said. "Where Kevin was concerned, however, it bordered on cruel."

Chase could not disagree. Much as he loved his uncle, there had indeed been a few consequences of that testament that appeared vindictive without cause.

"I suppose I should go greet them."

"Go to your apartment instead. Let them settle in. See them in the drawing room before dinner. Arrive last, and greet them as the duke, not as Cousin Nicky."

Nicholas laughed. "Sage advice."

"Do nothing to lose the upper hand or you will never get it back. We will have pandemonium then."

"I will inform them this evening that there will be no discussion about the estate until tomorrow afternoon. I have told the solicitor to be here at three o'clock."

Nicholas turned to make good his escape, but just then Kevin entered the library. To Chase's surprise, he beamed a smile and strode forward, the frown now gone.

Younger than Chase by four years, Kevin had always been a favored younger cousin mostly due to his vivid personality and unusual interests. Of their generation, he possessed the most likelihood of eventually displaying the eccentricity that marked his own father and Uncle Frederick, mostly because he had always trod his own path.

"It is good that you are back," Nicholas said. "You can help Chase keep them from killing me."

Kevin glanced out the window. "Having just come from the solicitor's chambers, I expect they want to kill someone and Uncle is no longer available."

Nicholas paused over that, but let it pass. "I did write and warn you."

"I didn't receive your letter before I left. I arrived two days ago, and my father informed me of the worst of it straight off. I would have seen Sanders yesterday, but my father wanted help repairing one of his automatons." He rolled his eyes at the mention of his father's ongoing obsession.

"An interesting one?"

"They are all interesting if you find worthless mechanical devices of no use to humanity interesting."

"Is he coming today?" Nicholas asked. "Did you leave him back on the lane?"

"He told me that none of his brothers were coming up to town, and he would not be oppressed just because he is always in London. They expected nothing from Uncle Frederick, so they have no complaints."

Chase gave Kevin a deeper consideration. For all the good cheer he displayed, shadows veiled his normally bright eyes on this allusion to the will. "Why don't you settle in. We'll talk later."

"I suppose I should see what chamber the housekeeper has allotted me. I could return to my father's house at night, of course, but he can be a trial and I want to keep an eye on all of them." He sent a sharp glance out the window.

Nicholas clamped a firm grip on Kevin's shoulder. "Let us go find Mrs. Wiggins, so I can make sure she does not put you in the attic. It is hell being a bachelor."

Chase let them go, and returned his attention to the activity outside the window.

Minerva knelt before the fireplace. She began arranging some fuel.

"Don't fold the dress that way, girl. It will become intolerably wrinkled. Hang it in the wardrobe." The woman's voice snapped out the complaint and command. Minerva kept her back to the room, doing her work.

The housekeeper, Mrs. Wiggins, had been desperate enough to hire her on Mrs. Drable's recommendation for the lowly position of chambermaid during the visit of all these guests. She had been sent up to prepare the fires in the guests' chambers, starting with the ladies. She had already concluded that Lady Agnes Radnor, tall, regal, buxom, and dark-haired, saw herself as the queen among the bees buzzing round the house.

A door opened. Soft steps paced until a person stood so closely behind Minerva that she felt the warmth on her back. The looming presence also hid her own body, however. She slowed her actions.

"I hope they gave you a better maid than I have," a new feminine voice said. Lower than Agnes's. Throaty in a pleasant way.

"Oh, dear heavens. Yours is a disaster too? I had hoped to steal her for myself."

"The best ones are gone, Mrs. Wiggins explained to me. Abandoned ship once they had their pensions. Handsome settlements they were too, if you remember. They left us to fend for ourselves with short-time riffraff while they enjoy *our* money. Only Mrs. Fowler, the cook, and the butler are still here among the senior servants, out of a sense of duty to the title's requirements."

"I assume that once they find their own replacements, they too will go off to grow legumes in the country."

"Once more, with *our* money." The voice turned brittle. "He did this to spite me. You know he did. After what happened he owed me better—"

"Enough of that, Sister. You are speaking like a madwoman. That was long in the past and Hollinburgh probably didn't even remember it."

Silence stretched, thick and full of an unspoken argument. Minerva wished they would continue voicing it.

"I think we are wasting our time. We should challenge the will's bequests."

"Dolores, you know what will happen then. It will be in the courts for years while we become all the poorer paying the lawyers, and in the end nothing will change. Allow me to lead the way in this. We will all meet before that solicitor comes tomorrow, in order to devise a plan that will avoid the courts."

The body behind her walked away.

"Girl, haven't you finished with that yet?" Lady Agnes's voice boomed across the chamber. "The damp in here will get to my bones before you are done."

Minerva turned her head sideways, to acknowledge the complaint. "Forgive me, my lady. Some of the fuel was damp and would not light. I had to rebuild."

"Be quick about it. We are going to live like barbarians here, Dolores. Even the chambermaids are incompetent."

Minerva finished quickly, stood, and, face down in deference, made a fast curtsy. Then she left to find the next fireplace. While she did she caught the eye of the young woman serving as lady's maid, and they shared a secret smile.

Chase made his way to a bedchamber in the northwest corner of the house. The door stood open and once Chase entered he saw why. A chambermaid knelt to build the fire while Kevin paced the small space, frowning.

Chase greeted him. Then he surveyed the chamber. Although comfortable enough, it lacked good light and was not much larger than those used by the servants. "Nicholas was right. It isn't in the attic, at least, but as bachelors we always end up with the smallest and darkest one."

Kevin looked around, as if he hadn't noticed. "It will do. I've lived in worse." The frown, then, had been about other things. Chase could imagine what they were.

"You could stay at your club. Or, if you prefer, stay with me."

"I'll be damned before I let the harpies out of my sight. Given half a chance Agnes would leave me penniless. Do you know how she greeted me? 'Oh, you are here, Kevin. I thought your trade would keep you too busy to join us.'" He imitated Agnes's shrill, imperial tone very well.

"She is old-fashioned in her thinking. Nothing new there. She is also ignorant of your achievements."

"They all are, except you and Nicholas."

"And Uncle Frederick, of course."

That stopped Kevin in his tracks. He faced Chase with a furious expression and let fly the emotion he had hidden when he entered the library an hour ago. "Have you any idea why he did it? It was such a betrayal that I can't—" He shook his head in a renewal of disbelief. "To have put forth the capital while I perfected the invention, to have become a partner in the enterprise, then this. I will confess that I am like a man who was hit too hard during a prize fight."

Chase wished he could explain their uncle's decision to leave his share of Kevin's company to a stranger. Not Miss Hepplewhite, either. One of those other women still to be found. "It could be that she will have something to offer, of which we are unaware. Another company that will enhance your progress."

"Or she might just be some whore he took up with and liked better than the others. Don't look at me like that. I think I am entitled to state the likely truth under the circumstances. When you go looking for them, try the brothels first. I will give you a list of his favorites."

No doubt Kevin could do that, since Kevin probably had been to all of them. Chase had long ago accepted that this younger cousin, whose intense curiosity led to *very* thorough investigations when his interest was piqued, had a vast experience in sexual matters.

"What makes you think I will go looking for them?"

"Who else can Nicholas trust? Or any of us, for that matter. If he has not yet put you to the task, then I will in his place. As bad as that will is, hanging in limbo is worse."

Chase did not acknowledge he had been put to the task almost immediately.

Kevin set his valise on the bed. "I may as well unpack myself. There is supposed to be some man serving as my valet, but who knows when he will show."

The mention of servants had Chase glancing to the one now lighting the fire. He could only see the back of her white cap and the dull brown of her dress. The hand that held the flint, however, struck him as quite lovely. Almost elegant.

"They are all green. Most are not from Uncle's time."

His tone had Kevin looking over. Chase gestured toward the fireplace and the woman there. Kevin nodded.

As if she knew attention had turned to her, the woman stood, lifted her basket, and, head lowered, hurried out.

"How long was she here?" Chase asked.

Kevin shrugged. "I did not see her arrive."

"I would be careful what is said in front of any of them. They are not household staff, and not beholden to the family. We can't expect the normal discretion from them."

Kevin strode over and shut the door. He turned to Chase. "Have you any idea what he was thinking? He favored you. Of all of us, you may have known him best."

"I can't tell you what you want to know. I have some ideas about it, but nothing more." His ideas would hardly placate the family, since they mostly had to do with a man tired of grasping relatives too dependent on his generosity.

"I thought you at least would have been left something."

"I, however, did not think that. He told me as much. I may be the only one who is not disappointed as a result."

"At least you and I have our *trades* to put food on the table. I can't imagine what will become of some of them."

"I expect they will live within their substantial means for a change."

Kevin laughed quietly at that. "Agnes and Dolores will buy only two wardrobes a year, instead of four, you mean. What a tragedy that will be."

Chase headed for the door. "Do not despair until you have reason to. He was not a stupid man. Perhaps he had a plan of which we are yet unaware."

* * *

Minerva finished with the bedchambers in late afternoon. By the time she carried her basket down the back stairs some of the family had begun their own descent on the front ones, all bedecked for the dinner they would soon enjoy.

She entered the little storage chamber in the cellar that held fuel and rushes. While she refilled her basket for the morning, the door of the chamber closed.

Startled, she looked up. Standing there, his back to the door and his arms crossed over his chest, was Chase Radnor. He did not look pleased.

"We meet again, Miss Hepplewhite."

She returned her attention to her basket. "What gave me away?"

"Your hands. They are quite distinctive."

She looked down at her hands, now dirty from handling fuel. She saw nothing remarkable about them.

"What in hell are you doing here?" he asked.

"I can use the money and they are hiring any able-bodied person available."

"Careless of the housekeeper."

"Perhaps she should have instead said you must all do for yourselves." She smiled as she pictured Lady Agnes's reaction to *that*.

He paced the few feet between them. He removed the basket from her grip and set it aside. Then he pulled out a handkerchief. He took one of her hands in his and wiped the soot from her palm. "It is not fitting that you do this. If you choose to, I have to wonder what you are plotting."

It is not fitting that I do most of the things I have done since the day I married. She almost said it, but the way he wiped her palm distracted her. So did the sensation of his own fingers pressing the back of her hand. Not gentle or careful. More commanding and efficient. She still found that touch, and her toleration of it, fascinating.

He dropped her hand, then lifted the other. "You are not here to earn some coin. You are watching the family. You hope to find a way to blame one of them."

Another arch response entered her head, but what he was doing to her hand garnered more attention. He had a firm hold on her, but she did not feel threatened. The time he took in removing the unsuitable soot charmed her, despite her dislike of him.

The soot gone and the handkerchief ruined, he did not release her right away. She looked up to see him gazing down at her palm and fingers.

She pulled her hand away. "You still consider me a likely object of accusation, if you assume I am looking to place the blame elsewhere."

"If it is determined he did not fall accidentally, everyone is a possible object of accusation. You are no more likely than any of the others. You do not need to devise a way to accuse someone else."

She would be much more likely to find fingers pointing at herself. Fortunately, he did not know that. Yet.

"I do not seek a way to accuse anyone. However, my fate for good or bad is now bound to this family's. I am naturally curious, as I said."

"Yes. As you said."

He had become irritating again. She moved aside, so she could step around him. "I must leave. I am expected to help in the kitchen after dinner."

She reached the door. His hand rose high on it, holding it closed. "If you, in your duties, should learn something of interest, you should inform me."

"They are your relatives. If I find something of interest, you will probably bury it."

He let her go then. She paused once she was away from the chamber, and pressed her back against the hard wall. She looked down at her hands. Some soot still showed around her fingernails. She felt again the gentle wipes on her palm, and the strong hand holding hers.

Chapter Five

Chase let himself into Nicholas's apartment. He found the new duke in his dressing room, preparing for dinner.

"You think to attend like that?" Nicholas raised his chin while his valet tied his crisp cravat. "Johnson, give my cousin a fresh neck linen."

Johnson, a middle-aged, small man with pale hair, finished the tie, then took another linen from a neatly ironed stack. He approached Chase, set down the linen, and reached up to untie Chase's neckpiece.

Chase allowed it. Johnson would be horrified if his attendance to his master's command were thwarted.

"Give his boots a quick buff too," Nicholas said.

If Johnson minded performing these duties for an additional person, nothing in his expression revealed it.

Finally made presentable enough for Nicholas, so presumably for the rest, Chase sat in one of the blue damask upholstered chairs set in a circle. Nicholas had already ensconced himself in another one.

"Who else among the old servants remains?" Chase asked.

"The butler and the housekeeper for now. I doubt they will stay more than another month. They are hoping to find the rest of the permanent staff, and their own replacements, in that time."

"No others?"

"It seems to me that the cook has not changed, nor a few scullery maids down there. I recognize two of the grooms as having served when I visited Uncle Frederick." He shrugged. "Does it matter?"

"There are too many strangers about for my liking." If Minerva Hepplewhite found employment here, so she could spy, others might have too. Chase regretted he had not thought to bring in a few extra eyes himself.

He pictured her building those fires, unseen by the chamber's occupants. Listening. "It might have been wiser to refuse to host this house party, if it meant so many strangers in the house."

"Too late for that advice." Nicholas's dismissive tone set the topic aside. "Kevin sought me out. He is bitter."

"They are all bitter. He only has more cause for it than the others."

"Hell of a thing, for a man to devote his life to something and have his benefactor remove his support upon death. It was uncle's to do with as he chose, but some of it is damned unjust."

Chase wondered if Nicholas included himself in the unjust part. When a man inherits a title he expects the estate to provide the income required to maintain the position. Nicholas would probably manage, but he would be gritting his teeth over the finances for years to come.

"You, for example," Nicholas said. "He liked you more than he did most of us. You indulged his whims and peculiarities. You spent time with him, whether on his expensive pastimes or riding with him. To cut you off without so much as a farthing . . . He defended you when you sold out your commission and others were saying—" Nicholas ceased talking like a man who had said too much.

"He told me there would be nothing."

"So you said. Still—"

Still. Had he thought in the end Uncle Frederick would drop a sentence into his will and surprise his favorite nephew? Had he hoped for it? Any man would. Yet, he knew in his heart it would not happen. The duke had many strange ideas, and some sound ones, and both kinds played a role in that will.

You will have to make your own way now. That was what he had said when Chase came back to England and left the army. *Not such a bad thing. Men get lazy when life is too easy. Good minds go slack and good bodies get fat. Nine out of ten men in the ton have achieved nothing but the pursuit of pleasure. The world won't stand for it much longer. France showed us that.*

He doubted Nicholas or Kevin could comprehend how Uncle Frederick thought making life harder for his nephews would be a valuable bequest.

Nicholas pulled out his pocket watch. "I expect they have all gathered in the drawing room now." He stood. "I depend on you to guard my back."

"I will join you soon, to do just that. First I need to speak to someone." Chase led the way to the door. "And in the future, do not talk freely in front of any of the servants."

The man was following her. Minerva noticed the young gentleman strolling about the house, using the same path that she did. Although her duties with the fires were finished, she still carried her basket while she took the very long way back to the kitchen.

His presence interfered with her plan to learn the lay of

the entire house, and who used which chamber. She had even entered some vacant ones and built fires to see if he would move on, but each time she moved on herself, there he was.

She went down to the library. No one had told her to build fires here, and on entering she saw why. The large fireplace already blazed, enough that the chamber had grown too warm. She set down her basket and lowered the upper sash of two windows, so the heat could escape. She would find out who had been so careless in preparing this room.

She returned to the hearth, picked up her basket again, and turned to leave. There he was suddenly, blocking her path to the door.

He looked her over, head to toe. He couldn't be much older than Jeremy, but she hoped Jeremy never examined a woman with such a wolfish gleam in his eyes. His slow smile made bells of warning sound in her head. He was a family member, she assumed. She could see a resemblance to Chase Radnor in him, buried in the youthful softness that still marked his face.

"You've a wandering way about you." His tone made it more an observation than an accusation. She could do without either.

"I am new here. I was given duties, but not a map of the house."

He appeared taken aback. "You've a way of speaking that is not typical of servants."

"I normally am not one. I am a widow who could use a bit of coin, however." She looked down at her basket. "Doing this for a short time does not require I eat my pride too much."

His expression cleared. A new one took its place. One she knew too well and wished she did not witness now.

He looked her up and down again. "There's all kinds of ways to earn some coin without relinquishing too much pride."

"A few. This suits me, however. I do not mind the labor." She inched to her right, so she stood close to the fireplace implements. "I should find my way back now. I'm to help in the kitchen."

He stepped along with her, so he continued blocking her way. "No need to run down there. There's so many of you here that it is unlikely the cook knows who should be working and who shouldn't." He cocked his head so he could peer at her face. "You are a handsome woman." His gaze drifted to where she held the basket. "Beautiful hands. Sad that they should be ruined by such work as this."

"As I said, I don't mind." A shiver crawled up her back. His intentions became more apparent in the way he crowded her.

"Ah, but I do. It's a pity for such elegant hands to do such work. There are far better ways for such softness to be employed."

Her blood froze. Her whole body did. She battled her immobility by finding a very hard place in her mind, one that had learned how to survive when she felt helpless.

She gave him her coldest, most impassive stare. "You must allow me to leave now."

"Must I?" He chortled, but a hardness entered his gaze. He knew she had looked at him with disdain. "I don't answer to anyone here, not even the duke. Least of all you."

I can do whatever I want in this house and no one will believe you if you complain.

Her entire body tensed like a plucked bowstring. She moved the basket in front of her body and her other hand behind her back.

He snatched the basket out of her grip, then stepped closer yet. His hand closed on hers just as her other hand gripped the iron poker in the holder behind her.

He held her hand and caressed it with his other. It echoed what Chase had done earlier, but this touch did not distract her. It repulsed her. His hold hurt her wrist. Algernon had held her that way.

His gaze rose to her face. "Lips just as soft, I'd warrant. And the rest of you too."

She struggled to keep her disgust in check, so as not to goad him. If he made any attempt to do more . . . She gripped the poker hard, ready to swing it.

"*Phillip.*"

The male voice startled Minerva, and the young man too. He dropped her hand and stepped back.

Minerva looked over his shoulder to see Chase Radnor right inside the door. Chase's glare bored into the other man's back.

"The family is gathering." Chase's conversational tone did not match the furious expression that Minerva could see. "You should join them."

Phillip turned to face Chase. "I wondered where everyone was. I thought we were meeting here."

"No. The drawing room."

"I will go there forthwith." He marched away, like a busy man with much to do.

Chase waited for the door to close. Then he strode over to Minerva and reached around her body. "I apologize for my rash, young cousin." He gently extricated the poker from her fingers. "He had no idea whom he importuned. If you had used this, you might have killed him."

Her body betrayed her, limb by limb, bit by bit, until her core shook. Waves of revulsion and fear inundated her.

She tried to reach down for the basket, but wobbled.

Two firm hands set her upright, holding her shoulders. Deep blue eyes examined her face. She tried to appear normal and calm, but her body still wanted to shiver from an inner cold.

His gaze locked on her eyes. Both curiosity and concern peered into her.

"Sit here." He turned her, his hands still on her shoulders, and directed her to a divan.

"I should return to—"

"Sit." He pressed her shoulders until she obeyed.

He dropped to one knee in front of her, watching her closely. "Did more occur before I arrived?"

She shook her head. "You must think me very frail for being disconcerted by such a small advance." She glanced down at the hand Phillip had held. The pleasant memory of Chase's gentle pressure had now been ruined.

"I think you sensed a bigger danger than you had to confront, fortunately. I'm sure he would not have . . . Still, you are too vulnerable here. You should not return tomorrow." He spoke it like a command. She had calmed enough to dislike that, but not enough to argue.

"If not me, one of the others. He is that kind of man," she murmured. "Trust me on this."

"Then let it be one of the others," he snapped. Then he inhaled deeply. "I will tell the housekeeper to warn all the women. You, however—"

"I will never be far from a poker or other weapon."

"That is one hell of an answer. Stay home. You will learn nothing here."

His manner raised her pique, and her spirits. "I assure you that I have already learned plenty. I appreciate your stopping your cousin, but do not think to command *me*."

He ran his fingers through his hair in exasperation.

He stood. "I must join the others. The fires there are built already, so your work is done." He held out his hand to help her up.

She accepted it, using the hand violated by Phillip. The texture of Chase's warm skin salved the insult more than she expected.

"Go down to the kitchen now." He herded her to the door, and parted near the stairs to the cellar.

She did not descend those steps. Instead she took the servant stairs up one level, to the service passageway that ran alongside the big drawing room. She found a door and cracked it ajar, so she might watch.

"The choice is simple," Nicholas said loudly, his voice crashing through the arguments filling the drawing room. Those other conversations dwindled in the face of his annoyance until silence faced him.

Chase hoped Nicholas would not rush to continue, because the interval of peace felt delicious. He surveyed the large chamber while the last of the voices died out. A panel on one wall that hid an access to the servants' corridor stood ajar. He strolled over and shut it.

"Choice one. The bequests are challenged by someone. Anyone. And nothing gets disbursed until Chancery rules. That means no one gets anything until that time. Except me, because the entailments are a separate indenture, as are the servants' pensions which are in trusts funded by the ducal holdings."

"At least we might get a respectable sum eventually," Dolores said before a disdainful sniff.

"Choice two. We listen to what the solicitor says tomorrow afternoon regarding the accounting done thus far.

There is the possibility that at least something can be paid out soon, even if the final figures are not secure yet. I have asked him to consider if half the estimated remaining funds can be divided among us."

"It will be half a pittance then," Phillip muttered. "It is tempting to go for more."

"Easy for you to say, Phillip," Agnes said. "You are such a pup that you might still be alive when it is all finished. However, I doubt your creditors will like to wait that long."

Phillip colored until his ears were red. At twenty-two, and the youngest cousin by five years, he did not like being called a pup. He also would not care to have his aunt mention the precarious nature of his debts. He had shown no mercy to the tradesmen of London in abusing his credit, all on unfounded expectations. Once word of this will's provisions got out, Phillip would probably be dodging bailiffs.

At the moment Chase hoped Phillip landed in debtors' prison. His youngest cousin had little to recommend him. There were a dozen reasons why Phillip had grown into a man without good character, but even a hundred reasons would not excuse his behavior with Minerva today.

"Yet if we accept even half a pittance, we have accepted the bequests as written," Kevin said. "Anyone who takes the money has given up the first choice. How good of Uncle to include a bribe in his will. For most of you it should hold appeal, since he owed you nothing."

"He owed you nothing too," Nicholas said, kindly.

Kevin's tight expression revealed his reaction to that.

"I say we take what we can get while we are still young enough to enjoy it." Claudine, wife of Cousin Douglas, spoke with emotional emphasis. "We have expenses now, and I don't think it will be a pittance at all, so not half a pittance soon. He was rich as Croesus, from the talk of it. I say we hear what the solicitor has determined about the potential amount left to us when all is said and done, and convince him to release as much as possible."

Douglas nodded obediently. Douglas never spoke much. Even as a boy he had been an observer of the world, not a true participant. As he had married a woman who talked a lot, the expectations placed on him for good conversation had decreased overnight. Chase guessed Claudine led the way in other things too, but Douglas did not seem to mind.

Over in a corner the eldest of the cousins, Douglas's older brother, Walter, bided his time while he helped himself to some brandy from a decanter set on a table against another of those panels, one that also rested ajar. Chase mused at how they all managed to remain predictable in this least predictable situation. Walter had always thought his position as the eldest gave him more authority than Nicholas, even though Nicholas was the son of the second oldest uncle, and thus heir presumptive to the title. Even when they were all boys, Walter would try to issue commands and make decisions that no one paid attention to.

Now, glass in hand, he went to stand beside his beautiful blond wife, Felicity. She looked up at him adoringly, like a nymph to a god. They cut a handsome couple, with Felicity's ethereal beauty and Walter's darkly handsome face. Walter waited for the others to have their say.

"We will wait for the solicitor to explain what he can tomorrow," Nicholas said. "I merely lay out the choices now, so that everyone understands that if even one of you issues a challenge, everyone will be affected."

Walter stepped forward. "We will wait to hear what the solicitor has to say before any of us decide anything."

Kevin smirked. "That is what Nicholas just said, Walter."

"Now I am saying it."

"How useful," Agnes said, sardonically.

"Thank you for agreeing with me," Nicholas said.

"I have concluded it is the right thing to do," Walter said.

"I want the damned money," Phillip said.

"Why? It is not likely to pay off your debts even by half," Dolores said. "You will squander it before a single hatter gets his due."

"At least I have the style to squander well, unlike the rest of you."

"Like father like son," Agnes said. "All style, no substance. Your father *would* be off in Naples during this crisis, spending money he does not have. He probably doesn't even know his brother has died."

"He knows, Aunt Agnes," Nicholas said. "Even in Naples the word spreads when an English duke passes."

"Then he should be here, doing his duty to the family. All of my brothers should be."

"They knew there would be nothing for them in the will," Nicholas said. "They may be angry for their sons, but not for themselves. This is not their battle."

"You mean they should be here complaining like the rest?" Kevin asked Agnes.

"I don't see you accepting the will as it stands," Phillip said.

"I have a reason to be angry. My expectations were not built out of air and greed."

"I insist everyone set this topic aside until tomorrow," Nicholas said, loudly. "We will go down to dinner and not mention it there. Talk about the theater, or fashion, or gossip about your neighbors, but not one word at the table about the will."

"These arguments will give us all indigestion," Walter said, as if Nicholas had not spoken. "None of this down there. Do you hear me, Phillip? Kevin?"

They lined up in a parade of negligible hierarchy. Chase waited until all were in place, then stepped next to Phillip. He gripped Phillip's arm, hard, and bent his head low to his ear. "If I learn that you again interfered with any woman in this house, in any way, I will thrash you within an inch of your life."

Phillip colored, but recovered and smirked at him. Chase left and took his own spot, with Douglas behind him. He could see Aunt Agnes bending Nicholas's ear as they began the march.

"So, do you know who did it?" Walter addressed him despite standing in front of him.

"At this point, I am not sure *it* was even done."

"I thought you were good at this. If a man takes to trade, he should endeavor to be the best at it."

"I am not conducting a formal inquiry, Walter. Do you want me to? I can discuss my fee with you after dinner."

"Well, someone should do one of those inquiries. If one of them did it"—Walter gestured to the line ahead of him and behind—"that is one fewer of us, isn't it?"

His wife gazed in awe as if he had just spoken words that should be memorialized forever.

Chase gritted his teeth. "Walter, I find Phillip childish in his demands, and Douglas stunning in his passivity, but you are intolerable. You have calculated that if one of your relatives hangs for murder, you will get more money out of the estate. Nor did you sound dismayed by the idea." He tipped his head close to the back of Walter's.

"If your avarice runs that deeply, I think I will advise the magistrate in Sussex to take a very close look at your dealings with Uncle Frederick."

Walter stopped dead in his tracks. His head snapped around and he glared at Chase. His wife's expression fell.

"Move along," Chase said. "The others are leaving you in the dust."

Chapter Six

"The housekeeper had a private word with us, one by one." Elise shared the information while she and Minerva walked back to Rupert Street. "She came up above to seek us out. Warned us about the gentlemen and male servants. That was good of her, not that I need warnings on such things."

"I received the lesson in the kitchen," Minerva said. "It was a general announcement there, since we were too busy for anything else." Her feet ached and her back rebelled at the day's labors. Her hands itched from being in soap too long. She yearned to arrive at her home, where she could rest and find the time to think about the day's events. Since she had to return to Whiteford House by seven in the morning, such reflection would have to wait.

Tomorrow she would hire a coach to take Elise and her both ways. This was an inquiry, after all. She would have money soon to replenish the household account that would have to pay for such coaches now, so it wasn't really an indulgence.

They trudged along, two women alone, moving from one pool of light cast by a streetlamp to another, like they experienced repeated dawns and dusks, days and nights.

She could see Elise's soft countenance clearly for a spell, and admire her delicate face and clear blue eyes, only to have a ghost beside her a few yards farther along.

Minerva had taken to Elise at once. Bright, animated, but also sensible, Elise had acquitted herself well when Minerva met her at Mrs. Drable's house. The idea of doing work for Hepplewhite's Office of Discreet Inquiries excited her. It would be occasional at first, but one day Minerva expected to be able to pay Elise regular wages.

Her first assignment had been easy to arrange. Minerva merely asked her to keep her ears and eyes open while she served Lady Agnes Radnor.

"It is the youngest gentleman you must watch out for in particular," she said, thinking about pretty, young Elise alone in the chamber where she served as lady's maid. "He is the sort to importune a woman, especially if he thinks she has no recourse against him. His name is Phillip."

"I don't think he would dare enter Lady Agnes's chamber uninvited."

"If he does enter, you are to leave immediately." She spoke it as a command, which had Elise looking over at her with curiosity just as another dawn broke.

"Perhaps you should not go back," Elise said.

"I am capable of dealing with such as he. You, however . . . Watch for him, do you hear?"

"Yes, ma'am." Elise smiled. "Dolores visited Agnes after the dinner while I prepared her for bed. Dolores intends to quiz the solicitor sharply tomorrow. She also shared the opinion that of all of them, if anyone harmed the last duke, it was probably either Kevin or Chase Radnor, since both of them are of questionable character."

"Did she say why she believed that?"

"Regarding Kevin, it had to do with his common interests. All that mechanical experimentation. Not even real science, she said. He might as well be a factory owner, she said."

It was not Kevin whom Minerva wanted to hear about. She slowed her steps a bit, to make sure Elise had enough time to explain the rest. When she did so, she heard a sound behind them. She looked over her shoulder. Nothing.

"As for the other Mr. Radnor, she said everyone knew the army threw him out. They let him sell out his commission, but the whole of it was highly suspicious and for her money he had probably been spared a public scandal only due to the duke's interference on his behalf."

"No doubt she had an opinion on why it happened too."

"She began saying something about that, when Agnes interrupted with a very firm 'We do not talk about that lest we give the scandal wings.' I was surprised that Dolores indeed stopped talking and left soon after."

Minerva wondered about the specifics that had remained unspoken. If it could cause a public scandal and if the family did not even refer to it, something serious had happened.

They reached the last lamp before Mrs. Drable's home. The door showed in the dusky light beyond. Elise climbed the steps when they arrived. "Wait and I will have the footman escort you home."

"No one is about and it is only another six buildings down the street."

Elise looked up and down the lane before touching the latch. "Tomorrow morning, then."

Once the door closed behind Elise, Minerva continued on her way. Again she thought she heard a sound behind her. A soft footfall. She did not look back this time. Instead she worked the tie of her knit reticule, and extracted the two long hatpins that she had woven into its side. Grasping them like the daggers they could be, she walked up the steps toward her door.

As she did so, a figure came out of the shadows. It stood ten feet away but did not advance. She looked at the silhouette, then turned to it. "You."

"Yes, me."

"You make too much noise. It is a wonder you can follow anyone in secret."

"I did not care if you knew I was there. The other woman, however—"

"She had no suspicion."

"Then I succeeded."

She jabbed her pins back in the knitting of her bag. "Why are you following us?"

"I wanted to ensure no one interfered with you."

"Do you worry about Phillip accosting women on the street? I hope he is not so stupid as that. I promise I will not kill him if he importunes me again, but I would make sure he regrets it."

A low laugh. "I'm sure you would." He moved a few steps closer. "I also was curious. What did you think of the family?"

"I have not had the pleasure of meeting all your relatives, so I have formed no opinions."

"You have not met them all, but you have observed them all."

He knew she had watched them in the drawing room, it seemed. That surprised her only because he had not stopped her from doing so. If he were the one who had closed the first panel, he had chosen not to close the second for some reason.

"Come in. We can hardly discuss this out in the street."
She set her key into the lock.

No sound behind her. She glanced over to see him still
standing in the same spot.

"I should not—"

"Are you worried about my reputation?"

"Aren't you?"

"When a woman decides not to marry, idle gossip
about her carries far less of a threat to her. Now, it is
almost midnight, the houses are all dark, and I assure
you I won't be the first woman on this street to have a
late visitor for unexplained purposes. My feet hurt, so
either come inside or I must bid you goodnight."

After what looked like a shrug, he came up the stairs
and followed her inside.

Far be it for him to worry about her good name more
than she did. Chase followed her into the dimly lit reception hall. The normal implications of such a visit made
him alert to the warmth of her presence in front of him,
and to the subtle scent that wafted while she untied her
bonnet. Lavender.

He knew she had met with the solicitor. He wondered
how long she would remain in this modest home. Soon
she could afford much better.

"Back finally, are you?" The older woman called Beth
peered around a doorjamb, a white cap hanging in droopy
waves around her face. She saw him and her eyebrows
drew together beneath the festoons.

"I am. I told you not to wait up this late."

"I was half asleep on the divan. I'll go up now." That
frown aimed in his direction. "Unless you want me to stay."

"There is no need. Mr. Radnor wants to compare ideas, not interrogate me."

"If you say so." Beth did not sound convinced.

"I will leave shortly, I promise." He tried an innocent smile.

"Is Jeremy back yet?" Minerva asked.

Beth nodded. "Came at least an hour ago. Could be more. I was dozing, as I said."

"I'll speak with him tomorrow then. Good night, Beth."

Beth carried her night candle to the stairs and began the climb.

"We can talk in here." Minerva led the way into the library that Beth had just left. "There is sherry in that decanter if you want some." She gestured to a table before falling onto the divan.

She did not wear an undressing gown like the last time, but her relaxed pose reminded him of the night she conked him on the head. He eyed the poker near the fireplace, much like the one she had almost used on Phillip. She probably did not need anyone following her home to make sure she was safe. It had been a nonsensical impulse on his part, a result of the anger at Phillip's behavior that had never completely calmed all evening. Her vulnerability in going to and from that house had pressed on his mind as a result.

The expression on her face during that confrontation had not left his mind either. Terror. He had seen that look before, on the battlefield. The men who wore it almost never survived the day. It was not a reaction one would expect from a woman who hit intruders over the head with bed warmers.

"Thank you for alerting the housekeeper about your cousin," she said. "Warnings were issued to all the women on the staff."

"I did not single him out, but I reminded her that there were a lot of men in the house. Some of unknown backgrounds, others with too much entitlement. The housekeeper was shocked to learn I had seen a servant being importuned by someone. From her reaction one would think she never before had experiences with that. Perhaps while the last duke reigned, she didn't."

"I am friends with a woman who places servants in households, and it is a common story according to her. The servants do not complain because they do not think they will be believed." She resettled herself against the side of the divan so she could bend her knees and lift her feet onto its cushion. "Forgive me, but I have been standing or walking all day."

Her shoes poked out from the hem of her dress. He wondered if her feet were as lovely as her hands. Probably. Delicate and pretty and soft—he imagined a foot like that sliding up the skin of his leg.

He killed the fantasy when the smooth caress reached his knee. The low light, the late hour, was sending his mind where it should not go. The intimacy of this library right now sang like a siren's song to his masculinity. She appeared lovely on that divan. Almost domestic in her ease and informality.

"If you want to go above and change into a garment more comfortable, I don't mind waiting."

Mild astonishment, then a laugh. "When I said I was not concerned with my reputation, I did not mean that I was so careless with it that I would host you while wearing an undressing gown."

"And yet you did so once."

"There was no choice that time. You broke into my home in the middle of the night."

"A precedent nonetheless."

"I must decline your kind, and somewhat naughty, offer."

He sat on one of the chairs, resisting the temptation to take the one nearest to her. "To repeat my question from the street, what did you think of them?"

"Are you asking because you value my perceptions, or in order to flirt with me through flattery?"

Now, that was direct. "Let us say I am truly curious."

Her small smile said she did not miss that he had not denied the flattery. She stifled a yawn behind her hand. "Since I need my sleep, I will not waste time being coy. I think if one of them killed him, it was either Walter or Dolores. I would add Kevin, but I heard he was out of the country. And Phillip may be a wastrel but I don't think he would have the courage to do it." She shrugged. "Or, of course, it could have been you."

"Me?"

"I can think of many reasons why. You also do not lack courage. I think that you lose your temper on occasion and this sounds like an act of passion, not a calculated crime. More a matter of opportunity calling."

"I had no reason. I knew he had removed me from the will, so I had nothing to gain."

"Perhaps you knew because he told you that evening, and you reacted with anger."

"He told me weeks earlier."

"If you say so." Another little shrug left the question open no matter what he claimed.

"You can't believe I did it."

"I said it is a possibility. Just as you believe it is possible that I did it. Now, don't you want to know why I pointed a finger at Walter? It is not only because he is pompous and clearly thinks himself deserving of everything, or that he resents that Nicholas has become the duke when he sees himself as far more qualified." She leaned in a bit. "It is because of his wife."

"Felicity?"

"She idolizes him. He loves her misplaced awe more than he probably loves *her*. If he has allowed her to have expectations regarding a fortune, and he learned he will have to disappoint her . . . Also, he is the kind of man who can probably rationalize anything. If he did it, he no doubt has a long explanation that eventually blames his uncle for his own death."

It did sound like Walter. He always found someone else to blame. He always had, even when they were all boys.

She had surmised all of this from an hour's eavesdropping. Anyone else would have accepted Walter's boring blandness and predictable correctness at face value.

"And Dolores?"

"Ah, the angry sister. Too angry. It isn't only about the will. She is bitter about something regarding her brother."

He had always assumed that Dolores merely possessed an unpleasant disposition. He had never considered there might be a reason for it, let alone one having to do with Uncle Frederick.

She smiled slyly. "I told you I had learned plenty already. Her sister knows. If you ever want to find out, browbeat Agnes. There was the smallest allusion to it while they spoke today, and I built the fire. It is something long in the past."

"I will not browbeat her, but I may cajole her to confide in me."

She laughed quietly, making a pretty melody in the quiet of the chamber. "She does not look to be a woman easily cajoled. Or charmed."

"You underestimate my powers at both."

She leveled her gaze on him. "Not at all." She watched him intently, as if she tried to read his soul. He refused to look away, and gave as good as he got. That increased the cozy intimacy hanging between them in the barely lit chamber.

"When did he tell you about the will? Before or after he had changed it?" she asked.

"It was about a month before he died. I can't be sure, but his words to me implied it was soon to happen."

"Did he inform each of them?"

"No."

"Only you?"

"Only me." *It is not because of that business with the army. I want you to know that. I'm removing all of you from the major legacies. There will be something left to share, but not a fortune for each of you.*

"I think he wanted to make sure I did not misunderstand why he was doing it." He did not have to explain, and cursed himself as soon as he did. Damnation, the mood in this chamber was putting *him* at the disadvantage, not her.

"Perhaps some of the others found out anyway. Someone may have hoped he passed away before a new testament was signed and encouraged that eventuality to take place."

That was his thinking, when he allowed himself to consider a relative at all. How much better if it turned out to be one of those women getting a fat inheritance. Like this woman here.

The notion did not appeal to him nearly as much as it had when he stole into Minerva Hepplewhite's house, looking for evidence of just that. The night and the mood probably had much to do with that. Come morning he would see clearly again, and realize she was still his best suspect.

"Did you tell any of them?" she asked. "Because if you did, then that person may have told another, and so forth."

"No, I did not." Yes, damn it. He had warned Nicholas.

"Commendable discretion. Unfortunately, that puts you quite high on the list."

"Almost as high as you?"

"Oh, not nearly that high. High enough to be a person of interest to any inquiry, however."

Meaning hers, he assumed. If it were afternoon and he were speaking to her in an office and the light were not so low and flattering to her face, and the night did not emphasize that they were alone, he might have turned the tables on her, and posed his own questions. He might have reminded her that few had as much reason to want the duke dead as she did because few had benefitted as much.

Only the mood right now did not require that, or even want it. Suspicion was not what simmered in him, causing a pleasant heightening of awareness of her sultry relaxation. She had done nothing forward or untoward, but he was well on the way to being seduced anyway. He could not tell if that was her intention, or if she even knew what was happening.

What would happen if he went to that divan and reached for her? Their connected gazes, the quiet conversation, the silence of the night all begged for something besides this talk of possible murderers.

Her lips parted slightly. Her gaze warmed as if another lamp had been lit behind her eyes. Her examination of him turned both cautious and curious at the same time.

She sat upright and returned her feet to the floor. "I think you have what you came for."

"Hardly."

His allusion was subtle, but she heard its implications. Her expression firmed just enough to discourage that line of thought. He had not held out much hope. It would be a bizarre liaison under the circumstances.

She stood, and he did too. "I must get some rest before I take up my servant duties again. You must leave now."

He did not want to leave. He wanted to talk all night, or better yet not talk at all but investigate her in all kinds of ways. Of course that was impossible, for many reasons, not the least being she would never have it.

He followed her to the chamber's door and out into the little reception hall. The small space caused a closer proximity to each other. She opened the door to usher him out.

"Do not walk to and from Whiteford House alone in the future," he said while he took his leave.

"Do you have any other unwelcomed instructions, Mr. Radnor?"

He stepped over the threshold. "Just one. Do not have male visitors in the middle of the night. They will get ideas. It is inevitable."

The smallest smile formed in the moonlight while the door closed.

Minerva felt the smile on her lips. She stood with her back against the door while she reconsidered the last five minutes.

It had not taken her long to recognize the male interest coming her way from this man. She no longer looked for such things, but the power stretching between them was undeniable. The mood had taken on a familiarity that could only be called intimate, and Chase Radnor had clearly been contemplating whether to explore what that could mean.

What had her piecing together her memories was the way she had reacted, not him.

Lively sensations had perked through her. His attention had flattered her. She had wanted more of that, and more of the intimacy. She relived it all while she stood by the door, fascinated. In hindsight it did seem that she had been at least mildly . . . fine, she would call it what it probably was . . . mildly *aroused*.

She had assumed that Algernon had ruined all of that for her. Destroyed her ability to trust a man enough to have such feelings for him. And Radnor? If ever she should not trust a man, it was he.

And yet . . . She looked down at her hands. Her *lovely* hands. His touch had not repulsed her or frightened her. Her reaction to Phillip's hold said her aversion had not disappeared either. For some reason, however, Chase Radnor was not provoking her usual responses.

She would not mind knowing a woman's emotions again. She hoped she did not grow old still suspicious of every man but guessed that she would. It would be nice to be touched at times, though, or even held in caring arms if any could be found. It would be strange to consider Radnor's arms appropriate, though. And yet . . .

For a few moments in the library, when that special warmth in his eyes arrested her attention, a fresh breeze had entered her, carrying the promise of spring.

Chapter Seven

The relatives rose late, so Minerva performed her duties late too. She made the rounds of the chambers while the family dressed and prepared for the day.

Kevin visited Lady Dolores while her maid dressed her hair and Minerva built the fire.

"Sit," Dolores ordered when he entered. "I summoned you because I surmise we may be allies. Agnes is going to press everyone to accept the provisions in the will as it stands. Half a loaf now, she says. Hardly half, I say. Surely you are not satisfied with what my brother did."

"It is half a loaf, but worthless with the other half of the company going to someone who is ignorant. We will be bankrupt within two years, is my guess. If he had left that to my father, or one of the cousins—"

"I am speaking of the money, not that company." A deep sigh. "That is the problem when men engage in trade. It becomes all they can think of. If we challenge the will and win, you will have enough to start ten companies if you want. Keep your eye on the main prize, Kevin."

Silence chilled Minerva's back. She made it a point to have difficulty lighting the fuel.

"Aunt Dolores, you may think of it as trade. I think of it as science, applied to the benefit of progress."

"Yes, yes. All well and good. You still need an old-fashioned legacy, just like the rest of us. Where is your father, by the way? The brothers should be here. I know they were informed."

"My father told me that Uncle Frederick had long ago informed his brothers that the portion they received from their mother, and the allowances over the years, had compensated his generation sufficiently."

"Did he indeed? What nonsense. I trust he did not include Agnes and me in that assessment. It is different with unmarried sisters."

"Perhaps you should ask my father directly for Uncle Frederick's view of that."

"I would, except he isn't here."

"He is in town. You could call on him and be back in time for the solicitor's arrival."

"I am asking you, Kevin. Stop being difficult."

"The duke did include you and Aunt Agnes. He believed you both could have married but did not because your allowances were so handsome you considered marriage a step down. To his mind, you also had—how did my father say the duke put it?—fed at the trough long enough."

"Fed at the—how dare they! He and Frederick were always too clever by half, and conceited about it as well. Two strange peas in a very odd pod."

"You are talking to another strange pea. Now I must bid you good day. I will not be at any family meetings today, other than that with the solicitor. You should seek your allies elsewhere. Cousin Walter, for example. Or young Phillip. The latter is so far into dun territory that he will probably take any bribe you offer."

As soon as the door closed, Dolores took to mumbling and sputtering. "Rude boy. Always was. Too proud for what little he is and has. Another one stepping down, like Chase. The humiliation of it is not to be borne. Girl! Fix this curl! I told you how to do it twice. Nicholas has us living like barbarians here, with such poor excuses for servants and—"

Minerva stood, grabbed her basket, and slipped away while the woman complained.

Hoping to learn more about Walter, she tended to that chamber next. Unfortunately, both he and his wife were not there. Minerva eyed the wardrobe and dressing table. It would be too risky to pry into either. Nor did she think there would be anything to find. She swallowed her curiosity, dealt with the fireplace, then moved on.

A half hour later she descended to the cellar and set her basket in its place. She visited the kitchen next.

"There's washing to do," the cook said, jabbing her thumb to the back of the house. "Was told to send anyone there who was not busy, and that appears to be you."

Minerva was elbow deep in soap water when the laundry door opened. Chase entered.

"How did you find me?" she said while she used the board to scrub a linen sheet.

"You said you help in the kitchen after your morning duties. I asked Mrs. Fowler, the cook, where you were."

His arrival raised her spirits, which had fallen considerably upon entering this chamber. "Do you want something?"

A slow smile formed. "Not at all, except reassurance my young cousin does not still pursue you."

Her femininity longed to hear other words. Y*es, your company, your kiss, your desire.*

What was wrong with her? "He has been invisible thus far today. Did you warn him off?"

"I promised to thrash him if he tried that again, with anyone here. I had rather counted on having an excuse to do so. A few thrashings would do him good."

"Perhaps I should reconsider his place on my list of potential good objects of inquiry."

"I am inclined to agree he does not have the courage, even if he had good cause to be worried and angry if he learned there would be no legacy. He has lived off his expectations for several years now, with impressive self-indulgence."

"He is not like you, then."

"Not like most of us."

She turned the sheet. Her hands, red and soapy, caught her attention. She paused to check her nails. They looked like a washerwoman's. Not surprising, since she had become one.

She began scrubbing again but noticed that Chase's attention had also been on her hands.

"Only one more day," she said. "They will heal."

"Could you not have found someone to spy in your stead?"

An awkward question. She scrubbed with determination.

"Ah, you *did.*" He ambled closer. "You have friends here, helping you. I thought you might have."

"I don't need anyone else to do this. I have eyes and ears."

"But more eyes and ears would be useful."

"Did you place some friends or employees among the

servants? Do you think I did because you did? How clever of you. I wonder if I can guess which ones." She made a display of pondering. "The footman Andrew? He is amiable enough to lure all kinds of secrets out of people."

"If I had placed him here, I would have made him a valet. There is much more to learn in the chambers behind closed doors."

Indeed there was. Elise had provided all kinds of information from serving Lady Agnes.

He blocked the stack of linens she needed to wash. After dumping her sheet in a rinsing tub, she gestured for him to move. He turned, lifted a towel, and handed it to her.

The water had cooled too much. She wiped her hands on the towel before dumping it in the vat, then strode to the fireplace where water warmed.

Other hands met hers on the big kettle's handle. Strong ones. "I will do it," he said.

He lifted the kettle and carried it to the tub and poured it in. He tipped his fingers in to test the temperature. "Too hot. Wait a spell."

She all but shoved him aside. She plunged her hands in and found the towel.

"Interesting that you mention Andrew. I saw you and him together this morning, out in the garden," he said. "I assumed you were learning what bits he had overheard. Or else just flirting."

She had been assessing Andrew to see if he might be a good addition to her enterprise once his short hire here ended. Amiable and not too young, the footman had a manner that put people at ease. "Andrew is not one of my friends, so you were wrong."

"About his helping your eyes and ears? Or about the flirting?"

She stopped scrubbing and looked at him. No teasing smile. No impish sparks in his eyes. It had been a serious question. A ridiculous notion flew through her mind. *He is jealous.* She almost laughed at herself for thinking it. Yet, the way he stood there, watching her, waiting for some response . . .

"As a well-born gentleman, you would not understand how servants are informal with each other," she said. "The best ones watch out for each other too. He insisted the cook give me some time to rest from my chores, and invited me to join him outside to escape."

Why was she explaining? He had no reason to know, or care. If she had been kissing Andrew it would be none of his business.

"Then I am left to guess who the others are." He smiled sardonically. "Only you considered how useful additional ears would be. A fine thing, isn't it? A professional investigator stands before you, and you were more clever than he was."

She had not confirmed that she had anyone here. If he thought to trick her into doing so, he would be disappointed. She did glow inside at his praise, though. Since she intended to make this her profession too, it was good to have another investigator call her clever.

"If I were truly clever, I would have bribed the family solicitor to spy for me. I can think of no way to eavesdrop on that meeting this afternoon short of that." She threw the towel in the rinsing tub.

He dropped another linen into her water. "I will be there."

"Of course."

"I mean that I can tell you what happens. Not spy as such. Simply pass along some particulars."

She obscured her surprise by twisting her current linen to wring it out. "Why would you do that?"

"Why not?" He watched the last linen fly to the rinsing tub. "Must you deal with that now?"

"I am due to check the fires up above. Someone else will have to rinse and hang."

He removed his handkerchief from his pocket and opened it. He took her hand and patted it dry. Then he did the same thing with her other hand. "In the army, when work made hands so raw that the skin cracked and bled, the men would use cooking fats to soothe them. Go to the kitchen and find some. Even if you wipe it off at once, even if you attempt to wash it away, your skin will be protected and will heal faster."

"Are you really going to tell me what happens at that meeting?"

"If you want me to. It will be no secret since so many will be there. I will pay a call tonight after you return to your house and give you the particulars."

He had warned her not to have late callers, hadn't he? Had said men would get ideas if they were allowed over her threshold that late. Yet here he was inviting himself to do just that.

It was no time to get delicate. Chase clearly was conducting an inquiry into the duke's death. If he convinced the authorities it had been no accident, she fully expected additional inquiries into herself. She might not have much time to find the true culprit behind the duke's untimely demise.

"I will leave here at nine o'clock," she said. "If you call at ten, we will talk then."

"There is only one condition. If I share with you, you must again share with me."

She nodded, then left him with the laundry. She would find a few bits to give him. She made her way to the kitchen. Cooking fat, he said. She took some while the cook was distracted.

Chapter Eight

"They streamed out of there like their rumps were on fire." Jeremy regaled his mother and Minerva in the house's kitchen while they each drank an inch of port. It was a celebration of the end of their duties at Whiteford House. Jeremy's pay sat on the table in front of him. The stack of coins would be shared with Beth for a bit of personal spending, but Minerva's pay would go toward household expenses.

It was the understanding that they had made when they joined their fates five years ago. She paid neither of them but she maintained the household. For several years the jewels she sold took care of that. The last year life became more precarious.

Her pay for the last few days did not amount to much, but would help until she could obtain some of the trust's income. Also, she had returned to find a letter from Mrs. Drable that contained the name of a woman who might be calling to seek out the services of Hepplewhite's Office of Discreet Inquiries. She hoped so, and not only because it would mean earning some money. She wanted to prove this was an enterprise in which she could succeed.

"None of them looked happy," Jeremy added. "We were

busy for over two hours and received many complaints about the wait. Well, only three of us getting the horses and carriages ready, so it couldn't all be done at once, could it?"

"Who looked the least happy?" Minerva asked.

"That young one who favors fancy waistcoats. He was not as angry as some of the others, like that dark-haired woman with the deep voice, but he appeared miserable."

"That would be Phillip. He needs money. He is profligate and runs up debts everywhere. He could end up in debtors' prison."

"If he went to the type who loan money, he might be worse off than that."

Minerva had not considered that Phillip's concerns were for his physical safety. That might make him very rash if he thought his uncle was going to change his will. After the way he threatened her in the library, she was inclined to find reasons to move him up the list of suspects.

She began to sip the rest of her port, then thought better of it. She already glowed from its warmth, and did not want to put herself at a disadvantage. Chase might flirt a little and charm her with his smiles, but he was no friend and she needed to have her wits about her.

"Did you come to know the footman Andrew?" she asked Jeremy.

"We shared a few words when I would bring horses to the front. Friendly sort. That Thompson fellow sent him over. I think they were both hoping he'd be kept on, but I don't think he was. He used to be in service, but for several years was an agent to a manufacturer."

"Then he has not been in service for years and probably has no recent references. Thompson placed him, you say?"

"I think he mentioned that. At my prompting. I asked if

Mrs. Drable had sent him. I thought it might be worthwhile to know where those servants came from, and if any were like us."

Meaning, if any had been placed there by Chase or some family member looking for information. Minerva had a high regard for Jeremy's initiative. He possessed a shrewdness that could be very useful.

"I wonder if he might take employment from us when we have need of an amiable man who makes friends easily," she said.

"My guess is he will take any employment that is legal." Jeremy pointed to the coins before he swept them up. "If this is what they paid him, it won't last long."

Jeremy downed his port and left. Minerva rose to leave too. "There will be a caller in fifteen minutes," she said to Beth.

Beth collected the glasses and set them in the washing basin. "Who might that be?"

"Mr. Radnor."

She received a pointed glance and frown. "You getting sweet on him?"

"Don't be ridiculous. You know I am not—" She let it hang there, because of all people Beth knew just how ridiculous it was. *You know I am no longer capable of feeling that way about a man.* It would not do to tell Beth that with Mr. Radnor she had begun to feel very capable.

"It has been a long while now. He is handsome and can be charming when it suits him."

"I do not need a lecture, Beth."

"Don't you? He broke into this house because he is looking to blame someone about that duke's death. He still is, no doubt. He is dangerous."

"I have forgotten nothing. At the moment, however, we have a common goal."

"The problem is *he* thinks to make *you* the means to reach *his* goal. I don't trust him and you should not either."

"I am not so stupid as to forget who and what he is, or the truth of his intentions. But for all I learned from Jeremy and Elise, and saw and heard myself, he is one of them and knows far more. You go up to bed. I will make sure the front door is locked before I follow."

Chase handed his horse to a groom at a public stable two streets from Minerva's house. It would not do to have his mount standing outside her home at this hour. She might dismiss the notion of gossip harming her name, but he knew better than most how people like to talk.

That thought conjured up memories of the meeting with the solicitor, and how Aunt Dolores, when seeing her battle being lost, spoke the unspeakable about one of her nephews. Him.

I find it odd that you are favoring his counsel, Nicholas. They probably would have shot him if not for my brother's intercession on his behalf. It was the closest anyone had ever come to voicing the belief he had been under suspicion of cowardice in the army. He wasn't sure if that was better or worse than the real reason for his departure.

Did you kill him? How often had he heard that question in his head? In the colonel's voice. In Uncle Frederick's. In his own.

He had become expert on closing the mental door on that question and the history that provoked it. He did so now with a slam. He walked the rest of the way to Minerva's house, lining up what he would tell her and what he would hold back.

Among the latter particulars would be his brief conversation with Sanders after the meeting. While the solicitor was quite sure that the correct Minerva Hepplewhite had been found, the lack of a documented connection to the woman known as Margaret Finley bothered him.

"The only two people who know her under both names are in her household," Sanders had explained. "How your uncle knew of her under either name remains a mystery. I am satisfied, but with the mood of the family, it might be best to find another person who is disinterested. You are still advertising for the other two women. Why not add a notice regarding her married name?"

She opened the door herself when he arrived, backlit by the lamplight in the reception hall. Immediately the intimacy of their last night meeting stretched between them. As if she felt it too, she backed away from the door and let him enter and close it himself.

She led him to the library again, but did not sit. Instead she appeared unsure of herself. That was unusual, and fascinating.

"I suppose we could have done this in the park," she said.

"It would have been very dark there."

"I meant in the morning."

"Then it would have been very light. It would be better if all of London does not wonder why I am strolling the park with one of my cousin's temporary servants."

"Of course. Yes." She sat on the divan, in her usual spot. She did not lift her feet onto the cushions. She did not lounge, but remained upright. Stiff.

He availed himself of a chair near the divan this time. She did not react to that.

"The meeting. You said you would give me the particulars."

"It began calmly enough. It ended in a rout. I think Sanders, the solicitor, feared for his life."

"What changed the tone?"

"Reality. Sanders explained that if anyone challenged the will it would hold up disbursement for all concerned. They knew that, but having a lawyer say it is more real. He outlined the various reasons a will might be successfully challenged, and pointed out that none of them applied to the late duke's testament. Well, they knew that too so had not done so. He explained the rare circumstances when a legal will might be challenged regarding the disbursement of assets. Only one might work for any of them."

"He explained that to me too. They would have to claim that they were dependent on the duke and had reason to believe his support would continue. He told me that did not apply to any of them either."

"That is his professional opinion. It would not be hard to find a solicitor who made a different case. That is the danger. He made matters worse by describing the accounting thus far, and how little there was to divide if all the legacies were administered. He did hold out the possibility that one of the two mystery women not yet found would be dead."

"How good of him."

"Several of my cousins brightened at that information. I heard someone mutter that whoever had done in Uncle Frederick had a few other jobs to complete."

"Yet it still was calm?"

"The storm broke right then. The factions declared

themselves, with Agnes and Dolores leading each one. Old resentments flew along with accusations and insults. My family can be as contentious as any, but this was a rare display. Unfortunately, Nicholas thought he could quell it all and end the dispute. He only made it worse."

"What did he do?"

"He assumed his most ducal demeanor and announced that if anyone challenged the will's execution as it was written that person or persons be cut off without a penny in *his* will."

"Oh, dear."

"It was injury upon injury. No hope for salvation. Poverty for life was how most of them saw it. Pandemonium erupted."

"Surely in such a family they have other resources than legacies."

"They do indeed. Each of my uncle's brothers received a portion from their mother and a share of their father's personal wealth. It was respectable enough, with careful tending, to keep gentlemen of their positions in style. Unfortunately, they could never, as younger sons, marry quite as well, so their own children would have much smaller portions in addition to dividing whatever survived of their father's legacy. You can see the problem. In several generations, after several divisions, little would be left for each person. My uncles were not present because they understood nothing would be left to them by the duke. But my generation sees the future too clearly."

"Which is increasingly diminished income."

"Or, heaven forbid, employment."

She considered him intently, as if his amiable tone had revealed too much. "Do you resent that? Were your own expectations thwarted more than you admit?"

"Are you still trying to build an argument that I killed

my uncle?" The evidence that she was disappointed him, although his reaction could not be justified. Still, he rather wished . . . he was not sure what he wished, although right now kissing her kept tempting his mind. The night begged for it. He was not the only one who experienced that special magnetism that men and women feel when arousal altered the senses and delirium waited one kiss away. The way she met him already on her guard as much as announced she felt it too.

"Of course, I am still considering you a likely culprit. Better you than me. My question was more generous than that, however. I am truly curious how a man like you, the nephew of a duke, reconciles taking such a step. Gentlemen do not seek employment."

He normally avoided the reflection that an honest answer would require. Right now, however, flattered by this deeper interest she showed, and beset by a desire that made his blood spark, he found himself looking inward. A hard cock can make a man do many foolish things.

"I am of two minds," he admitted. "The gentleman tells himself he is no more in trade than a physician or a barrister, both acceptable endeavors. Even more acceptable, since I can claim my inquiries are favors to friends, or an avocation."

"And the other mind?"

"The soldier is grateful for something to do other than gamble and drink. I suppose I could occupy my time investigating some obscure ruin and writing its history, as some do to fill their days, but I prefer more interesting searches."

"I think your second mind is the one that matters most. You do not really need this employment, after all. You could cease it anytime you chose."

"You sound sure of that, when possibly only my next inquiry will keep me from being out on the street."

"Nonsense. You spoke of portions from your grand-mother. Your father received one like the other uncles. And you do not have to share what is left with a brother or sister, since you have no siblings."

"How do you know that?"

She laughed lightly. "Little about your family tree is not known to the servants who worked in that house the last few days. A bit here, a bit there, and a total picture comes together. I daresay that if I were willing to visit the others who left today as I did, I could have learned most of what transpired at that meeting without your visiting to tell me."

He watched how the low fire sent golden patterns across her form. "Yet you had me visit anyway."

That caught her up short with a smile half formed. He took the pause as an opportunity to move over to the divan and sit beside her, turned in so he could watch those patterns more closely.

She scooted away a few inches. "I allowed you to visit because learning about the meeting from you was more efficient."

"Is that what this is? Efficiency? It is not a word I would use to describe the mood in this chamber tonight. Or the last time."

Flustered now. Charmingly so, mostly because she never showed anything but self-possession. "I cannot trust you," she murmured, to herself more than him.

"You do not have to trust me yet. You only have to kiss me."

"You came to my house looking for evidence I killed the duke. I could never want to kiss you."

"And yet I think you do."

"You don't even deny your dangerous suspicions."

"I will explain all that in a moment." He leaned in, noticing how deeply dark her eyes looked in the low light. "Later." He touched his lips to hers, ignoring the inner voice warning of impossible complications.

She did not veer back, but allowed it. It entered his mind that she was too stunned to resist, but the softness of her lips and the warmth of their closeness diverted his attention from that idea. He lingered in the kiss, and when she still did not object, he gathered her toward him and into an embrace.

She waited for the sad, dull emotions that ruled her whenever she seriously considered intimacy with a man. They did not come. Instead his kiss enlivened her. She dared not move lest she ruin it. She wanted to both laugh and weep at the irony that this man could evoke excitement with his embrace instead of loathing.

It would not last, of course. It couldn't. For a moment, however, she allowed herself to pretend that she did trust him. She ignored all the warnings her mind tried to shout, and permitted her body to respond if it could.

A quiet bedazzlement that she had known long ago sparkled in her blood, far better than what she experienced in those recent dreams. The girlhood she had lost in every way possible raised one hand above the dank waters that submerged it. Her spirit took hold of that hand and held tight so it would not disappear again.

That meant letting the kiss continue. She noted every second of it. Every warmth, every touch. How it changed to something deeper and the way his hands rested on her back and side. She relinquished confusion and just floated in the sensations, amazed.

He took her face in his hands and looked in her eyes. Not frowning, but with an intensity that made the beauty pause.

"You have not kissed me," he said. "Do you not want to? If you don't, if I misunderstood—"

She placed her lips on his to silence him. She must have done it right because he took over again and there were no more words.

It could not go on. Soon, it would be ruined. A corner of her mind waited for the moment that would happen while the rest of her relished the brief rejuvenation while she could.

True desire worked its ways with her, transforming her, starting a strange hunger that only seemed to grow. She lost hold of her thoughts, her judgment . . . herself. His hands moved in a caress that spoke of his own desire and rising passion.

That possessive hold should alarm her, but didn't. A part of her awoke to what was happening, however. To the time and place of it, and who he was. His dominating presence provoked her vulnerability. Her desire actually enjoyed that. A primitive inner voice urged him on. Rationality spoke louder. How they had met, what he might seek besides pleasure, pressed itself onto her consciousness.

Regretfully, she moved her head to break the kiss. Battling a preference to embrace and hold him close, she placed her hands on his chest, stopping him. "You should go."

He did not cajole or reveal disappointment. Whatever he had thought to have tonight, he seemed to accept that this was all there would be.

One more kiss, a sweet one, and he released her. "Of course. You should sleep. You were too long a servant and should stay abed until noon tomorrow."

"Yes, I should retire." Alone. She did not have to say it. She released the hand she clutched above the water and let it sink again.

After Chase took his leave, Minerva sat on the divan, eyes blurring, finding herself amidst the chaotic reactions those kisses had caused. It had been stupid to allow herself to taste that which she dare not enjoy in full. She was well along on a good scolding when she realized that his "later" explanation had not come.

Glad to have something to do so she did not weep from disappointment, she marched down the stairs and hurried through the garden to the small carriage house in back. She knocked on its door. "Are you asleep?"

Jeremy opened the door. "Have you been crying?"

He was still dressed. She stood aside. "Hurry. Radnor just left and I want you to follow him. His horse was not outside, so it must be at the stable around the corner. You can go through the garden and mews and be there when he arrives if you are quick about it."

Already he had pulled on his boots. "Follow him where?"

"I want to know where he lives. Take some coin and hire a horse from the stable if necessary."

"Won't need it. Unless he gallops I can keep up on foot. It will be more obvious if I follow on a horse. He'll hear me for sure then, and there's no shadows to hide in." Still, he swept up the coins on the table from his pay before he ran into the night.

Chapter Nine

Chase finished his meal just as his manservant Brigsby brought in the mail and paper. Brigsby insisted on doing it this way. A leisurely breakfast was a gentleman's ritual, to his mind, and he refused to provide the reading material while Chase ate.

Chase flipped through the mail, then distracted himself with the paper. His mind did not really notice the words he read. All night his thoughts dwelled on those embraces at Minerva's house. He still tried to make sense of what had happened.

He was no lothario, but he was not green. He liked to believe he understood the mood between them, and its potential. He had never importuned a woman, but he had never been refused either, because his instincts had proven to be excellent.

Except last night. Perhaps. Or not. That was the devil of the problem. He had kissed a woman who wanted to be kissed, he was sure. She had also allowed the warmth of those embraces. He had felt her rising passion. He had good cause to expect more, even if he did not expect everything.

Then, nothing. She was done. Most done. Thoroughly

finished. He might have been tested and failed, her retreat had been so abrupt and complete.

He thought she looked sad or perhaps embarrassed when he took his leave, but that might have been the low light playing tricks. Or his mind finding excuses.

He set aside the paper, remembering that he had some business with *The Times* today in order to insert another set of advertisements. He pulled over the portfolio he had carried downstairs and opened it. He reviewed the notes he had added last night when he could not sleep.

Brigsby entered the chamber and cleared his throat. "Sir."

Chase turned a page. "Yes?"

"A caller, sir."

Chase looked up. There beside a fretful Brigsby stood Minerva Hepplewhite. She wore a vague artificial smile and a brown dress and orange pelisse. More brown and orange decorated a bonnet that framed her face nicely, showing her dark hair and darker eyes.

Chase stood and gestured for Brigsby to leave. Minerva's gaze speared into him. She did not appear either sad or embarrassed this morning. She looked determined.

"Good morning," he said. "How did you know where to find me?"

"I had you followed."

"Did you now? By whom?"

She pretended she had not heard him. "May I sit?"

"Of course." He walked around the table and held out a chair for her. "It is early. Would you like some breakfast?"

"Some coffee would be nice."

He strode to the door and found Brigsby very close on the other side. He sent him for more coffee and another cup. He returned to the table, and closed the portfolio.

"You should not be here," he said.

"If I let you in my house late at night, I am not going to worry about coming to yours in broad daylight. If gossip starts, we will tell them all that I came to employ you in a discreet inquiry."

"Which you did not. Something else sent you through town at nine o'clock. I might have still been asleep. Mayfair does not awaken until noon."

"I assumed you were not the sort to lie abed all morning. My concern was that I would arrive to find you already had left this house." She gazed around the chamber that he used for dining, taking its measure, lingering on the Turkish carpet and the dark wooden Indian table against the window. As her gaze returned to him, it first paused a moment on the portfolio.

"It appears a comfortable house," she said. "Of course on Bury Street it should be."

"It suits me." The whole house was not his, but he assumed she knew that since she had climbed the stairs to his front door. His apartment occupied the third level, which gave him good air and fine prospects of the street and nearby St. James's Square.

The coffee arrived. He waited while Brigsby served her. His manservant said nothing, but a worried little frown expressed how irregular Brigsby found the situation. On a few occasions he had served women breakfast, but they had stayed the night. Apparently, Brigsby found that more acceptable than a woman arriving before calling hours.

Chase waited until the door closed again. "Why are you here?" *To kiss you again. To apologize for throwing you out. To tear off this brown dress and beg you to take me.* He could fantasize, but he knew better than to hope.

"You left before explaining."

"You want an explanation? Fine. You are a lovely woman. I am a man. I wanted to kiss you. You seemed agreeable. So I did, and you allowed it. Until you didn't. There is no other explanation than that."

She just looked at him. He looked back. The silence stretched.

"Not an explanation about *that*," she said with exasperation.

"Too bad. I wouldn't mind talking about it. I have a few questions of my own."

"Before you—that is, just as you were about to—I mentioned that you thought I killed the duke and you said you would explain all, later. Only you didn't."

"I pride myself on knowing when it is time to leave a party."

"I understand. Truly. You could hardly—but I want to hear the explanation, so I came here."

She must want to hear it badly if she tracked him down and arrived at nine o'clock. Fool that he was, that flattered him. Only now he did have to offer some explanation that appeased her, or at least satisfied her curiosity. Since she appeared so earnest and attentive, he found himself wanting to give her an explanation that put himself in a very good light.

"You are merely one person of a long list of people with excellent motives where he is concerned."

"A list that includes you," she reminded him.

"I know it was not me, so for my purposes that does not signify."

"Have you concluded I did not do it, if it was even done?"

Tempted though he was to lie, he would not with her. "I did not conclude that at all. I merely considered it unlikely. I am counting on the evidence—"

"Oh, tosh. Evidence." She pressed forward against the table. "Do you think I did it? Do you? What does your inner sense tell you?"

"I do not rely on any sense other than my mind in these matters."

"You are so objective?"

"I must be. One's inner sense, as you put it, is influenced by . . . emotions and . . . other things." Intent, direct gazes. Light that reflected intelligence in a woman's eyes. Desire to possess.

He had learned the hard way to judge important matters without passion or prejudice. Long before he met Minerva and found himself wanting her, intuition had betrayed him badly. Using his inner sense had made him horribly wrong once.

She stood. "I suppose I can't blame you too much, what with your refusal to simply *know* the truth, instead of requiring hard proof. Unfortunately, it is difficult to prove one did not do something. I have no choice but to continue to see you as dangerous to me."

In other words, no more kisses. "Do I get to ask my questions now? About last night?"

"No." She began making motions of departure, but stopped. "What is that?" She pointed at the portfolio. "I could not help but see my name on the top page when I arrived."

"It holds my notes on this inquiry."

She cocked her head. "You make notes to yourself?"

"I do. Mostly lists of matters to address and things to inquire about and information acquired. I do it for all my inquiries."

"Lists?" She laughed. "We have spoken of a list of suspects, and who is on it. Are you saying there *really* is a list?"

"There is."

She seemed to find that peculiar. "So that is where you list all the hard proof and evidence that you need in order to know anything. Do you have a bad memory?"

"I have an excellent memory. This encourages me to progress through an inquiry efficiently."

"Hmmm. I would think that one thing would lead to another in a natural way. That is how it has worked for me. I can't imagine drawing up lists about it."

"That is because it is not your profession."

"Ah, yes." She stood. "I will take my leave. Good day to you." She turned on her heel.

"Since you can simply *know* the truth, in ways I am denied, what does your inner sense say about me?" he asked.

She looked back over her shoulder. "It says that you did not harm your uncle, but that you think learning who did will bring you pain."

Brigsby arrived to escort her out. Chase heard her last words echo in his head. She was good. Very good.

"It was kind of you to offer to call on me, but it is better that I see you here." Mrs. Oliver possessed a deep, quiet voice. She sat in Minerva's little study, on a chair placed right where Chase Radnor had stood before the warming pan crashed down on his head. Deep into her middle years, Mrs. Oliver was a buxom, blond, proud woman with exacting posture. She imposed herself on the small chamber, her body tilted forward just enough to impose on Minerva as well.

Mrs. Oliver had been referred to Hepplewhite's Office of Discreet Inquiries by Mrs. Drable. She was their first *paying* client.

"Tell me how we can assist you."

Mrs. Oliver licked her lips. "It is complicated."

Minerva had hoped it would be a simple matter that could be solved quickly, like proving a husband had a mistress. She needed to devote time to her own inquiry. This afternoon she had intended to do just that before Mrs. Oliver's letter came in the morning mail. She hoped that staying busy on this matter would at least distract her from continually dwelling on what had happened in the library with Chase.

"It involves my husband's business affairs. He imports mercery from France, then sells to shops and warehouses in London and other towns in the south. He has been very successful. He took on a new agent five months ago, however, who I believe is stealing from him."

"Would that not become obvious to your husband? The accounts—"

"Not stealing in the normal way. I think he has been taking the information regarding where James—my husband—buys his stock and to whom he sells it. I think he has been using my husband's contacts to trade for himself. I suspect he sought his current position specifically to learn what he needed to know in order to do this."

"What does your husband think?"

Mrs. Oliver lowered her gaze. "I have not mentioned it to him. It is really not my concern. It is not my company. He would not like me meddling."

This was what was wrong with marriage, Minerva thought. One of the many things wrong with it. Here this perceptive woman had suspicions of activity that would harm her husband, but their union was such that the man would not want to hear her out.

"Tell me why you suspect this?"

"I visit my sister in Brighton frequently. I went down there two weeks ago. We visited the shops and, as I always do, I made it a point to pass by the one that buys from James. That is one of the towns that this new agent sells to, you see. I'm not checking on my husband's trade, mind you. Just being curious."

Keeping an eye on matters, was more like it. Mr. Oliver would do well to make his wife a partner.

"I don't meddle," Mrs. Oliver emphasized. "I just pay attention because if something ever happened to James, I'd have to do it all myself, wouldn't I? There's some money put away but not enough and I'd have to live on something."

"You were telling me about Brighton?"

"So I was down there and passed by his patron shop and all appeared normal. I kept going, chatting with my sister, when ten doors down there was a shop that does not buy from James. In that shop there were the exact same lace collars and cuffs that he sells. Identical. Only one family in the Loire Valley makes them quite like that, and he never reveals their name. Well, in I go, pretending to want to buy some, and I learned this other shop had a price far below the one up the lane that James sells to. I knew then that something was wrong."

"Shops can sell at any price they choose. Are you very sure that your husband did not sell this other shop the collars?"

"Asked, didn't I? Not directly. When I returned home I mentioned how nicely the lace was shown in that shop he sells to, then asked if he has other shops down there. What a stupid question, he says. Such merchandise is cheapened if sold in too many places. That Loire lace is exclusive to one shop per town, he says, so that shop can sell at a good price and in turn pay him a good price. I knew that, but pretended I didn't. I want you to find out if I am right about that agent. I want clear evidence if it is him. Proof that can't be questioned. Then I will bring it to James."

Clear evidence. Proof. She reminded Minerva of her conversation with Radnor yesterday morning. Mrs. Oliver already *knew* the truth, but she needed evidence before she confronted her husband.

That conversation had stayed in her mind since she all but ran from his apartment. He had wanted to talk about those kisses, and probably about the ones that never happened. What a conversation that would have been! Not that she would ever explain any of that. It would be too humiliating. What could she say? *It isn't only that I can't trust you. As it happens, these feelings are so new to me, so unexpected, that I can't trust myself, either.*

"I don't think this should take long," she said, forcing her mind to Mrs. Oliver's problem and making plans on what to do. "I will need some information from you if you can get it. I want the names of both of those Brighton shops, and I also want the name of the agent and of other shops the agent calls on."

"I'll write to you this evening."

"Then we will begin in the morning. Now, I must be indelicate and explain our fees."

Five minutes later she brought Mrs. Oliver to the door where her carriage waited. "Leave it all to us. I will give you a report in five days and let you know if we are successful or need more time."

Chapter Ten

Chase entered Nicholas's apartment to find him reading in bed.

"Adopting the habits of your new position, are you?"

Nicholas looked up from his newspaper. He set it aside on the breakfast tray. "All that waits for me on rising are the complaints in those." He gestured to a little stack of letters set neatly on the side of the bed, unopened.

"Not dunning letters, I hope."

"I should be so fortunate. If you look closely you will recognize the hands. One is Phillip, who wants to borrow money and writes me daily. He even made it a point to chance upon me at my club."

"Tell him to go to hell."

"One is from Dolores, who still tries to persuade me to be less strict about challenging the will. And one, unless I am mistaken—it has been so long since I received a letter from him that I can't be sure—is Cousin Walter."

"What does he want?"

"I have no idea."

Chase lifted the letter. "Let us find out. May I?"

"Enjoy yourself."

He unsealed the letter. Walter had the practiced flamboyance in his penmanship that one would expect of a man with a high opinion of himself. Lots of flourishes and unnecessary ink decorated the capital letters. Chase read the one-page missive.

"Hmmm."

"I don't care for that *hmmm*," Nicholas said.

"You won't care for this letter either." Chase waved it in front of Nicholas's nose. "He feels the need to advise you on your duties, which he proceeds to do in a very Walter sort of way. In particular, he scolds about your lack of a wife and heir."

"Odd, since if I die today he becomes the duke."

"Frightening thought. You will endeavor *not* to die today, or soon, I trust."

"If I do, assume he did me in."

"Anyway, he scolds. He reminds you of that duty. And, you will be overjoyed to learn, he has even helped out by finding a potential bride for you."

"Hell to that." Nicholas threw off the bedclothes and strode to his dressing room.

Chase positioned himself outside its door. "She is a lovely girl, he writes. Sweet and demure and of course virtuous in the extreme. Well-bred and better raised."

"Of course she is," Nicholas's voice said. "She sounds boring."

"Walter would think that a virtue. Let me see what else he admires in her. Ah, here is more. Apparently, she is related to his wife. Her niece. Her brother Viscount Beaufort's daughter."

Nicholas's face showed around the threshold. "I have seen this girl if she is that relative. We met. She had the temerity to ask when I thought my uncle would die and I would become duke. Not in so many words, but that was the question being broached. When I said Uncle was so healthy he would probably live to ninety, she suddenly lost interest."

"Well, she wouldn't want to wait too long, would she? Clearly you have become interesting again."

Nicholas's response came garbled. Chase entered the dressing room to find him being shaved by his valet.

"I wonder what Beaufort has promised Walter if this marriage occurs."

Nicholas pushed away the valet's razor and tilted his head up to look at Chase. "Knowing Walter, I would assume enough to set up a trust that brings him at least a thousand a year."

"At least."

Nicholas submitted to the valet again. "Any news on the inquiry?"

"I have continued advertisements in *The Times*, and added some county papers, searching for the other mystery women. If any by those two names sees them, I should hear within the week."

"Not everyone reads the papers."

"Most people at least know someone who does. I am hopeful. In the meantime, I pursue other ways."

Face wiped and clothes ready, Nicholas rose. "I will be going down to Melton Park tomorrow. Perhaps you should come with me."

"I may do that." Chase wandered over to the window. A little row of men stood beneath it, waiting to enter the side door. The butler must be inspecting possible servants today.

While he watched, another person arrived and walked right past all of them, then on along the house. Not a servant.

Chase aimed for the apartment's entrance. "We will

talk again soon. Come to my chambers this evening, and we'll go to the club together."

Minerva marched past all the hopeful men awaiting inspection, then continued to the kitchen door of Whiteford House. Since she would be leaving town for a day or so, she needed to take care of this now.

She let herself in. Mrs. Fowler stood with her back to the door, peeling onions.

At her footstep, Mrs. Fowler looked over her shoulder. "What you doing here? Not hoping for work again, I hope. You won't do. Too many airs."

"I'm not looking for work. I was nearby and thought I would call on you."

"Call on me, is it? I've food to prepare. I have no time for callers." She returned to her onions. "Call on me, indeed."

Minerva went over and stood beside her just as the woman wiped her eyes with her apron. "I will cut those if you give me a knife and a board. Then both of us will cry but be done quickly."

Mrs. Fowler shrugged. She set a board and knife in front of Minerva. "Strange one you are."

"I know." Minerva began slicing the onions. Mrs. Fowler inspected them, nodded, and went back to her peeling.

"You've no one here to help you." The kitchen quaked with silence.

"Up above they are today, tending to the chambers. Tomorrow more start, so I'll have them back, plus another. Mrs. Wiggins has been taking on new servants fast."

"Has she found her own replacement?"

"I fear so. I don't like the woman. Came down here

poking around, asking too many questions, telling me my business. Next week she starts."

"It has been difficult, I suppose, having so many of the staff leave. Of course, with those pensions, one would expect it."

"Didn't see me leave, did you? I have one too. A nice trust with a good income. What would I do with myself? No point in cooking a big stew for one person."

"Do you still get to see some of them at times?"

Two more onions awaited slicing now. Minerva blinked against the film of tears and kept her knife moving so Mrs. Fowler would keep talking.

"Most are gone from town. I've a few letters, but that will stop soon as they are settled. It's like family here, but it isn't really family, now is it?" She paused and thought. "Only one surprises me. Never wrote, and we'd served here together a long time. Of course he was all but a gentleman himself, what with being valet to the last duke. I suppose he's living on that spot on the water that he found and is happy to be done with all of this."

"I love the sea. I have always wanted to live in a coastal town. One with beaches, not cliffs like Dover."

"He didn't go to Dover, or the sea. He spoke of Sussex a lot, where the duke has his big manor. Mr. Edkins likes to fish and said there were some good places to do that near there. Mrs. Wiggins said he bought himself a cottage on a little lake near Stevening down there. Can't say I can see him fishing, what with his coats and cravat and such."

"Perhaps now he won't dress so formally."

"Can't picture it since he always did. Nice for him to not have to stay in service though. He was young still. Too young for a pension. Kind of His Grace to leave him enough, though I expect that family thought it too much."

She sent Minerva a sideways, critical glance that indicated her feelings about the family.

"Will you stay on even with this new housekeeper you don't like? Does the new duke suit you?"

"Suit me? What a question." She set the last onion in front of Minerva, and dipped the corner of her apron into a water bucket. "He's no trouble. He'll marry now, though. That wife will be worse than the new housekeeper, what with having opinions about food and such." She wiped her eyes. "Well, we will see. Can leave whenever I want, can't I? I like that."

Minerva finished her slicing. Mrs. Fowler dipped the other corner of her hem in the water and offered it. Minerva availed herself of the damp cloth, but knew leaving the kitchen would help more.

"It was nice visiting with you, Mrs. Fowler. I hope the new housekeeper appreciates the fine cook she has in you, and does not interfere too much."

"You stop by anytime you want to work for free. Saved me crying another ten minutes, didn't you?" She swept all the onions into that apron of hers, walked to the big hearth, and dumped them into a big cauldron.

Minerva let herself out and climbed the five stairs to the garden. That had gone better than she had hoped. She now knew the valet's name, and the vicinity where he now lived.

Her smug satisfaction disappeared as soon as she began walking toward the garden gate. In her path, lounging with his back against the building's stones, stood Chase Radnor.

"Are you always here?" she asked.

"Are you?"

What an exasperating man. "I visited a friend."

"I visited my cousin. And how did Mrs. Fowler become a friend? Isn't she the one who made you do all that laundry?"

"She is a kind soul."

"She is also a talkative woman. What did you want from her?"

"You are so suspicious. You should find a diversion to occupy your mind on occasion."

His hand stopped her progress along the path on the side of the house. She looked down at the hand on her arm, then up at him. He did not look suspicious. He looked annoyed.

"I was going to call, but we may as well have this out now," he said.

She tried to appear interested instead of perplexed, but he made no sense.

"I am speaking of Mrs. Oliver."

"Who is she?"

"Do not dissemble with me. You know very well who she is."

"The question really is how do you know who she is?"

He folded his arms and looked down at her. "She approached me about conducting an inquiry for her."

Oh, dear.

"We were to meet this morning. Only instead I received a letter in which she explained she had engaged another to do the inquiry instead."

Again Minerva tried to appear interested. And innocent.

"Imagine my surprise when she wrote that she decided to hand her problem to Hepplewhite's Office of Discreet Inquiries."

"For a woman who desires discretion, she is not very discreet herself."

"Then it *is* you."

"Of course it is. How many Hepplewhites are qualified to conduct inquiries?"

"*None.*"

That was not fair. "I am eminently qualified. For her purposes, perhaps more so than you."

"*More* qualified? I conducted inquiries for the army. I was trained by experts. I uncovered spies in France and in London have conducted inquiries for five lords and a half dozen members of Parliament. Other than Mrs. Oliver, for whom have you conducted them?"

"Another woman. And myself. You are only annoyed because you don't want competition."

"You are not competition."

"Then why are you so vexed? If I am not competition, you have nothing to worry about."

"I am worried for Mrs. Oliver. She requires a professional."

"She requires someone who can walk into shops that cater to *women* and learn information that requires *a woman's sensibility* and knowledge of fashion. That does not sound like you. As soon as you arrive the shop owner will know something is afoot. Tell me, what do you know about lace cuffs?"

He frowned harder.

"As I suspected. You know nothing about them. I am clearly the better choice for Mrs. Oliver since the path of inquiry goes right through a stack of lace cuffs. She thought so too, it appears. Now, I must ask you to move aside. I am very busy and cannot dally here chatting with you."

He did move, but when she walked on he again fell into step with her. "Is it your intention to try and make a profession of this?"

"I don't intend to *try* anything. It is now my profession. I even have cards."

He looked to the sky in exasperation. "Other than a few women who are misguided, no one will employ you."

She strode all the harder and turned onto Park Lane. "I think many will, especially women. If you were a wife hiring someone to do inquiries on your husband, would you want to discuss such indelicate matters with such as *you*? Of course not. If you were a woman who had written indiscreet letters and needed help getting them back, would you hire—"

"If I were a smart woman I would, in every case."

"Then I will make my living serving the stupid ones. With time perhaps the stupid men will find me too. I daresay even if I limit myself to stupid clients, I will be very busy."

Again that hold stopping her. "Minerva—"

She glared back at him. He released her arm. She faced him squarely. "Do not insult me by implying I am incapable of such simple inquiries when I have done harder ones very well in the past."

A flicker of curiosity entered his eyes. "What ones?"

She had been careless. She pretended even more vexation with him. "Never you mind. Just believe me that I have."

His expression softened. "As a woman, there are places you cannot go. Society you cannot join. People who will not hear your questions. There are those who will notice if a woman follows them."

She threw her hand to her forehead and feigned shock.

"Truly? Oh, my. What a fool I have been not to think of those things. Whatever will I do?" She walked on, amazed at the small opinion he had of her. "I learned where you live, didn't I? You had no idea you were being followed."

His damned boots matched her stride. The mood pouring off him changed to one of thought. "You are not doing this alone," he said after twenty paces. "You have others helping, including men. You had others at the house as servants and now they will aid you in your future inquiries."

She just let him chew on that.

"How long has there been an Office of Discreet Inquiries?"

"Not long." She would never admit just how *not long*. Let him wonder.

"I trust you will not be doing anything dangerous. There have been times when I barely got out of a bad situation alive. I would not like to think of you—people can become vicious if they believe themselves cornered, Minerva. Domestic inquiries can be the most volatile. If you persist in this, you must take care."

His voice, honestly troubled, touched her. That drained her belligerent indignation. He sounded truly concerned.

"I will be careful," she said. "I doubt I will ever face what you have. Those who need a soldier will seek out a soldier, not Hepplewhite's."

He stopped walking. His slow smile offered a truce.

"Let us enjoy a ride in the park. Nicholas will give us a carriage to use, so we can do it right now."

She gazed up at the blue sky and bright sun. A ride would be delicious. Only, she wondered if he intended to try and kiss her again. He looked as if he might. Would that she could keep it at just that, a few kisses and some sensual warmth that ended soon after it started. They were neither of them innocents, however, and she doubted he would treat her like one. Nor could she afford herself the luxury of an hour in the park.

Yet he looked so appealing in the bright light. Handsome and dashing, his stern face softened by that smile that quirked up on one side, forming an adorable and unexpected dimple in that one cheek. She would not mind gazing at him for an hour or so during the ride he proposed.

"It sounds lovely, but I must be on my way," she said. "I have much to do and the day is passing."

He accepted that, but the look he gave her made an ember glow at the bottom of her stomach. "Another time, then."

She walked down the lane. She felt him long after she had parted. Felt his gaze on her, and his spirit stretching toward her.

"The first thing you must do is sell those urns." Kevin voiced the opinion while he drank port in Chase's sitting room.

He spoke to Nicholas, who had stopped by to collect Chase and brought Kevin along, to distract Kevin from his brooding. Brigsby had fed them, and they now lubricated their senses in preparation for a few hours of gambling.

"They are very valuable," Nicholas said. "And very numerous. It will take some time to sell them if I decide to."

"Then at least move them. The way he set them up on that landing, in close rows—I almost knocked one over today, when coming up to your chambers. Who would present precious items in such a precarious manner? One can't even appreciate their beauty, they are so tightly packed."

Chase chuckled. Those urns formed a forest on the first

landing, interfering with easy access to the drawing room. "I have to walk among them sideways, to make sure one of my shoulders does not send one crashing to the floor."

"If I move them, then I lose the joke of watching you slide along like that, Chase. Or of men of more girth inching along." He grinned. "Or of Aunt Agnes being flustered by their fragility."

"It is a strange sort of joke," Kevin said. "I hope you are not going to assume his habits as well as his title."

"That danger more likely lies with you, young man."

"Uncle Frederick never had to slide, of course," Chase said. "He set them out perfectly measured so his own shoulders could pass with an inch to spare. He could stride through them, then wait and watch others try to navigate their ways. He never smiled or laughed, but he enjoyed the show."

"They have been there a long time," Nicholas said. "Do you remember how we would tempt fate as boys and play tag among them? I did break one once. He made me repay him by cleaning out the stables the next time I was down at Melton Park."

"They came over with the Chinese village," Chase reminded him. "Kevin was probably too young then to now remember that."

"Not entirely. I have vague memories of many people visiting Uncle at one point, none of whom spoke English. They wore colorful robes."

"He decided to learn Chinese," Nicholas said. "And he concluded the fastest way was to either visit China, or have China visit him, so he would hear the language all the time. He arranged to have an entire village stay in Whiteford House for almost a year." He shook his head, smiling at the memory. "He sent a man who negotiated with the emperor's people for six months to get permission. Women, babies, children—the whole damned village picked up and moved. The chambers above were full. My father stopped visiting, so I did not see much of it. Our one meal here at that time was long noodles in broth. I think that is why father chose to avoid more calls."

"He ate like them. He dressed like them," Chase said. "He made the servants learn enough Chinese so his visitors could make their needs known. One youth who came over in turn learned English, as part of the agreement with the emperor. Anyway, those urns came with the village, purchased on his behalf by the factor he sent there to arrange all of it."

"Did he learn the language in the end?" Kevin asked.

"I assume so," Chase said. "He spoke it frequently over the next few years. Or at least it sounded like he did."

"Who would know?" Nicholas said. "He could have been speaking nonsense."

"Unlikely," Kevin said.

Yes, unlikely. "I am sorry to say that this is the first time since he passed that I have reminisced with anyone about him," Chase said. "The conversations have all been on other things."

They both nodded. No one had to itemize those other things. The manner of death. The will.

"At the risk of alluding to that again, I just remembered that I have a request from my father," Kevin said to Nicholas. "He wants to know if you have found the mechanical man. He wants it, if you are willing to let it go."

The mechanical man was an automaton. Uncle Frederick had purchased it, and actually used it, because it could move on wheels. It carried a salver in one hand, like a butler. Uncle liked to place glasses of drink on it, and have it carry the glasses to guests.

"I haven't seen it in years," Nicholas said. "Chase?"

Chase shook his head.

"You are welcome to come to the house and look for it. When it ceased amusing Uncle he probably put it in an attic."

"I may do that, since it started my own father's fascination with the damned things," Kevin said. "Father has asked me to attach a little steam engine to it, so it moves faster. I have advised against it, but . . ." He shrugged the shrug of a son never heard by a father.

"It did move very slowly," Chase said.

Kevin gave him a look of forbearance. "Which meant it stopped if it hit a chair or a person. Imagine it with a steam engine. An automaton stops working if the mechanism unwinds, which happens fairly quickly. A steam engine works quite differently."

Nicholas started laughing. "I think you must find it and do as your father wants. Please invite me to the demonstration. I am seeing that little butler crashing about the library like a marauder in high blood."

"I think a better site would be among those urns, not a library." Kevin set his glass down. "Let us go. The two of you can further distract me from my brooding by losing lots of money to me at cards."

Nicholas looked at Chase, with mock astonishment. "Was it your plan to distract him from brooding? What an odd thing for him to suggest."

"Not me. You? Nor is he given to brooding." He opened the door. "You are too suspicious, Kevin."

Kevin crossed the threshold, shaking his head and sighing.

* * *

Due to her early morning errands the next day, Minerva did not read the newspaper until afternoon. The day had turned fair, so she brought it outside to the small garden and sat on a stone bench. Her quick scan of the advertisements stopped abruptly when she saw her own name.

Desire information on Margaret Finley, widow of Algernon, of Dorset County. To report or inquire, write to John Smith, care of Montgomery Stationers, Montagu Street.

Chase Radnor must have inserted that query in the paper. The scoundrel was inquiring into her past, and her story. She had thought the solicitor satisfied, but remembered Sanders referring to perhaps firming up the particulars. She had not thought he meant the ones about Margaret Finley!

After swallowing her dismay, she noted that two other notices, with two other names, followed the one regarding her.

Her mind immediately lined up who if anyone could respond to the notice. Beth and Jeremy, of course. No one else, since she had never been Minerva Hepplewhite while living in Dorset. She had become Minerva Hepplewhite while they journeyed to London. The only possible connection between the two names might be the hired coachman who took them from her home in Dorset and brought them to the coaching inn where they found transportation. If he had dallied at the inn he might have heard her new name used. It had been five years ago, however, and she doubted anyone would remember something hardly worthy of note to begin with.

The kitchen door opened and Beth came out to her. "Elise Turner is here."

"Send her out to me."

"I still think it is I who should go with you."

Beth renewed a contentious conversation from the night before.

"I need you here in case Mrs. Drable sends anyone else to us. I can hardly ask Elise to do that." Minerva did not want to hurt or insult Beth with the real reason she preferred Elise. Her young friend would simply be more plausible entering shops and examining lace cuffs.

"Jeremy could do it."

"If women come looking for a business run by women, it would hardly do to have their first meeting be with a man."

Beth pursed her lips. "I hope you don't expect me to only open doors and such with this Office of Inquiries, or sit at that desk listening to possible patrons. I want to have some of the fun too."

"There will be many times when only you will do, Beth. Times when I can only depend on someone I trust with my life."

Flattered and a little chagrined, Beth returned to the door and opened it to allow Elise entry to the garden.

Minerva had asked Elise to wear her best dress, so she might see just how good that dress might be. Examining the blue muslin now approaching, she mentally added her own fawn pelisse and dark blue bonnet.

She bade Elise sit with her. "Are you currently engaged in any employment?"

"Mrs. Drable tries, but so far nothing, not even another short-term hire."

"I have something that should last a few days. I will bring it to Mrs. Drable if, after hearing about it, you are interested. First I need to see if you have the temperament."

"I'm considered very even tempered, if that is what you mean."

"Not entirely. In this assignment you will have to act. You must be someone other than you are. I want to see if you can do that. I'll ask you to show a mood or emotion, and you try to do it."

Elise nodded, but her puckered brow indicated she thought this very odd.

"Good. First, I want you to show sadness."

Elise thought about that. Then she closed her eyes. When she opened them she threw back her head and began wailing. Loudly. Her moans and cries rang through the garden.

Minerva veered back, startled. Beth threw open the kitchen door. A head poked out the upper window of the neighboring house. Jeremy came running through the garden. Elise continued wailing so loud the whole street must have heard. Minerva half expected the girl to tear her hair and rend her clothing.

Minerva grasped Elise's shoulder. *"Not like that."*

Elise quieted. "You said sad."

"Yes, but not grieving sad. Disappointed sad." She waved for Jeremy to go back to the carriage house. Beth closed the kitchen door. "Let's try this instead. Pretend you are a lady of high breeding and I am a shop owner. Ask me if I have any better muslin than you have seen."

"Am I rich?"

"Fairly so."

"Am I conceited?"

"No. You are nice."

Elise thought about it. She smiled vaguely. Kindly, but a bit patronizing. It was not the smile one gives an equal. Her eyes sparkled with good humor, but also expectations of deference. "These muslins are quite nice, but do you have anything better? With primrose sprigs, perhaps?"

Minerva was impressed at how well she transformed herself. Elise Turner was a natural actress. She would do very well.

"I will speak with Mrs. Drable."

Chapter Eleven

Chase dismounted in front of the inn. Beside him Nicholas did the same. A groom took both of their horses to be rested, watered, and fed.

"I'm glad we rode," Nicholas said while they entered the coaching inn. "It has been both faster and more leisurely, since we make these stops. I think at this one some food is in order."

Chase was hungry too, and he accompanied Nicholas into the large public room. A busy crowd filled the inn, with the tables occupied by the people traveling in the stagecoach having its horses changed in the yard.

Nicholas led the way over to a counter where the publican dispensed beer. "They should leave soon."

"I don't mind standing a while." A couple of hours on a horse and his body begged for some stretching.

They bought pints and lounged against the counter while they watched the quick movements and quicker eating of the patrons.

"I called at the Home Office," Nicholas said. "I asked Peel what theories were being considered about Uncle's fall. I received much attention and deference, but no information. Perhaps they are not looking into it at all."

"While we are at Melton Park I will take a better look

at that parapet. My examination after the funeral was necessarily quick and cursory, but perhaps more can be determined."

"You do that, but—he went up there regularly. He probably knew every stone and slate tile. Even if he tripped, going over that wall would take some doing."

Those were Chase's thoughts too. It was one small step after that to debating who had done it. To avoid that conversation he shifted his stance a bit away from Nicholas and watched the stagecoach party collecting themselves to leave.

One passenger caught his eye. A pretty girl with very light brown hair, she wore a blue muslin dress and a darker blue bonnet. Something about her looked familiar, but he could not place her. Her companion wore all gray and her back was to him. While he watched, the companion reached over to slide her reticule on her arm and her hand came into view. It was an especially lovely hand.

They filed out with the others to retake their spots in the stagecoach. Chase leaned toward the publican. "Where is that coach going?"

"Brighton. There's two of them stop here every day."

Nicholas pushed away to claim one of the tables that the coaching party had used. Chase joined him, wondering why Minerva Hepplewhite was traveling to Brighton.

"Do not be worried. You can do this. If in your mind you become a young woman of some substance, that is exactly who you will be. It will be just like in my garden." Minerva gave the instructions to Elise while they strolled down the lane in Brighton. They passed fine shops as befitted neighbors of the shop that sold Mr. Oliver's wares. They had just visited that establishment to confirm that those lace cuffs and collars resided there.

Now they advanced on the other shop reported to have the same merchandise. The one that should not have it.

An obvious change occurred when they made their way through a small crossroad. The shops became smaller. The goods offered appeared less luxurious. Minerva doubted the ton, when visiting Brighton, passed the crossroad when shopping.

Mrs. Oliver had provided the name of the other shop, and they found it easily. The window displayed some nice linen and ribbons, but no cuffs. She and Elise entered.

The owner, Mr. Seymour, stood behind the counter showing a patron a box of silk braids. Minerva browsed the wares and squinted at the shelves behind Mr. Seymour. No cuffs.

"They are not on display," she murmured to Katherine. "He may have had cause to tuck them away. Let us find out. Pout and look disappointed."

As soon as the other patron left, Mr. Seymour turned his attention to them.

"It appears your friend was wrong," Minerva said to Elise. "I did not think we would find such as that here."

"She was most specific," Elise said.

"Well, she was wrong."

"Can I be of service in some way?" Mr. Seymour nipped out from behind the counter.

"My friend Mary said that you had lace cuffs here, beautiful ones," Elise said. "Are they in a drawer, perhaps?"

"I regret they are not." Mr. Seymour beamed while he gave the bad news. "They were all purchased. The last sold three days ago. There was a line waiting to buy them. Some very fine ladies availed themselves of my stock in order to obtain them, so even some of my usual patrons were disappointed."

Elise pouted all the more. "I wish we had come down from town last week."

"I am sure there are equally nice lace cuffs in other shops," Minerva said.

"Only one other," Mr. Seymour said, making a face. "You will pay far higher there, I'm afraid. Same cuffs, same lace, all from the Loire Valley and imported. Only the price is different." He gave Minerva a meaningful look. "Very different."

"We can't buy what is not available to buy," Minerva said to Elise. "We will find something just as good in London."

"But I had so wanted to get the cuffs for myself, and cuffs and a collar for Aunt Charlotte." Elise looked ready to cry. Minerva saw that with alarm, remembering the wails in the garden.

"Well, not quite just as good," Mr. Seymour said. "As I said, these are from France. Exquisitely made. And—" He leaned closer to share a confidence. "I had one set that even a certain other shop did not have. A new set that proved very popular."

"You will have her in tears soon," Minerva scolded. "My own disappointment I can accept, but you know how young women can be."

"Your own disappointment? Did you intend to purchase some as well? We are talking about three sets?"

Minerva shrugged. "If the new ones are as good as you say, I think it would be four or five. Unfortunately, you do not have them and we leave for town tomorrow."

Mr. Seymour chewed his lower lip. "The man who brings them to me is expected this afternoon. I should have more tomorrow if you can—"

As if distracted, Minerva fingered some gloves on a table next to where they stood. "We leave soon after breakfast, I'm afraid."

More chewing. "Could you—if you came by this evening, say at six o'clock, I think I would have what you want by then."

Elise brightened. "Oh, could we?" she begged Minerva. "We would be back well before dinner, and surely Lady Talbot would give us use of the carriage again."

Minerva chewed her own lower lip. "Six o'clock, you say?"

"I am confident I will have all that you want then."

"I suppose so. I hope this lace is as wonderful as you say, since this will be a lot of trouble."

"You will think it some of the best lace you have seen."

Minerva nodded at Elise, who grinned and clapped her hands.

With the appointment arranged, she and Elise left the shop. "We will return at five thirty, and hope that we see that agent here." She looked over at Elise, who had played her role very well. "Lady Talbot?"

"He seemed impressed with the way the lace had brought him finer patrons. I think he would wait all evening for our return now."

"We have both come up in the world. I suppose now I will have to hire a carriage too, since you said we would arrive in one."

"You probably should."

"Are you enjoying this assignment, Elise?"

"Oh, yes. Very much, thank you."

That night, washed and dressed for bed, Minerva sat at her chamber's writing desk in the coaching inn outside

Brighton. In the reflection of the looking glass Elise sat on the bed, brushing her long hair.

She dipped her pen in ink and began writing a letter to Mrs. Oliver.

I have all the proof that you will need to convince your husband that his agent is betraying his trust. I saw the agent myself at Mr. Seymour's shop, when he delivered at least two score sets of cuffs and collars. Mr. Seymour sells them for 2s 5p, which is far less than the 3s up the lane. I bought four sets, including one that your husband does not import. This indicates that the agent is importing on his own or has found another wholesaler of which your husband is unaware.

I will provide a full report, along with the purchased sets upon my return to London.

She remembered how Mrs. Oliver kept saying she was not interfering. Mrs. Oliver might need more than a written report to garner her husband's attention. He would probably mock her if the proof were not overwhelming.

She wished Mrs. Oliver did not have to live with a man who did that. Algernon used to mock too, anytime she voiced any kind of opinion. The nasty sarcasm meant that in a short time she never spoke to him unless he asked her a question. It took several years to realize that had been his goal all along.

She continued writing. *If you desire it, I will also meet with your husband to describe my visit here and what I saw and learned. With such testimony I do not think he will disregard your concerns.*

Let the lout try and mock Minerva Hepplewhite.

You can tell your husband I am an acquaintance who frequents Brighton to visit my elderly mother and chanced

upon these other cuffs, if you prefer. He need never know
you engaged my services.

I expect to return to town by Friday. Another inquiry
will keep me away until then.

She signed, folded, and sealed the letter. Tomorrow she
would post it.

She stood and carried the lamp to the bedside and
folded back the covers. Elise scrambled under them.

"Where are we going tomorrow?" she asked. "You
were examining the county map very closely at dinner."

"We are going to a town called Stevening. It is perhaps
an hour or two carriage ride away."

"We don't have a carriage."

"I will hire one."

"Such a lady I am these days, with your nice pelisse
and bonnet and now a hired carriage."

"Do not be too excited. The carriage will be no more
than a gig, and you will sit in the back." She climbed into
the bed and turned out the lamp. They lay side by side in
darkness pierced by a filmy ray of moonlight slipping
between the window drapes. The white plaster walls reflected that light so that the ceiling beams showed black
in contrast. Two men had the chamber next to them and
from the sounds were enjoying a bottle together.

"Mrs. Drable told me that you left your last position
because the husband importuned you," Minerva said.

Elise did not respond, but her head nodded.

"Was it more than that?"

She shook her head. "I feared him getting me alone,
though. He touched me in ways he shouldn't and I feared
one day he would—not stop."

Probably so. Eventually. "It is good you left. I know
without references that obtaining another position is

very difficult, but things will be right soon, I'm sure." She hoped that Hepplewhite's became successful, and that there was enough work for Elise to keep herself.

"If necessary, you can return to your village," she added.

"I wouldn't want to do that. There is no place for me there, except with relatives who don't want the keep of me. There was a man who offered to marry me, but I did not want to marry him. So I came up to town."

That twisted Minerva's heart. She knew Elise's situation all too well. When her uncle decided to emigrate to America, he had not offered to bring her too. He let her know the cost of it, and how taking her would delay how he established himself and his two daughters. Her future had looked bleak then, adding to the sorrow she felt at losing her cousins who were her girlhood friends. She saw herself as a governess, perhaps, or maybe in service.

Then Mr. Finley had offered for her hand, to everyone's astonishment and relief. A love match, her uncle called it, since she had no fortune. A miracle.

She had convinced herself she wanted that marriage. In reality she embraced the idea because there was no alternative that appealed to a girl of seventeen years. Algernon was older. Thirty-seven when they wed. If she thought him handsome in a brittle, sharp way, and somewhat unctuous in his manner and speech, those were small objections that she assumed would soon pass.

For a few months their marriage had been almost normal, except in the marriage bed. He blamed her for his frequent failures there. With every attempt he treated her as if she were some lifeless vessel for his seed, and in truth that was all she felt like. His anger about his impotence infected their whole marriage and turned violent.

Eventually life with him became impossible to bear. Yet bear it she did, for too long, because she could see no way out.

She calculated the fees Mrs. Oliver would pay, and how much she could give to the young woman falling asleep at her side.

Chapter Twelve

After two days at Melton Park, joining Nicholas while he rode through the farms and otherwise performed lord of the manor activities, Chase decided it was time to pick up the duties that had brought him down from town.

Since the day was fair, he rearranged the list in his head to take advantage of the bright sun and dry roads. He called for his horse, and sent word to Nicholas that he would probably not return until morning. Before he left he drew the butler aside.

"Has the local magistrate been here since the funeral, to investigate?"

The butler shook his head. "No one has been investigating here, sir."

"I need you to take a few minutes from your duties and write down which servants accompanied my uncle down from town on his last visit. Also I want to know if he had any visitors, even neighbors. Include everyone who was here for any reason his last three days."

The butler nodded. "A bad business, sir, if I may say so. Both shocking and sad. No one could have foreseen it."

"Foreseen it? What do you think happened?"

The butler flushed. "I'm sure I don't know. I was only

referring to his death itself, not—that is to say, I wasn't implying—"

Of course he was, but to say it would be to invite more questions when one of his duties was to see there were none at all.

There could be only two ways Uncle Frederick went over that parapet. Either he fell by accident. Or he was pushed. So why did he think the butler believed it might have been a third possibility, and the one no one considered—that Uncle Frederick had jumped?

No, he was wrong. One other had considered it. Peel. *A conclusion that casts aspersions on your uncle's good name.* He had not paid much attention to that vague allusion, but he now realized just what Peel probably meant.

It took him half an hour just to ride to the border of the estate, and another to reach the nearest village. His destination lay beyond that, so he passed through the town down its main lane. While he circled the churchyard, he noticed some color amidst the plantings. A spot of dark blue bobbed in and out behind the branches of the shrubbery. He paused his horse and waited for the blue to become more visible, but instead it disappeared.

He scrutinized the garden, searching for not blue, but gray. No other unexpected colors showed. He moved on, laughing at himself. Minerva was in Brighton. It was ridiculous to see evidence of her wherever he went, like some green boy infatuated for the first time. Still, that blue had looked much like the blue worn by her companion, so he could be partly excused.

He wondered what she was up to in Brighton. A brief holiday, perhaps. Or she could be getting into trouble. Why did he think the latter more likely?

Outside the village he stopped and consulted his pocket map. A mile farther, and two turns off the main road, he approached a cottage of respectable size. Behind it he could see the bank of a small lake. In front of it rested a horse hitched to a gig.

He hoped that gig did not mean Mr. Edkins had a caller.

He dismounted, tied his horse to a fence post, and strode to the door. Just as he was about to knock, it opened. He found himself facing the crown of a gray bonnet.

"You have been so generous, sir. I will be sure to give Mrs. Fowler your regards." A lovely hand rose to wave good-bye and the gray bonnet turned. One step brought the owner of the gray ensemble close enough to almost bounce off his nose.

She looked up, startled.

She glanced over her shoulder and gave Mr. Edkins a dazzling smile. "It appears you have another caller."

"Odd that. Normally I have none and now it is two in one day." Mr. Edkins, a man of middle years and closely cropped brown hair, adjusted his spectacles and gave Chase a good examination.

"I have indeed called," Chase said. "I hope that you will receive me even if you have already been intruded upon."

"I suppose I can spare a bit more time."

"Give me a few minutes with your last guest, please, before I ask that of you."

Mr. Edkins closed the door. With nary a greeting, Minerva walked toward the gig. Chase followed.

"What are you doing here?"

"Bringing this good man greetings from Mrs. Fowler. They shared the same household for years." She untied the horse's ribbons and moved to the gig's side.

Chase looked back at the cottage. Mr. Edkins could be

seen watching from a window. He turned back to Minerva. "Do not move this gig until I come out."

She pursed her lips. "I hope that was not the command it sounded to be."

Damnation, the woman was infuriating at times. "Just. Don't. Move."

She climbed onto the gig and took the ribbons in her hands. "I think it will look very odd to Mr. Edkins if I sit in this gig for however long you are in there. There was a nice, sunny spot near the last crossroad, beside a pretty stream. If you ask nicely and do not dare command, I may wait for you there."

He gritted his teeth. "Would you be kind enough to wait so I may have a few words with you?"

She began to turn the horse. "Perhaps. Now you should attend to Mr. Edkins. He intends to go fishing soon."

She moved the gig down the lane. With one more curse under his breath, he presented himself at the door with card in hand.

What did you tell that woman? Chase could not ask outright, much as he wanted to. Instead he asked his own questions and looked for signs that Mr. Edkins had heard them already, recently.

They settled into a pleasant sitting room with good light from handsome windows on the front of the house. The entire cottage had an appealing if spare appearance. This chamber held good proportions and a distinctive, carved mantel on the fireplace. The furniture, such as it held, showed quality. Mr. Edkins had spent wisely and well, and not been especially frugal. Of course with the pension he received in the will, he did not have to stint.

The man was younger than Uncle Frederick had been, perhaps fifty years old. The large pension he received had surprised the solicitor, and angered the family. *He's another fifteen years of service in him before a settlement like that,* Dolores had complained. Uncle Frederick had thought differently, and now Mr. Edkins lived like a gentleman on a nice spot of land on a lake.

"I picked this cottage because I can fish whenever I want to." Mr. Edkins waxed eloquent about his property when Chase complimented him on it. "Never could all those years. Missed it. Now I go out there whenever I fancy." His thumb jabbed toward the back of the house.

"I am glad my uncle afforded you that ability," Chase said. "Have you had much contact with his family or the servants from the houses?"

Edkins shook his head. "It is an odd thing. Hard to explain. When it is over, it is over. The people that filled your days—the family are employers, and the other servants are . . . like other monks in their cells, laboring in the monastery beside you." He grinned at the analogy. "The friendships are all very formal."

"I would have expected the longest serving of you to remain in contact. Letters and such."

"I've sent a few and received a few. It was all so sudden and recent, wasn't it? I expect in a few years we will write when something of interest leads us to."

Chase resettled himself in the upholstered chair. "I have come to ask you some questions. I hope that you will share some information with me."

Did he imagine that Mr. Edkins glanced to the window and out to the yard where Minerva had so recently been?

"Has anyone else already quizzed you about that night?" Chase asked. *Damnation, what did you tell that woman?*

"There was a man at the house, soon after His Grace died, before I left. He came for only a day and asked questions of many of us."

"The magistrate?"

"I think so. I was so in shock that I did not much pay attention to his name and such. I didn't care for his manner with us. He did not ask questions so much as bark them, if you understand me."

"Did you answer his questions?"

Mr. Edkins assumed the bland expression that all servants knew how to wear. "Of course. Such as they were. He wanted to know what I knew about my master's death. The answer was nothing at all. I was asleep at the time. He also wanted to know my master's movements that day. I told him what I knew for certain because I had seen it. When he rose from bed, when he went below. I did not think it wise to report what I was told he would do, such as ride out or such as that. If I did not witness it, I did not tell this man it had happened."

"Wise of you. What you heard would happen or did happen may not have happened, and including that could complicate the information."

"Thank you, sir. Although I confess that I did it out of pique at this man's manner. I admit that my goal was to give him as little as required."

Chase stood. "Will you show me the lake? If you want to fish, you can. My questions will not take long, but they may be more specific than the magistrate's."

Mr. Edkins led the way through the house. He removed a rod and some equipment from a tall holder near the garden door. Together they exited the garden through a back portal and walked the fifty feet to the lake. Edkins set about preparing his rod while Chase took in the peaceful scene.

The valet cast his line. Chase sat on a large tree stump.

"Mr. Edkins, were any family members at Melton Park that day, or during the three days before?"

"I saw none and heard none. The butler would know better than I."

"The duke may have mentioned it while you tended to him, however."

Edkins moved his lure in a long, deep circle. "He mentioned no relative's name to me."

The man was answering the way he had answered the magistrate. Guarded. That alone piqued Chase's curiosity. Had Minerva received more forthright answers? She had no standing to ask, which alone may have garnered her more.

"Did anyone visit? Anyone at all? A neighbor, perhaps. A business associate. Even if you did not know the name and did not serve them in any way, were you aware of anyone like that being on the property?" He could find no other way to cover all eventualities.

Edkins studied his line. He made the lure bob. He appeared not to have heard the question.

"One," he finally said. "That afternoon. I looked out into the garden and saw His Grace with someone. A woman."

"One of his sisters?"

"I can't say. I don't think she entered through the house. I think perhaps she came in the garden from the back. I could not see her well. I only know it was a woman from the bonnet and such. They were among the trees in back, strolling."

"Do you think he expected her?"

"I wouldn't know. He talked with her, though. He did not make her leave."

A woman. Damnation. "Have you ever seen someone who you think was this woman? In London, for example?" He added the last to appease his conscience that he was not really asking if Edkins had seen that woman a half an hour ago, in his own sitting room.

"I can't say that I have, sir."

That was not the same thing as saying he hadn't.

"That evening, after dinner, did the duke return to his chambers? Did you serve him?"

"No. I was in the dressing room dozing as was my habit. He came up very late most nights. I rarely prepared him for sleep before midnight. Then suddenly it was morning and he had never come. We soon knew why." Sadness flexed his expression. He squinted behind the spectacles.

"What do you think happened?"

"I think he fell. It is not safe up there. That wall would not protect him much if he slipped. I don't know why he went up there at night like that, with it so dangerous."

He went because up there at night, nothing existed except him and the vast night sky. Uncle Frederick had not been an especially spiritual man, except for his habit of taking walks under the stars.

Chase could think of nothing else to ask for now. He stood to take his leave. Just then the line tensed and dipped down. With a big smile Edkins began pulling in his catch.

"It will be a small one," he said. "Small lake means small fish. But I don't need much for my supper."

"I will leave you to it. I will see my way out. Thank you for seeing me." He let himself into the garden and strode to its front portal. A woman had visited the duke on the day he died. Hell.

Minerva let the horse eat grass while she sat on a felled log and watched the stream bubble past her. In spring this spot would be lovely, with wildflowers making broad ribbons of color. Now some yellow and orange felled leaves kept the growth from being only barren branches.

She heard the horse coming toward her. She probably should not have stayed the way Chase had demanded. She would not have either, except she hoped to discover if he learned more than she did, or even quite as much.

Mr. Edkins had not been very forthcoming, but then her questions hardly were pointed enough to get good answers. Unlike Chase, who probably announced he was conducting inquiries, she had used her friendship with Mrs. Fowler the cook as a pretext for her call. She'd had to weave her curiosity about the family and the duke and the death into general chatting and gossip. That might have not been such a bad thing, however. The one bit of useful information that emerged from Mr. Edkins had slipped out. A startling piece of information. She debated whether to share it with Chase.

The horse stopped near her gig. Chase dismounted and tied the reins to the back of the conveyance. He walked over to her and offered his hand. "I will bring you back to the village."

She allowed him to help her to stand. "What makes you think I need to return to any village?"

"I saw your companion there. I assume you need to collect her at least."

He handed her into the seat, then took the reins and

climbed in beside her. They rolled down the lane with his horse in tow.

"What are you doing here?" he asked.

"What are you doing here?"

A sigh of strained forbearance breathed beside her. "I came down to Melton Park with my cousin for a few days."

"The duke is in residence?"

"He is."

How inconvenient. Her plan to ask the housekeeper for a tour of the house no longer would work. She might as well return the gig, and find transportation back to London.

"What did Edkins tell you?" he asked.

"Very little. We mostly talked about old times and his memories."

"Memories of what? How old?"

"Fairly old. Mrs. Fowler, and his master. He admired the last duke an inordinate amount, seeing as how as valet he would see him in very human terms, what with bathing and such. He told me the man was a genius. That was the word he used. Eccentric, quite odd at times, but a genius who did not suffer fools gladly and most men in comparison were fools."

"My uncle was very kind about that. Fools rarely knew he thought them as such. Did he talk about my uncle's businesses?"

"In a general way. I'm not sure Mr. Edkins understood what they were. Inventions, he said. Financial things. Buildings. Shipping. He mentioned that there could be arguments over all of that. Some of the other investors could become demanding." She did not mention the specific example he had used.

"One of those business partners may well have had

cause to want to see him gone. If one had cheated, for example. I will be looking into that."

"When you get to it on the list, you mean." If business partners needed investigating, she would be at a disadvantage, since she did not even know what businesses the duke had invested in. She did not think it was one of those business associates, however. Not exactly.

He drove the gig faster than she ever did, so they approached the village soon. He slowed it when the roofs came into view. "Are you staying at the inn here?"

"Only one night. We will leave this afternoon."

"Yet you surely intended to do more than chat with the duke's old valet. I expect you had some plan for gaining entry to Melton Park."

"Why would I want to do that?"

"That was not your plan? You came all this way only to carry the cook's well wishes to Edkins. You are a good soul."

"Thank you. I try to be. Although I hear Melton Park has a grand house, and wondered if the housekeeper ever gives little tours when the family is not in residence."

The gig rolled for at most a ten count. "I can get you in, of course," he said. "As my guest. Your companion too."

"I expect it is worth seeing, being such an important house."

"I did not know you had an interest in architecture. If so, you really must see it. Why don't you stay there tonight? We can examine that parapet together. It is of great architectural uniqueness."

She turned to see if he was serious. "How will you explain who I am to your cousin?"

He thought about that while the gig entered the main

lane of the village. "I will tell him that you are one of my agents, who aids me in inquiries on occasion."

"Your employee, in other words. I would prefer if you told him I am a partner on occasion. A woman who conducts her own inquiries but who partners with you when you require help."

"I am not going to say that I need help, least of all from you. If we do this at all, you are an occasional employee or you are not coming."

"If you are going to be so prideful, I will do it that way. It might be best. As a partner I might have to eat with you and the duke and be bored. As an employee I can eat with the servants and actually learn something."

"As my employee you must inform me of anything you learn."

"Are you going to pay my fees? If not, I am not an employee. We are only pretending."

He thought about that. "If your fees are reasonable—"

"Twenty pounds."

"*Twenty pounds*?"

"A day."

He laughed. "No one is going to pay a woman that much for *anything*."

"Is it too much? Oh, dear. I should have learned the expected amount, I suppose. What are your fees?"

He didn't answer. Not twenty pounds, apparently.

"It might be best if we left it at pretending," she said. "I will inform you of anything I think you need to know."

That was not what he had demanded. "We will need a name for you. It would be best if you are not known to my cousin as a legatee, just yet."

"I will be Mrs. Rupert. That will be easy for all of us to remember, since I live on that street. Ah, there is Elise in front of the church, waiting for my return. I will keep her from being with others, lest she give away the ruse."

They collected Minerva's friend, Miss Turner, from the churchyard, and their baggage from the small inn. Chase hired a man to return the gig to its owner, then hired a carriage to take them all to Melton Park.

There he handed the women over to the housekeeper, calling them guests so they would receive good chambers. Once they were gone, he headed for the library. He found Nicholas standing in its doorway, watching the skirts go up the big staircase.

"Who are they?"

"One is Mrs. Rupert and the other is her companion, Miss Turner. Mrs. Rupert does some small inquiries for me on occasion. The sort it is better to have a woman do."

"I assume she is the gray ensemble with intelligent eyes, and not the pretty one in blue."

"The pretty one in blue is not for you, if you were thinking that way. Mrs. Rupert would not look kindly on any interference with that girl."

"She looked to be at least twenty. Hardly a girl, although she has a freshness to her. It was charming how she gawked at the reception hall's appointments."

"Whenever I see all those African masks, I'm inclined to gawk too." He threw himself onto a divan and stretched out his legs. "I visited Edkins today."

"Uncle's valet? How is he?"

"Flourishing. He has a fine property on a good bit of land with a lake in back. He spends his afternoons fishing for his dinner. He did well."

"One more person who benefited handsomely. Between

those who came into money and those who didn't, the list of motives only gets longer."

"How much easier if he had done it the normal way and left it all to you. No one would have liked that, but it is so commonplace I doubt the family would be arming themselves for battle now."

"Perhaps he wanted to spare me the effort to figure out all the allowances they would all expect of me. Did Edkins have anything of interest to reveal?"

He saw a female visitor here that day. He did not know why he chose not to share that yet. It felt disloyal. He knew in his blood that whatever had happened, Nicholas had played no role. Yet he had been equally sure of another man once only to learn he was wrong. He hated how being disillusioned once had him guarding information now.

"I will invite Mrs. Rupert and her friend to dine with us," Nicholas said. "It will be a distraction from all of that." He gestured to a stack of papers on a desk.

"Tomorrow, perhaps. Tonight she dines below so she can meet the servants."

"Do you think she will learn something new? The magistrate was most thorough in questioning them."

"If you were a young footman or chambermaid and you thought you might have heard something in the night but were not sure, would you admit as much to that magistrate? After he questioned them, most of the women left the study in tears."

"Do you believe they might confide in Mrs. Rupert instead?"

"Possibly, if there is anything to confide to begin with. She has a way about her that seems to encourage it."

"You speak of her with admiration in your voice."

"She is very useful."

"Useful, is she? How practical. She is also very attractive.

Captivating eyes. You must have admired them as well as her wits." His gaze turned inward, as if he conjured up the memory of her. "Yes, most attractive."

Chase did not care for the tone of that private musing.

"Have you kissed her?" Nicholas asked.

"No." Yes, but she wasn't interested in more of that. But then Nicholas was a duke. Presumably any woman would be interested if a duke kissed her. Even Minerva.

"So that means you do not have a tendre for her. If you did you would have at least tried to kiss her." Nicholas clasped his hands behind his head, splayed his bent arms on the back of the divan, and sent a hooded look to Chase. "We will definitely invite them to dine with us."

Chase knew that look. "I must leave you. I have matters to address here. By all means invite them to dinner. To-morrow night."

Nicholas just smiled. Chase went to the door.

"Just one thing," Chase said before leaving. "I said her companion was not for you. Neither is Mrs. Rupert."

Nicholas laughed. "I can't believe you are warning me off."

"Believe it."

Chapter Thirteen

Minerva tried not to gawk the way Elise did, but it proved difficult. Algernon had been well-to-do, even wealthy by most standards, but dukes lived a different existence from what that old life had experienced. Not only was the house impressive in size and appointments, but Chase's uncle's own taste had crowded it with strange, exotic items such as she had never seen before.

The masks and spears on the walls of the reception hall were only the beginning. A zoo of stuffed animals filled the first landing. A tiger, a giraffe, an animal she did not know the name of—the finest taxidermy she had ever seen growled and strode.

The housekeeper, Mrs. Young, noticed her attention. "Most of them were once alive here. He had a section of the park for them. The last duke was very fond of such exotic creatures. Not so much the usual kind, except horses. So when one of them died—these sort, not the horses—he had them made up to stay here."

It sounded almost sentimental, as if the late duke had truly cared for his menagerie and it had not merely been the indulgence of a man who could buy anything. She wondered if he had named each one.

"I trust this will suit you," Mrs. Young said when she

opened the door to Minerva's chamber on the third level. They had reached the second story and this door was tucked into a nook at the back. "Your companion will have a similar one on the other side. Mr. Radnor told me to put you here, not above."

"Above would have been fine," Minerva said. "As an employee I am accustomed to making do and eating with the staff."

"He said here. Not a servant as such, are you, even if you are in employment." The housekeeper gestured and a girl slipped in. "This is Sarah. She will serve the two of you. She has a way with hair, even if she is not a lady's maid."

Sarah beamed a smile before assuming a demure demeanor.

"I'll leave her to settle you in." Mrs. Young turned to Elise. "If you come with me, I will show you your chamber."

Minerva waited until they left, then gave the high mattress a subtle press. Very nice. She peered out one of the windows. A bit of garden showed below, then a paddock, and beyond that some fields.

Sarah lifted her valise and set it on a stool. Minerva noticed. "I'll unpack myself. There isn't much there." She had only planned to be gone from town three nights, so she had few garments.

"Would you like me to prepare a bath, or help you undress for a rest?"

She wanted the maid to leave so she could look through the house while she had the chance. "No, but I'm sure Miss Turner would enjoy that bath. Tell her I said she should rest afterward. Also, while I will dine with the servants, Miss Turner will take her meal in her chamber."

Sarah left. Minerva was just about to check that the

landing was clear when a knock sounded on her door. She opened it, expecting Elise.

Instead a footman stood there. "For you, Mrs. Rupert." He offered her a folded paper.

Minerva opened it. *There is a back stairs behind the doors at the end of each landing. Take it to the top. I'll meet you there. CR.*

"Do you want to send a reply?" he asked.

"No."

Minerva waited until the footman was well gone. Then she slipped out to find the back stairs.

From the parapet walk one could see for miles, even beyond the low hills that flanked the estate's land on the north. Dark clouds gathered there. They appeared to be moving east, not south, and Chase doubted storms would ruin this fair day.

He kept one eye on the door that gave way to the interior of the house, wondering if Minerva would come up here. He assumed so. She would want to see the spot where Uncle Frederick had gone over. It was the only reason she had left London.

She had not liked hearing Nicholas was in residence. She had probably planned to ask the housekeeper for a tour. He imagined the housekeeper showing two young women the public rooms, and not much noticing when one of them loitered to admire the appointments. He pictured Minerva rejoining the tour twenty minutes later, apologetic about getting lost or distracted. That would give her enough time to find the stairs to the roof, run up them, examine the parapet, and run down.

She was resourceful, he had to give her that. Clever. He wondered what the valet had told her while she visited and chatted about old times in his master's home. If Edkins had mentioned that woman in the garden, she would be on her guard. After all, she could have been the woman in question.

Did you kill him? He did not think she had. She was going through too much effort to try and determine if anyone had, and if so who.

He could simply ask her, and assess whether he thought she spoke the truth. He had been tempted to several times after their conversations became familiar. He hadn't because—he laughed to himself. He hadn't because if he did, she might speak lies that he was only too willing to believe. That was what wanting a woman does to a man.

So he was left to his own judgment. If he did not want her, he would trust it more. He would not suspect he found excuses for her, or put too much faith in his intuition and instincts—his inner sense, as she called it—instead of hard facts. Any investigator became worthless when feelings trumped information.

Did you kill him? He all but heard his uncle's voice that day seven years ago, up here behind this parapet, while they looked down on the land and discussed some new investment the duke had made. Right in the middle of a small pause, as if it were part of the conversation, the question had come. He had been waiting for it. If anyone had the right to ask, it was Uncle Frederick.

No, not exactly. But also, yes. There had been no choice but to explain it then. He found some relief in doing so. Perhaps his uncle had known he would.

"It took me a long time to find the door to the staircase. It is well hidden." The voice sounded right by his shoulder, pulling him out of the reverie. He had not even heard Minerva arrive. Behind her, the door to the stairs stood open now. "Where did it happen?"

He propped an elbow on the parapet and looked at her. She still wore her gray ensemble. It did not flatter her, but it did not hurt her either. If anything its lack of color and decoration allowed her own presence to dominate. Instead of noticing some bright hue or embroidery, the only thing to admire was the woman herself.

He allowed himself a moment to do so, watching her dark eyes light with interest while she gazed out over the land below and beyond, distracted now from the mission that had brought her up here.

"What makes you think I invited you up to see where it happened?"

She tore her attention away from the vista. "There could be no other reason, and you did say you would get me in."

"There could most definitely be another reason, and you know it."

Her gaze went back to the vista. Her cheeks took on some color.

"Come with me," he said. "I will show you."

He led her along the parapet to a place above the back of the building. "You can walk all the way around," he explained. "As you can see the walkway is narrow, but not precarious. It was built to be walked upon by members of the household. Since my uncle came up here frequently, he ensured it was kept in order."

"There are even these benches here, for viewing. That must be pleasant on a summer night."

"At parties, young gentlemen often invite young ladies up here for that purpose." And others.

"It appears secure and well maintained. I do not feel in danger of tripping over loose stones. Was the weather wet that night? Was there snow or ice?"

"It was fair."

"Have you been up here before?"

"On occasion."

"With him?"

"At times on my own."

"Or with a young lady during a party?"

"That too."

He stopped. Someone had painted a thick line on the parapet wall above where the body had lain. Probably the magistrate. It had been done that day before they moved him.

He looked over the wall. His mind imagined his uncle's body, and blood.

Minerva peered over too, but being shorter could not see much. She rose on her toes and stretched her neck. He stepped around her, grabbed her waist, and lifted her until she sat in the crook of his arm. She turned her body so she had a good seat and held on to his shoulders while she peered down.

Which brought her breast onto his face.

"It is a long fall." She veered back, as if noticing her own vulnerability, or perhaps the position of her breast. "You can put me down now."

He did so. She smoothed her skirt, then stepped away from the wall and gave him a good look. "Was he as tall as you?"

"Almost."

"That wall is far less protective of someone your height than it is of a person like me. I am very secure behind it. But while it ends at my chest, it ends at your waist. It is a critical difference." She frowned. "I don't suppose I could entice you to see if it would be possible for you to fall over."

"Entice me how?"

"Excuse me?"

"You said entice me. I am curious how you would do that."

"With reminders that you want to know as much as I do."

"How boring." He turned to the wall, pressed against it, and tested his balance. He hung his arms over, as if trying to catch something that fell. He leaned farther, seeing if he even felt insecure, as if one more inch would send him over.

Suddenly the edge of the wall slammed his body and he found himself desperately grabbing it while his feet lost contact for an instant with the walkway.

A weight dragged him back. He took a deep breath, staring at the ground below while panic subsided. He stood upright and the weight disappeared.

Furious, he swerved around. "*What the hell.*"

She dared to look innocent. "You were in no danger. I had hold of your coat the entire time."

"As if a woman of your size could stop a man of my size from going forward."

"I did not push you nearly hard enough to send you over the wall."

"*Why did you push me at all?*"

"So we would learn what we needed to learn. We now know it is possible to push a man of your size over. No fisticuffs would be needed. No struggle. No need to hit him over the head first. Just one good push when he is at the wall and it could happen. Oh, it might require a bit more help, but a push alone would move his weight forward enough to unbalance him and make it possible."

"You could have informed me of your experiment first, damn it."

"We also know," she continued, as if she did not notice his anger, "that a woman alone could probably manage it.

I say probably because if I had really wanted you to fall over, I think I would have had to help more and I don't think I would be big enough. A woman with more weight and height and strength than I have, however . . ." She just let that hang there.

"You had no idea whether your little push might be more effective than you supposed. I could be dead right now and you would be looking down at my body thinking *Oh, dear, it appears I pushed too hard.*"

"I would not be thinking that at all."

"No. You would be thinking of how to convince the magistrate that it had not been deliberate."

That sapped the confidence out of her expression. "That is not true. I would be too distraught to recognize my own peril. However, you are correct. I should have warned you. You would have been on your guard then, and it would have been a much poorer experiment, but at least you would not believe that I put you at risk with nary a thought about it."

She appeared very sorry. So much that he felt bad about scolding her. He had to check the impulse to embrace her and reassure her that he had never been much at risk.

"We also learned something else," he said, by way of appeasement. "We know that it is most unlikely that he could go over without that push. There is no chance that he tripped, say, and lost his balance and plunged over."

"No chance at all, it seems to me."

In other words, the duke's death had not been an accident.

She walked away from the spot, taking the long way in so she would navigate the entire roof before returning to the door. He trailed right behind her. She felt him there. Still angry, but not as much now.

She stopped on the front of the house. The prospect was magnificent. Not many hills here, and beyond the stand of trees along the approaching lane she could see the road, and even villages and farmhouses in the distance.

"It is remarkable up here," she said. "I understand why he favored it. If I lived here I would come up several times a day."

Chase said nothing, just looked out as she did. She liked how sometimes they shared a companionable silence like this.

"Distraught?" The word came to her quietly, in a tone of amusement and curiosity. "I am flattered."

She would have to watch every word she spoke to him, since he apparently did.

"No matter what you think, I do not kill men with nary a concern."

"Concern is understandable. Distraught, however—"

"We did share some kisses. I would have a cold heart if I did not feel at least somewhat distraught."

Fingertips brushed down the side of her face, making her cheek quiver with a pleasant little shock. He took careful hold of her chin and turned her face so she could see him, and he her.

"About those kisses," he said. "Did I in some way frighten you?"

Her soul sighed. He wanted to know why she had reacted as she had.

"It was nothing you did. There is no blame on you."

"I don't understand."

Of course not. How could he? She had never talked about this with anyone. She never had to, because she had not been touched or kissed in years. She gazed down, because she could never speak of this if she looked at him. "I am not like other women. It is not in my nature to know that kind of pleasure or desire. Please accept this explanation. To say more is too embarrassing."

Putting it into words made it more real. She had long ago accepted and lived with the sad truth, yet admitting this out loud almost took the breath out of her.

That touch lifted her chin. "That is not true, Minerva. You were no more unmoved than I was. Do you think a man cannot tell what a woman is feeling?"

For a while she had known that pleasure with Chase. The renewal would only make the final result more disappointing. At some point, if matters progressed, she would again be the empty vessel tolerating a man's imposition. She never wanted to experience that again. Ever.

She should tell him he was wrong, that she had taken a taste to see if anything had changed for her, but only learned it had not. It would be a lie, but it would avoid more explanations.

"Perhaps you misunderstood because you wanted to."

His thumb stroked her lips. "Did I? Tell me I did and that those kisses moved you not at all and I will never again do it."

Never again. One word and that part of her could go back to sleep. A real anguish gripped her heart. That soft stroke on her lips raised a rebellion in her spirit against speaking. *Maybe . . . perhaps . . .*

His lips replaced his thumb. Warmer. Firmer. She closed her eyes and tried not to hope too much.

Wonderful how the sensations absorbed one, so there soon were no thoughts or fears. The pleasure was too physical and the intimacy too spiritual to allow for distracting worries. A wave of sensual wonder crashed through her, soaking the parched areas of her soul.

She did not mind the embrace. She welcomed it. She did not object when he moved her to one of those benches and took her on his lap. His increased ardor and the consuming kisses and firm caresses did not frighten her this time. She even enjoyed the way his exploring tongue made all of her tingle and sent delicious spirals down her insides. *Maybe . . .*

A madness took hold of her, one that craved more of this pleasure that seemed to get better with each moment. She reveled in the amazing freedom delirium created. She did not want to control herself. She did not know how. She lost hold on the final tether to her normal self, and accepted the wildness of her senses.

His hand on her chest made her ache for more. His fingers working the buttons of her pelisse created an exquisite impatience. Only his touch on her breast made the wonder pause. For a moment old memories, tired and sad, tried to claim her. She refused to allow them. *Not now. No.* He caressed her breast and an incredible pleasure aided her, overwhelming the caution and fear.

Glorious then. So glorious that she almost laughed from the joy she experienced. He knew just what to do, how to touch her and caress her body so she lost herself. She opened her eyes to the beautiful sky and felt as if she flew up there. She turned her gaze to his taut expression, so hard and firm in his passion, and kissed his face in a dozen places. It surprised her, then, when his hand stilled and his kisses ended.

"We cannot continue like this here."

She rested her forehead against his while the tightening spiral inside her slowly began to unwind. No, they could not. She rather wished they could.

He held here there for a long while. She did not want him to let her go. Eventually, however, she found the presence of mind to slip off his lap, so he would not have to ask her to. She rebuttoned her pelisse.

They stood and he took her hand. "Come with me."

Down those stairs they went. Past the attic level where the servants lived. She wondered if they came up here at night, to enjoy the cool air in summer or to have assignations. Down again, past the door she had used to get to the stairs. Down one more level. He opened a door.

"These are the family chambers. That one is mine." He pointed to a door visible from where they stood. "A few steps and here I am. A few more above and there you are." He closed the door, then took her face in his hands. "I want to visit you tonight. Will you permit it?"

"Yes." Right now, with the pleasure still echoing in her, she would have agreed to anything.

"At ten o'clock then. Be sure your maid is gone." He brought her back up the stairs. At the door to her own level, he kissed her deeply, then turned to retrace his steps.

Chapter Fourteen

"A most unfortunate accident." Mrs. Young kept saying that, whenever Minerva raised the matter of the duke's death. It proved effective in ending the topic for a spell, until she raised it yet again. Between failed attempts, she chatted about the grounds, the manor building, and other simple topics. It kept her from thinking about tonight.

The sensual stupor had passed over an hour ago, leaving her to question whether she should have encouraged him. Could she do this? Should she? The usual cautions about pregnancy and heartbreak did not occupy her mind. What did was the chance for horrible disappointment, in herself.

Her own failings might be overcome by courage alone. The man she had chosen for this initiation was the bigger question. Even now, sitting at this dinner, she had to force her mind not to dwell on the questionable wisdom of taking such a step with him of all men.

The housekeeper's quelling look at the other servants sent them back to their dinners. Silence reigned. Minerva was losing her patience. So much for trying to glean information through casual chatting. More directness would be required.

"No one is sure it was an accident. How likely is that? The walkway up there is wide enough, and in good condition. The wall is high enough. The weather was fair. The duke was familiar with that roof walk, and not going to do something stupid that would make him fall."

Big eyes turned on her, shocked that she pursued the subject.

"We don't speak of it," Mrs. Young said sharply.

"Perhaps you should. Eventually there will be those who demand you do. I am sure the new duke would want you to cooperate with them."

"We were all in bed," Sarah said.

"Were you all asleep? Did no one hear anything? Your chambers are right below that parapet. Whose are on that side of the building?"

More determined eating. She looked at each of them in turn. One red-faced blond girl finally raised her hand. "Mine is. Joan and I are right there."

Joan, a dark-haired young woman, barely paused in her meal. "I was asleep, as was you."

"That's true, Mrs. Rupert. I was asleep too. I heard nothing until there was all the noise in the morning down there. I looked out and—" Her eyes teared.

"That is enough, Susan." The housekeeper speared Minerva with a glare. "*We do not talk about it.* You can see how it upsets the servants. I will thank you to show some respect for the dead and not insist on treating this tragedy as a bit of common gossip."

Minerva gave up and spooned into her stew.

Meal finished and duties calling, the servants rose to leave. Minerva joined them. While bodies grouped and jostled, a subtle tap touched her arm. Beside her Joan averted her eyes but gestured toward the storeroom.

Both of them lagged behind the others. With Mrs. Young gone and the kitchen empty of all but the cook and her helpers, Joan nipped into the storeroom. Minerva followed and shut the door.

"I wasn't asleep like I said," Joan whispered.

"Did you hear something? An argument or altercation?"

"Not that. But maybe I heard something. I may a seen something too." She licked her lips. "I've been walking out with one of the footmen, and sometimes, we go up there when it is dark. To talk."

Minerva nodded encouragingly.

"Everyone knows the duke was fond of doing so too, so we go much later than he would. Only this night, we were up there—talking—and I thought I heard someone else, around the corner, over my chamber. Like a groan, then steps. I told my friend he should finish what he was, um, saying. So we were going back to the stairs, and when we were about to turn the corner the shadows moved there, like the door opened and closed. We waited a good while before slipping back down ourselves."

"Do you know the time of this?"

"We agreed to meet up there at midnight, and we had talked for a spell."

"I expect since you had broken house rules you did not tell the magistrate any of this."

"Not just that. I can't swear to it, can I? A sound I barely heard and my friend did not, then what looked like someone maybe going to the stairs. The magistrate kept asking if any of us were up there that night and I was scared if I said I was that he would think—he was talking like he wanted to say one of us had done this. I worried that my friend would be accused and hanged on nothing more than what maybe I heard and saw."

It was an understandable fear. One Minerva sympathized with. Didn't she herself worry that she would make a convenient person to accuse if her history were known?

Joan reached for the door latch. "Everyone says it was an accident. None of us think it was, but we all pretend it happened that way. I'm telling you this because you are the first to say maybe it wasn't. But I can't swear to any of it. I'll not repeat this even if you ask me to."

"You may have to someday, but for now I will not ask you to. I thank you for confiding in me, however."

Minerva pulled her little watch out of her pocket. Eight o'clock. In two hours she would see Chase and could tell him about this, without naming Joan. Only he wasn't coming to her chamber to talk about the duke's death, was he?

A mixture of excitement and foreboding gripped her stomach whenever she allowed herself to think of that assignation. She made her way up to her chamber, with little else on her mind.

Chase bided his time in the library with Nicholas, but the back of his mind ticked away the minutes. They had ridden out in late afternoon, and hence eaten late. Now they sprawled on divans and drank port.

"I think you are right. I need a better land steward." Nicholas spoke like a man reviewing thoughts on which his mind dwelled often. "Surely I can find one who will not press me to enclose. Or, if we must, have the imagination to find a way to do that without displacing too many families."

"Why not speak with Brentworth? His family's handling of it is often admired by the more generous among us."

Nicholas accepted that and drank more port. He looked

to the ceiling and the invisible beyond. "Did you go up there today?"

"I did." He would have to tell his cousin eventually. "I am convinced it was not an accident."

"Convinced?"

"I ran an experiment to see how hard it would be to push someone of his size over. If a person were determined and waited for the right moment, it would not be difficult at all."

"What kind of experiment?"

"I used my own body."

"Risky. I'm not sure I approve."

"It is the sort of thing those who conduct inquiries sometimes have to do."

"How did you manage it? Pretend you were pushed and allow physics to take its course? You might have gone over. I am sure now that I do not approve."

"I was never in danger. I had help. Someone held on to my coat to counterbalance the forward movement."

"Did you drag a footman up there? He might have done it wrong."

"Not a footman. Mrs. Rupert aided me." *She pushed me herself, damn it.* He glanced to the clock on the table. Fifteen minutes past nine. Any residual annoyance he felt about the experiment disappeared while his anticipation rose several notches.

"You trusted a woman's strength? That was not risky, it was reckless. You must promise me that you will never try anything like that again without having me present."

"There will be no need to repeat the exercise. As I said, I am convinced it was possible. He would have to be caught unawares, though. If he saw it coming, it would never work."

"I suppose anyone in the house could have done it."

"Or anyone who entered the house unseen. The family has not been removed from the list." How hard would it be to slip in? He would have to check tomorrow. Not tonight. *Twenty-five past nine.*

Nicholas downed the rest of his port, then sank low in the divan's cushions. "Hell of a thing. I look around this house, amazed it is mine. I assumed he would eventually remarry, and sire his heir. Everyone did."

"The reason you inherited still weighs on you. With time—"

"With time I will long for simply being a man about town, without all these obligations and responsibilities. I will miss attending balls where no one takes my expectations too seriously and I can flirt with women without having them calculating the riches that marriage will bring them."

"You can still do that. You just have to pick different women."

"Married ones, you mean. Or courtesans."

"Or ones who know you will never marry them."

Nicholas brightened a bit at the various options enumerated. "Ah, I forgot to tell you at dinner. I received a letter from Sanders today. He had been called upon by a solicitor engaged by Aunt Dolores, who took two hours to explain that I am duty bound to provide for her the way her brother did. He handed over a long list of everything she received in the last five years, even above and beyond her allowance which alone was handsome. It was down to the shilling."

"You are under no obligations."

Nicholas laughed. "As if you would be so brave as to say that to them."

"I'd be brave enough to explain that my situation did

not match Uncle Frederick's, so my generosity could not either." *Thirty-five minutes past nine.*

"Dolores will never listen to reason of that kind."

"You will find a way to settle with her in a way she accepts, I am sure. Deciding about the cousins will be harder."

Forty minutes past nine. Chase set his glass down with finality. He stifled a feigned yawn and added a stretch for good measure. "I think I will retire. There are things I must do in the morning."

"It is early for you. I hope you are not getting too old to drink the night away with me. If I am to pursue inappropriate women, I will expect your company."

"No, no. Merely tonight I keep yawning, so some sleep is in order."

"You aren't planning any more experiments with Mrs. Rupert tonight, are you?" He asked ever so blandly, but his eyes glinted with humor.

"No need. We are done with that," Chase said, just as blandly.

"Ah. Well, I trust you will have a good night."

Chase took the stairs two at a time. He threw open the door to his apartment and strode into the dressing room. Hot water already waited. He cast off his coats and made use of it. Then he sent away the servant assigned to act as his valet, and checked his pocket watch. Fifty minutes past nine.

They were the longest ten minutes he had ever experienced. He kept seeing her standing by her door, flushed and bright-eyed from passion, still vaguely amazed. He heard her deep sighs and felt her tentative kisses. He was half mad by the time his watch showed ten o'clock.

Up the back stairs he walked, reining in the desire that wanted to break in him like a tempest.

* * *

Ten o'clock. Minerva braced herself.

It had been a hellish hour. One of introspection and relentless rationality. She so wanted to be some other woman right now. A woman with a different history or at least a different desire.

Was there anything more cruel than to want something after years of not wanting, and to know you cannot have it?

The deciding factor had been picturing it. Seeing him here, and imagining being in that bed with him. Only it had not been Chase whose face hovered over hers. It had been Algernon's, and her whole spirit turned cold at the memory.

After that the madness of even considering this overwhelmed her.

She wiped her eyes. Stupid to have cried over this. Childish. Ridiculous to have allowed herself to let matters get this far. She had lost her mind.

The rap on her door came softly. The temptation not to open it almost won, but she rose and walked over. She would not be a coward now, when she had learned never to be in matters that really counted.

He stood there in the dimmest light, his shirt glowing and his face planes of shadows. Handsome. Strong, but in good ways. His strength never frightened her. He never used it the wrong way. She saw him take in that she still wore the gray ensemble. Then he looked in her eyes. His stance altered slightly. He knew.

She walked back into her chamber. She thought he might not follow, but he did. She looked out the window into the dark because she found she could not look at him. She felt him there, though. His presence filled the chamber, touching her invisibly.

"I am sorry," she said. "I am not sure I can do this. I regret letting you think that I could." It was not how she had rehearsed it. She had planned to say something absolute. This tentative rejection came out instead, due to the tingles emerging in her against her will.

"A lady always has the right to change her mind." She heard his steps and glanced over to see he had moved closer to her. "Have you? It isn't clear."

She had hoped he would be so angry that he just left. She faced him, intending to enumerate all the reasons she should not do this.

The sight of him silenced that argument before she spoke one word. He looked unbearably handsome, so much so that her breath caught. His gaze compelled her own and a low, tight thrum started in her body.

"Have you?" he asked again, lowly.

"I don't know." She barely got the words out. She glanced at her bed. "This is not the same as this afternoon. This is . . . different. I am afraid I won't . . . enjoy it the way I did the kisses today." She gritted her teeth, and forced herself to be honest. "It is not you. It is me. The way I am."

He cocked his head, as if trying to understand what she meant. She thought she saw some comprehension enter his eyes. "I think you are wrong about that. However, if you don't enjoy it, we will stop."

They just stood there for what felt was forever. He waited for her to decide. She remained incapable of thinking clearly enough to do so. Where had all those sensible conclusions from the last hour gone? She didn't even try to remember them.

"Perhaps," she said. "If you were to kiss me, maybe . . ."

"It sounds like you want me to seduce you. It would be better if the choice were yours without persuasion,

Minerva. I want to kiss you. I want you to the point of madness right now, but only if you want me too."

Lies. Just his eyes were persuasive. And his lean form and handsome face. Without a touch or a word, he had established sensual bonds with her, that he seemed to pull. "I only thought that a small reminder . . ."

"I will gladly remind you of the afternoon, but I would like you to come here to me, so I know you are sure."

She wasn't sure. Not really. Even her arousal could not obscure her mind and memories so thoroughly as to make her certain. Yet she wanted this. Very much wanted it. Right now, with his power reaching out to her, she believed that maybe this would be a wonderful thing, so wonderful that nothing could ruin it.

Nervous, she took one step. She took another and, oddly, much of her trepidation disappeared. Resolve took its place. He had asked her to make her choice explicit. Had he guessed that doing this would exhilarate her? More secure with each step she walked to him.

With one long stride he intercepted her before she finished, and pulled her into an embrace. The first kiss was careful and sweet. The next one less so. Excitement spun through her and she was glad when their embrace tightened and their passion brought more kisses, dozens of them, shared and separate, while they released some of the madness descending. Somehow, while still holding her and kissing her, he shed his shirt. The sensation of his warmth, of his skin under her hands and lips fascinated her so much she had to press kisses on his chest, just to experience it again. While she did he kissed her neck and brought one hand to caress her breast.

One note of reality plucked in her. One instant of hesitation followed. He must have sensed it. He moved his hand away. Furious with herself, she moved his hand back where it had been and kissed him hard.

His slow smile formed against her lips. He caressed her breast. The sensation had her rising on her toes. The most subtle touch, yet her whole body responded. Titillating pleasure trickled down her core, more compelling than an overwhelming onslaught. It increased slowly, absorbing all of her attention. She wanted to moan from how good it felt.

"It is better if stays, petticoats, and dresses are not in the way," he said in her ear while he nibbled and kissed it.

"We will have to stop. I don't want to stop." She dared not stop.

"We won't stop. I'll do it."

"I hope you know how to—oh, I see you do." Her dress loosened. She had not noticed his hand at work back there. A few minutes later she stepped out of it.

Good to his word, they did not stop. Even the stays caused little delay, considering she found it hard to stand now. One touch on her bare breast and she did moan in an exhale of wonder.

She did not remember actually moving to the bed, but then they were there, his caresses moving down her body, his mouth finding her naked chest and breasts and stomach. Nothing could enter the small place she existed in. Nothing in her head or her past. Only he and she and astonishing sensations lived there. And joy. Each new pleasure brought a smile to her spirit.

"Come here." He rolled onto his back and brought her with him, so she was above him. She straddled his hips, feeling his phallus between her thighs. She gazed down at his face, then bent to kiss him. He took her breasts in his hands, then moved her forward and used his mouth. She was relieved that she would not have to worry about the moment he covered her, and imprisoned her with his body. It entered her besotted mind that sparing her that might have been his intention.

Their position caused his phallus to prod at her suggestively. "Do people ever . . . like this, the way we are . . ."

"Yes."

"Perhaps . . ."

"If you want. When you want."

She bent her head and looked down between their bodies. "I don't know how I . . ."

"I will help, but you will control it. You can stop if you want. If you find that you don't enjoy it." When she nodded, he lifted her, and positioned her body so he began entering.

The sensation intrigued her. She had never welcomed that fullness before. Her body ached to absorb more of him and bind him to her. She slowly lowered herself more, then more yet. He exhaled deeply when finally they were joined.

"That was too slow for you, wasn't it?"

"Tonight is not about me. The rest is up to you too."

She nestled down, so he was deeper yet. She pulsed where he stretched her, making her squirm. His expression tightened. Her movements created profoundly deep pleasure that kept increasing. Her sense of herself narrowed only to that demanding sensation. Soon she was rising and falling in an effort to take him deeper yet. Her whole body ached for more even though surely there could never be more. Her mind stretched toward something just out of reach. Something frightening in its power.

He grasped her hips and helped her rise and fall. The fury engulfed them both. Time and place disappeared until she tasted a rare moment of bliss before her spirit gave up the quest.

He pulled her into his arms and held her while her deep breaths feathered his ear. They lay entwined while he became aware of time again. He luxuriated in the press of her body on his, and the silken strands of her hair on his shoulder.

Her head moved. He opened his eyes a slit and realized she was looking down at herself. She shifted slightly.

"Are you uncomfortable?" he asked.

"Not uncomfortable. Just very . . . naked."

He moved her aside, sat up, and rearranged the bed-clothes so she would be covered. For good measure he got up and grabbed her chemise, in case she wanted that too. He turned back to the bed with the garment in his hands to find her wide eyes examining him.

He returned to her side and tucked the covers around her. "You have never seen a man undressed before, have you?"

"Not totally."

"And yourself?"

"Not totally."

"If you had not wanted—"

"I rather enjoyed your undressing me, and being like this. I liked feeling you against me. It seemed a bit wicked, and since I am being naughty I thought I might as well get full benefit of it."

"That was your thinking, was it?"

"When I was thinking at all." She rose up on one arm so she could see his face. "Of course I am thinking now, quite a bit. Your restraint on my behalf was heroic. I did not even know men could hold back like that. I just assumed their need required quick resolution."

He did not know what to say to her. Not what his mind cursed out, that was certain. It sounded as if nothing more than quick resolutions occurred in her past. He had suspected as much. Her claims of not being normal when it came to sensuality had made no sense, since the evidence showed she was very normal. She had merely not known pleasure because no man had given her the time or made the effort.

She poked at his side. "The truth now, so you get full credit."

"If you must know, it was damned heroic." He smiled when she laughed. "It almost killed me."

"Thank you." Such depth in her eyes when she said that. "I will always be grateful that you showed me I might . . . that I was not so different."

"So you enjoyed it after all?"

"Oh, yes. Couldn't you tell?" Her brow puckered. "Did you?"

"What a question. Of course. Couldn't *you* tell?"

"Well, you seemed to. You were able to finish. I did not ruin it for you."

Her words stunned him. He flipped her onto her back and looked down at her. "Forgive me, but . . . are you saying your husband could not finish?"

She nodded. "Other than a few times at the beginning of our marriage."

"He was impotent? And he blamed *you*?"

She just looked at him.

The scoundrel. Real anger gripped him. This man had made his young wife think his own physical problems were her fault. From the sounds of it, he hardly helped matters with his expectations of a *quick resolution*. He had probably turned the marriage bed into a place of nightmares.

"Listen to me, Minerva. You had nothing to do with his problem. He knew it, too. It did not start with you, I would wager. His ignorance in how he treated you probably made it worse, but that is not your fault either. It was ignoble of him to blame you in any way. Stupid and unforgiveable. It was not you. It was never you. It was him."

He could picture those nights, much as he would rather not. The anger. Her dread. No wonder she experienced arousal like a girl. Of course those first kisses in her library had confused her so much she abruptly ended them. For years she had been told she was so cold she made a man impotent. If the man were not already dead, he would thrash him senseless.

She caressed his face. "It is in the past. It may take me a while to appreciate just how thoroughly it is now. I assumed something about myself, and now I know I was wrong. That is a great gift."

"No. You have it wrong. Backward. You gave me yourself. You gave your passion. That is the gift. You owe me nothing, least of all gratitude." He kissed her deeply, then gathered her into his arms and a peaceful silence.

She fell asleep soon. He waited until she dozed soundly before leaving. He looked down at her before going to the door. No wonder she had changed her name.

She awoke in the earliest hours to find herself alone. His presence still drenched the chamber, however. And her bed. She felt him there as if he still embraced her.

She rose and pulled the drapes so she might watch the dawn. A new day would start soon, in so many ways. She looked out the window, waiting for it.

It was never you. It was him. At first she had regretted that they had allowed Algernon's specter to shadow their night. However, when Chase said those words, so forcefully, with such certainty—it had crystalized her own thoughts and reactions, and given voice to something she had dared not claim. She had long ago realized that all the rest had been his fault too, but with her utter absence of passion or pleasure—she had no experience, and could not know. Her deadened responses said the blame had indeed been hers. That she was lacking in the most essential part of femininity. Inadequate. Deformed.

It had taken five years to even begin to wonder if maybe she had it wrong. Dreams at first. Then her attraction to Chase made her truly hopeful. Now she knew for certain. Algernon had robbed her of many things, but this had been the worst. This was the one repercussion of that bad marriage that she had not been able to escape on her own.

She had not lied. She would forever be grateful to Chase. But, as she watched the black of night change to the misty silver of dawn, and saw the trees begin to take form, she knew that while he had been the right man for tonight, he was not the right one for anything more. Not even another tonight.

All those arguments against him that passion had obscured presented themselves again, fully clothed in their rationality. Worse, he may now be curious about her marriage, and ask her about it. Or ask others. Any chance that her old life would escape inquiry had just become less likely.

She left the drapes open, but returned to her bed, to await the sunrise. She inhaled what was left of his scent, imagined his embrace, and dwelled within the night's magic for a few minutes more.

Chase wore the happy mood of a man well sated when he descended the stairs and entered the morning room. Nicholas looked up from his mail upon his entry.

"You have risen early," Nicholas observed. "My excuse is I barely slept. What is yours?"

"I retired early. Remember?" Chase examined the sideboard, then filled a plate. Coffee already waited when he sat.

Nicholas continued perusing his mail. "Early though you are, you are too late to see off Mrs. Rupert. Rude of you. However, I took your place. I promised her that dinner when I return to London."

The news caught Chase while he was raising his cup. He paused a second, surprised.

"You did know she was leaving, I assume."

"Of course. Just not so early."

"She sent her maid down to ask for a carriage to be hired and brought for her and her friend. The butler had the sense to offer one of mine instead, so off they went." Nicholas turned another letter. "She said she had another assignment waiting and could not dally here, since her assistance to you was finished."

"She said all of that, did she?" Chase dug into his breakfast.

"Well, I asked. Her departure seemed hasty to me. And I was planning that dinner tonight." Nicholas set the stack of letters to one side. "She was most emphatic that we not disturb you, the way I suggested. I would suspect the two of you had a falling out, except she appeared not the least bit vexed. In fact she looked very contented. As did you when you entered this chamber."

Chase kept eating. Let Nicholas probe, in his unsubtle way. Minerva's assistance *was* over, for all intents and purposes. She had met with the servants. She merely had not told him what she had learned. And they had both concluded the duke had not fallen accidentally. In short, Melton Park no longer was of interest to her. She had learned all she probably would ever learn from it.

It thus made perfect sense that she had left. So why was his contentment much diminished now, replaced by a sharp annoyance? He had expected—he wasn't sure what. A few words at least. A secret smile. If she needed to leave, a note perhaps.

Hell, whom was he lying to except himself. He had expected far more than any of that. Another night, at least. Additional *contentment,* for both of them. Perhaps talk of even more, once they returned to London. He had no right to expect any of that, but it had seemed to him that one night was not adequate, to say the least.

He looked up to find Nicholas watching him. He set his fork down.

"I am going to make some of my own inquiries of the servants today. I should get to it." He made to leave.

"Sit a moment longer, if you will. You see, the oddest thing happened while they were leaving. I had handed them both into the carriage, and the young one, Miss Turner, examined the carriage's appointments with those pretty blue eyes of hers. 'Oh, my,' she said. 'Have you ever seen anything like it, Minerva?'" Nicholas leaned in. "What a coincidence, that Mrs. Rupert's given name is the same as one of our legatees. The one you have found. It is not a common name."

"It is not an uncommon name either. If the name were

Polyhymnia or Terpsichore, that would be a most peculiar coincidence. Now, I must be on my way, so I can—"

"Not yet. Please, indulge me lest I wonder all day."

Chase settled back in his chair.

"Was that in fact Minerva Hepplewhite?"

Nicholas *would* ask bluntly and leave no room for dissembling. "Yes."

"Ah."

Chase began rising again. Nicholas again gestured for him to sit.

"Why was she here?"

"She has a pointed interest in Uncle's death. Understandably, since it affected her so completely."

"If it was not an accident, she might be seen as a likely object of inquiry herself, I assume."

"That too. So she wanted to see for herself where it happened."

"And you arranged that. How good of you. Here I thought you had brought that woman here, no matter what her name, so you might seduce her. I thought perhaps she had not departed this morning so much as run away from your intentions."

"I do not importune women, if that is what you are saying." *I am not Phillip, damn it.*

"No, you don't. Her contentment, and yours, convinced me that no importuning was involved. I am relieved. I have some responsibility to women under my roof. I'm not sure I like that you are taking up with one of the women from the will, though."

"I am not taking up with her. She left, didn't she?"

"She did indeed."

"Then we are done here." Chase stood and gave his cousin a quelling frown.

"For someone who conducts inquiries, you do not like one when it is aimed at you," Nicholas said.

"Is that what you call this? It sounded to me like a drawing room matron's idle curiosity. Leave the inquiries to me, Cousin. You lack finesse." He strode out, not at all contented anymore.

"Are you feeling well?" Elise asked. "You appear sad and have been silent since we left the estate."

Minerva had been dwelling on the night before, fixing the memories securely in her mind. She was not sad, so much as wistful. She gathered her emotions so she might not show them so much. "Let us pass the time discussing what we learned at that house. You can tell me what you saw and heard."

"I'd rather talk about the house itself. Such space and luxury. I don't think I'll ever see the likes of it again."

She indulged Elise for an hour, then they retreated into their own thoughts.

She rarely spoke again, all the way back to London over the next three days. She accepted by the first evening that it might take a while to overcome her feelings about Chase, and what she had briefly known and now rejected.

As soon as the coach stopped in front of her home, she sought out her own chamber.

"Are you ill?"

The question pulled her out of a reverie in which her time at Melton Park repeated over and over. She looked behind her to see Beth closing the door. The image proved filmy. She had not even realized she'd been weeping.

"Elise said you have not been yourself."

The emotions started rising in her body, almost taking her breath away. "I have been very foolish, Beth."

"That man? Did you let him kiss you?"

To admit it had been more than kisses would only upset Beth. "Do not blame him."

Beth sat beside her on the edge of the bed. "Not the best choice on your part, under the circumstances. Not the right man to try that with."

"I know that."

"Not a man to get sweet on, I told you."

"You did at that."

An arm came around her. "Well, there's no sense to these things, is there?"

That embrace, so familiar and caring, broke her. Soft arms enclosed her while she wept onto Beth's shoulder.

Chapter Fifteen

Chase remained at Melton Park two more days. One night he left after dinner, then pretended to be a person entering the house without anyone's awareness. He left his horse down the lane in the trees, and approached on foot. Even with the servants up and about, he managed to get all the way to the parapet without being seen.

He had long conversations with the land steward and the grooms. Minerva had pursued the other servants for information. He would have to find out what she learned.

Which meant he would have to see her. She might not welcome that. He could all but hear her putting it into words. *We should not have done this*. Probably not, but he did not regret it for a minute, no matter what complications it brought.

She might, however. No matter what drew them together, the situation meant they should stay apart. He knew that, damn it. But what existed between them had nothing to do with reasoning.

He still simmered when he thought about her. Even upon his return to London she was not far from his mind.

His third morning back in town he left his chambers to go claim his horse in the stable in the nearby mews. As he approached the stable a tall, young, blond man blocked his path. He looked the fellow over.

"I know you," he said, searching his mind. "You are one of the grooms at Whiteford House."

"Was one, for a few days."

"Have you taken employment here?"

He shook his head. "I'm to give you a message from my mum. She said to meet her in Portman Square today at three o'clock. She wants to talk to you."

"Who is your mother?"

"She is Miss Hepplewhite's housekeeper."

He meant Beth. This was Beth's son. "I will be there."

The young man slipped down the mews and seemed to disappear. Chase went into the stable to get his horse. This fellow had been another one of Minerva's sets of eyes in Whiteford House during the house party. He wondered how many there had been.

He found Beth strolling along the park's perimeter. He recognized the big cap with its deep brim even before he saw how her stout form fit his memories. He swung off his horse and approached her.

She looked around. "I guess we can talk here. Not too many others about right now."

They walked a few minutes in silence.

"I'm of two minds about this," she finally said. "Minerva came home in a state I have not seen in years. She blames herself. I blame you."

"I accept the blame."

"Do you now? Won't do much good, will it?" She walked on, her steps heavy plods on the path. "That husband of hers ruined her. She didn't tell you that, did she?"

"She told me some of it."

"He was a brute. He got cruel when he drank and he drank a lot. I only stayed in his service because of my boy. Not many houses will let you have a young boy with you."

He reached out and touched Beth's arm so she stopped walking. He looked down at her. "A brute, you said. He hit her?"

"Hit her? He *beat her*. He brought this innocent girl home as his wife and for two months or so it was normal, but then——" She lifted a corner of her apron and dried her eyes.

Innocent, and all but orphaned. No family to turn to. Finley went looking for a victim. That is why he chose her.

"She blamed herself. She tried to please him. She became quiet and fearful, shrinking away like a dog that's been kicked. Nothing would stop him though. I would go to her and find her all bruised, weeping. Then one day she stopped crying, like that part of her had died. She told me she believed he liked to see her crying and pleading. That he enjoyed it, and she would not give him that satisfaction. He only got worse after that, but she didn't seem to care."

His mind recoiled at what she described. His jaw clenched so hard he couldn't speak. If Finley were not already dead, he'd——

"She grew up fast," Beth said. "It changed her, not all to the good. Then the miracle happened."

"Miracle?"

"One night when we were in London—he rarely brought her up here, and even then never let her go out. We were up here and he got drunk and took after her. I feared he would kill her. The next day, after he'd left the house, a boy come to it, asking for the woman of the house. She was in no condition to be seen, but she went to the threshold and this boy hands her a box, then left. It contained money. Gold coins. We neither of us could imagine who sent it. We waited for someone to arrive and say there'd been a mistake, but no one ever did. If that weren't a miracle I don't know what one is."

"And so she left?"

"As did I and my boy, as soon as we returned to Dorset. We lived in one chamber together at first, while she found a way to get a separation. She bought a pistol and learned how to use it and took it everywhere, even to bed, in case he tried to come and get her and force her back. Fortunately he died soon after he was made to agree to her living apart, so she was safe then.

"I thought you should hear some of this," Beth said. "She told me some of what happened with you. She doesn't trust men much anymore. Especially ones that can hurt her. She is better off left alone by such as you."

Beth's expression turned belligerent when she warned him off. He could hardly blame her. He could hurt Minerva with this inquiry. He had broken into her house to see if he could, hadn't he?

Minerva knew that when one got down to it, her inheritance made her an excellent suspect. High on the list, as she put it. That she had permitted their passion was a testament not to his great skills as a seducer, but to her indomitable spirit that even now wanted to be free of that horrible time, completely.

"Is she at home now?" he asked.

"She'd think it odd that I went out if she were. She left to go to the City. Had to visit some office about ships."

"Do you remember which office?"

Beth shook her head and began retracing her steps. "She mentioned it, but I don't remember. In the City, though. Something to do with packets."

"I thank you for telling me this."

"There was more, but not fitting for you to hear." With that she walked away from him.

He didn't need to hear it. He could imagine it. Finley had probably been a brute in bed too. A man looking for a victim would not stop at that.

He remained where he stood for a long time, looking out over the park but seeing nothing. Anger came in waves, and each time he had to force control on it. He should have known this. Should have guessed, or at least suspected, especially after she told him about her husband's failures in bed. If Minerva had been timid or fearful or other than the self-possessed woman she was, he might have at least wondered. Instead she had defeated the mouse that Finley had tried to make her, and turned into a tigress. Margaret Finley had indeed become Minerva Hepplewhite, even before she assumed the new name.

He swung up on his horse and turned it toward the park's gate. She was looking into ships. Packets. Hell, maybe she was planning to leave England.

Minerva closed the tome and sat back in her chair. Normally she was excited when an inquiry yielded the results she expected. This time she hated it.

She should tell Chase about this. She would not, however. Soon enough he would look into where everyone had been that night the duke died. He would want to confirm their stories. Then he would learn what she had just learned, that Kevin Radnor had not been in France that day. He had been right here in England.

She could not spare Chase that discovery, but she did not have to be the person who told him, either.

She thanked the clerk who had aided her and stood, brushing the dust off her dress and pelisse. She removed her bonnet and gave it a good shake. She made her way out of the building only to find her way blocked. Standing just outside the portico, his arms crossed and his face set in an expression of concern, stood Chase Radnor.

He saw her emerge and stepped up to where she had paused. His presence made an exquisite, sad yearning flutter inside her.

He looked down at her, his blue eyes dark like lapis lazuli, his rough features refined by the patrician angles they formed. His gaze demanded her entire attention.

"I do not think you had anything to do with the duke's death," he said. "I know this as surely as I know I'm standing here."

"Yet you have no proof of it, and some evidence that disagrees."

"I *know*, Minerva. I have no doubts about it."

He did know. She saw the truth of that in him. Her throat tightened. To be believed by anyone was not something she ever counted on.

"Come with me," he said, offering his hand. "I would like to talk with you if you will permit it."

They strolled along the City's streets until they arrived at Lincoln's Inn. The gardens there offered some privacy and they sat on a bench. Barristers walked by in their robes and clerks hurried back and forth.

He took her hand, discreetly, so anyone walking by would not see. Glove on glove their interwoven fingers nestled between their hips on the bench.

"Beth spoke with me."

"I wish she had not."

"I am glad she did. Everything she told me fit with what you had already let me know. I was just too stupid to see it." He squeezed her hand. Again that frown, and a troubled expression. "Beth said he hurt you badly."

To speak of it, to give particulars, would revive memories she had learned to forget. All the same a chill ran down her back, like the old days. "We both feared one day he would go too far. It seemed a high price to pay for the satisfaction of knowing he would hang."

"I am grateful that he did not have that chance. Relieved and grateful."

"He didn't have the chance because I found a way to leave him."

"Was that when you came here?"

"I left before he died." She lined up what she needed to explain, and what she might avoid. "I left Algernon and went to live on my own, with Beth and her son. He kept trying to force me back. He began some court proceeding that would obligate me to do so. I decided I could not accept that. So I found the information that would stop him."

"You conducted an inquiry."

"My first. Beth helped. Even Jeremy helped, boy though he was. We learned that Algernon was not always impotent. On occasion he could be most potent. With another woman, who played peculiar games with him."

"Did that stop him?"

"He laughed at me when I threw it at him. He wasn't even ashamed that his lover was a relative. An aunt, for goodness' sake. A blood relative at that. So I arranged to catch them at it."

"I trust you brought witnesses."

"Of course. I found where they met. I waited until they were together, paid off the innkeeper, and up we went with the key. There they were, doing something he would not want described in a courtroom. He tried to bribe my witnesses on the spot, but they held firm for me. He agreed to a separation a week later. That helped, but not as much as I had hoped."

"You are uncommonly brave, Minerva. Brave and resourceful and smarter than most men. I have never seen the likes of you."

She would have given him a kiss if they were not in a public park. Admiration from this man counted for something.

She sensed more questions. He did not speak them, but his deep thought and the vague dismay shading his expression told her what they were.

"Yes," she said. "What you are wondering. Yes. It all started with that, you see. His anger about his impotence is what turned violent first. Eventually nothing between us, no conversation or any connection, was not touched by violence. The only way to survive was to feel nothing at all."

He closed his eyes. "If I had known I would have never—"

"You would have never kissed me or touched me." She did kiss his cheek then. "And I would never have known that he had not completely ruined that part of me."

He raised her hand and kissed it. "Let us spend the rest of the day doing better things than talking about this. We will go someplace where you can smile and laugh and be Minerva Hepplewhite. Only Minerva Hepplewhite." He smiled. "I'll even go shopping with you if you want."

"I was planning to order a new ensemble. Perhaps you know of a good modiste."

"I know of one or two, so that is what we will do."

They strolled through the gardens and back to where he had left his horse. He hired a carriage and tethered the

horse to it, then climbed in with her. She hoped that this
modiste would take the commission based on her expectations. He appeared so pleased with his idea that she didn't
want to ruin it by being practical, however.

"It was an exorbitant self-indulgence." Minerva voiced
her thoughts while the carriage took them toward her
house. The self-scold could not blight the fun of buying
not one, but two ensembles. She smiled whenever she
thought about it.

"It was not a self-indulgence at all," he said. "The
owner of Hepplewhite's Office of Discreet Inquiries requires a suitable wardrobe. It was a pity you did not order
that dinner dress as well."

"It was too expensive."

"You forget that you are an heiress now."

"You should not have told Madame Tissot that. It was
very bad of you." The modiste had been merciless after
learning that, tempting her with luxuries. Like that dinner
dress.

She saw that dress in her mind. Raw silk with a subtle
shimmer, the hue reminded her of primroses. Pearls bedecked the neckline and waist, and more discreetly studded
the lower skirt's floral embroidery. The cost of it all would
have left her too dependent on her expectations, however,
and for a dress she might never wear.

"The wool ensembles will be enough for now," she
said. Their purpose, and rationale, had her mind returning
to her inquiries. She tucked away the one she had pursued
today, and raised another.

"I never had a chance to tell you, but something was
revealed to me at Melton Park by a servant," she said.

She repeated what the servant Joan had said to her,

about being on the roof and seeing and hearing someone. "She said she could not swear to it, but I think that was her way of trying to avoid ever being asked to."

"It might have been another servant, of course."

"It might have been, but I do not think it was. Do you?"

"I don't know yet. Nor do you. It is one more piece of information that might one day form a link in a chain, however."

"Something to note in your portfolio, you mean. To put on a list."

"Yes. The possible evidence list, not the secure facts list."

They had almost reached her house. He made the coachman stop two streets away. When he turned back to face her she knew they would no longer speak of investigations.

He reached over and lightly caressed her face. "I want you to come to me, Minerva. Send me a note first if you like, but pay a late call, or an early one, or anytime you want. We can sit and talk or go out about town again, if you like. We will do this however you want, darling, and at no time should you ever feel obligated, even by your own words or agreement."

He told the coachman to move on. A few minutes later the coach stopped at her own door. He jumped out and turned to hand her down. She gazed at his face, and at that hand reaching toward her. She screwed up her courage and leaned out. Before stepping down she quickly kissed him.

He smiled and helped her down. "Beth is watching from the window."

She looked past him and saw the bright white cap at the glass.

"Her son is watching from the garden alley."

She noticed Jeremy's blond hair amidst the shrubbery

beyond the garden portal. "I suppose I may have some explaining to do."

At the door she looked back to see him untying his horse from the carriage. She remained out there, watching, until he rode down the street and the carriage went on its own way. Then she went inside, to have what would probably be a long talk with the only two people she had dared trust for five years.

Chapter Sixteen

Foils whistled. Men lunged. From behind his mask Chase eyed his opponent. Dark eyes peered back.

They had been at this for close to an hour, both of them slashing and clashing out their individual angers. Thus far it had been an even match.

A lunge. A whip. A pause. Chase looked down to see the tip of a foil on his chest.

He pulled off the mask. "You have improved."

"I took lessons from a master while in France," Kevin said, removing his own mask. "This is an art there."

They started unbuckling equipment. "If it had been sabers you would never have won," Chase said.

"Only it wasn't, so I did." Kevin said. "I appreciated this match, but it is not your weapon."

"It served its purpose." The exertion had dulled his black mood to a dusky gray. He no longer wanted to go looking for a fight with his fists, the way he had at breakfast.

It had been two days since he had seen Minerva. No letter had come from her. He could not blame her, of course. Only the most conceited of men would.

He kept turning it all over in his mind, however, alternately trying to convince himself that he had handled the whole thing as well as any man could, and must reconcile himself to total retreat, and damning himself for being an ass.

He had half-heartedly read a few of the letters that *had* come this morning. A request from Nicholas to provide Miss Hepplewhite's address so he might make good on his promise to have her dine with him got set aside for response. A long letter full of complaints from Aunt Dolores went to the stack he had no intention of answering soon.

A short missive arrived from Peel, asking for a preliminary report in the next week. Damnation to that. He and Kevin went to wash and dress. Chase noticed that Kevin's attire appeared a bit unkempt, as if he had dressed himself and done it carelessly. "You weren't at home last night?"

"What makes you ask that?" Kevin worked at a cravat that had already been tied twice too often.

Chase glanced pointedly at that neckpiece, and the wrinkled shirt.

Kevin shrugged. "I was out and about. Conducting inquiries, if you must know."

"How so?"

"I saw your notices in the papers. Again. I don't think you will find those women that way. So I'm looking for them, or rather the one who gets my enterprise."

"In the brothels, you mean."

Kevin fixed his cuffs and settled his coat on his shoulders. "I was serious when I said that was where they can be found."

"The one I located was not in a brothel. Ever. Uncle Frederick paid well for those services. He would not feel the need to leave fat legacies for any of those women."

"Then I am wasting my time. It is mine to squander, and I've quite a bit of it at my disposal right now."

"Have you had any success?" If Kevin wanted to search

in brothels, Chase wasn't going to stop him. For one thing, his cousin knew those establishments and their owners far better than Chase did.

"I have discovered the annoying truth that some of them exercise extreme discretion where he is concerned."

Chase led the way out. They walked around the edge of the main hall, past other fencing matches taking place. "Well, he was a duke. I expect he demanded discretion."

"I can't imagine why. Anyway, last night I tried a different path. I presented myself to the madam and informed her I was his nephew. I then said I would like to be introduced to his most recent favorite, so I might enjoy her favors as he did."

Chase laughed. "A memorial fuck? It sounds almost sentimental."

"I thought so. My thinking was that this favorite might know about prior favorites, and even their real names. They rarely use real names in those houses."

"I am not green, Kevin. I do not visit brothels with your or Uncle's regularity, but I know the basics."

"Of course. So that was my thinking—to get into a room with his latest favorite, and get her talking."

"Clever."

"Are you being sarcastic?"

"No, no. How did your plan fare?"

Kevin led the way out to the street. "The madam informed me that it would be most inappropriate if one of Uncle's male relatives partook of the same wine he had recently drunk. Have you ever heard of such a thing? She was most severe too. I felt like I was being scolded by a vicar. She all but accused me of incest."

They stopped at their horses, and Kevin's frown suddenly cleared. "Damnation. I'll wager he told them to say that, to refuse any of us his women. Don't laugh. You know he could be selfish about some things. He didn't always share nicely."

"I am not laughing at you, or your idea. I think maybe you are right."

Kevin untied his horse. "He probably did not want to be compared with anyone so close to home, as it were."

Chase laughed again.

Kevin swung up. "I am going to Whiteford House to look around. Do you want to join me? We can drink some of the excellent wine Nicholas inherited."

"I have another engagement, I'm sorry to say. Are you going to look for the mechanical butler?"

"That and other things. Our conversation about it conjured up many other memories." He turned his horse west.

Chase mounted his own horse, but headed east instead.

Mr. Oliver was not a happy man. Round of face and body, sparse of hair, he kept looking at his wife with an expression of strained forbearance. Minerva sat with her across from him at the dining room table at their house, untying the thin package she had brought.

"Miss Hepplestone, my wife should have never wasted your time."

"Hepplewhite. I think that in a few minutes you will be most grateful she did."

"Unlikely. Women have no head for business nor any ability to conduct it. That is why I do not tolerate their interference."

"It was not interference as such," Mrs. Oliver said.

"What do you call it then?" he snapped.

"Your wife noticed something was amiss," Minerva said. "She asked me as a friend to confirm what she suspected.

I do not seek to interfere any more than she did. If you would prefer to be robbed and have your affairs compromised, just say so and I will take my leave."

Robbed raised an expression of alarm in him. *Compromised* brought forth a deep frown. He did not tell her to leave.

She described what she had learned in Brighton. She laid out the lace cuffs she had bought from Mr. Seymour's shop. She explained how she was told that they came from a town in the Loire Valley, and that the owner of the shop was well aware that he sold something that in the past had been available exclusively at a competitor.

"Quite smug he was," she said. "Furthermore, he had already sold out his stock and was getting more." She lifted one of the cuffs. "I arranged to be there when he did, and I saw your agent enter his building. A half hour later, I procured these cuffs. I thought this one unusually fine."

He snatched it out of her hand. He put on his spectacles and bent low over it. "Hell and damnation." He looked up with a chagrined smile. "My apologies. Only this is new. Not one of mine."

"He was very proud of that one. He anticipated much profit from it."

He rested back in his chair, fingering the cuff. "The thief," he muttered. "Who knows what else he's done."

Minerva stood. "I will indeed take my leave now."

"I will see you to the door," Mrs. Oliver said.

At the door Mrs. Oliver leaned in and whispered. "Well done. Write and let me know what I owe you for today."

"You owe nothing. This is part of my report." She looked toward the dining room. "He is not the sort to somehow turn this around to blame you, is he?"

"In two days my role will be forgotten, and the entire discovery will be his doing."

Of course. What other choice did he have? Admit that his wife had been right to involve herself?

"Hand delivery," Beth called. "A big one."

Minerva went to the stairs to see a large rectangular bundle hovering above the middle step. The package was too large for Beth to carry. It all but tipped her over, and obscured her sight. Minerva rushed down and helped her bring it up to her chamber.

Beth poked at the unbleached muslin and ribbon tie. "A gift?"

"I expect it is my new ensembles. They finished them very quickly."

Minerva plucked at the ribbon and it fell to the sides. She unfolded the muslin. Her woolen ensembles were not inside. The luscious dinner dress, the one she had not bought, glimmered up at her.

Beth's sharp intake of breath filled the chamber. "You said day ensembles. Not this."

"A mistake has been made. The woman must have not heard me correctly."

She lifted the dress. The simple raw silk far surpassed the more elaborate fabrics available. A subtle sheen rippled over it when she moved it in the light.

"What is this here?" Beth reached for the package and moved another piece of the muslin wrapper.

Minerva had been so distracted by admiring the dinner dress that she had not noticed something else had come with it. Beth lifted the garment high. An undressing gown unfolded and its hem dropped down. She had admired this at Madame Tissot's too, and only declined it after much thought.

Beth peered around the white lace, suspiciously.

"I will send it back with the dress," Minerva said.

Beth laid the undressing gown on the bed. "It is very pretty. The one you have has been mended five times over."

"It is lovely, isn't it?"

Beth ran her palm over the very fine lawn fabric. "Maybe it wasn't a mistake. Perhaps that dressmaker just wanted you to have it."

"Dressmakers do not make gifts of such as this, to patrons such as me. Pack it up and I'll ask Jeremy to—"

"Could be that Mr. Radnor wanted you to have it, as compensation for all the help you have given him."

If she had given him much help at all, she might convince herself of that. Still . . . She joined Beth in gazing at the garment. "If he did, it would be inappropriate for me to keep it."

"Very inappropriate." Beth fingered some lace, rubbing it. "I never thought to call such a thing delicious, but the word fits."

Minerva marveled at the tiny pearl beads on the neckline of the dress. "Sad to return them, but I must."

Beth gave a subtle shrug. "That all depends, doesn't it? You listened to my long scold about having no more to do with him, and seemed to agree. But you didn't actually do so, nor have you avoided him like you should."

Minerva felt her face warming. She doubted her old friend would place a wager on how matters would develop with Chase. Minerva had no idea herself, especially now. Last night she debated at length with herself, weighing her ache for intimacy against all the reasons ever going to him would be a mistake. For both of them now.

"I don't blame you," Beth said. "I just wish he were a

merchant or a fishmonger or doing anything other than these inquiries that seem to touch on you."

"As do I, Beth. As do I."

Beth lifted the undressing gown and carried it to the wardrobe. "Why not wait a few days, and see if that dressmaker writes to tell you they were sent by mistake. If she doesn't, you can always send them back next week if you choose to."

Chapter Seventeen

The letter from Chase contained one terse sentence. *I demand that you explain why you had cause to inquire as to my cousin Kevin's whereabouts last month.* Nothing indicated when and how she was supposed to provide that explanation. By letter, presumably.

He had reached the point on his list where he checked his relatives' stories, apparently. On learning about Kevin, he had realized her own reasons for visiting the packet office.

Their conversation after he found her there had not been one that any decent man would conclude with an interrogation on her reasons for that visit.

She rather wished she had blurted the lie she had devised as an explanation, should he ever ask about that. *I was wondering if I could find out where my uncle and cousins landed when they left England.* He would never know that she had looked into that when she first came up to London five years ago, to no good conclusion.

She sat down to write to him, but after a few jottings her pen paused. How cowardly to give bad news this way. She was about to hand him a problem worse than he imagined. He had a right to ask his questions and have quick answers.

She pulled forward a clean sheet of paper. *I will call at eight o'clock this evening to tell you what I know.*

She sent Jeremy off to deliver the note, then tried to concentrate on the rest of her day. A new client called, sent by Mrs. Oliver. This woman, Mrs. Jeffers, wanted to find her cousin, with whom she had been long estranged. Minerva was glad for the new inquiry, and grateful for the distraction. Once that meeting ended, she had nothing but thoughts about her next one in her head.

She ate dinner with Beth and Jeremy. When it ended, she went to her chamber to wash and change her garments, and to settle the errant strands of hair that had escaped during the day. For some reason she became all thumbs and did a poor job of it. All the signs of nervousness plagued her, so much that she almost left without her reticule. Finally she went down and asked Jeremy to go out and bring her a hired carriage.

"I don't need to," he said. "One will be here in a few minutes. It came half an hour ago and has been waiting. The coachman decided to walk the horses a bit but will be back soon."

"How thoughtful of you. Such foresight."

"Not my doing. I didn't know you were leaving, did I?" He gave her appearance a suspicious scrutiny.

The carriage rolled to a stop in front of her house. Jeremy accompanied her outside and helped her in. "Don't you be walking home late at night," he said.

"I expect to be back in an hour at most, and I think my return will be accommodated just as my departure has been."

"Let's all hope it happens that way." He stepped away and gestured for the coachman to go.

* * *

He paced the library. It was not a large one, so he kept pivoting and retracing his steps. His agitation threatened to create a valley in the carpet.

Anger sent him on this hike to nowhere. So did a different kind of fury. Upon receiving Minerva's note, his first thought had been *Finally*. Only she was not coming for the reason he had hoped. She wasn't even calling out of friendship. He had demanded an explanation and she intended to give it to him. Nothing more.

If his body did not accept the truth of that, it probably had to do with the way in which anticipation over the last few days had primed it to ache for relief. Telling himself he was an ass hardly helped. Desire did not have a logical mind.

"Sir, I prepared some negus. I will keep it warm until your caller arrives." Brigsby appeared out of nowhere to announce that. "Should I plan for two for dinner? I have some fowl that would not take long to cook."

Would she have eaten already? Hell if he knew. He doubted she had invited herself to dinner, though. "I don't think so."

"Perhaps you would like me to cook it for you, then. For after your caller leaves."

"Do whatever makes sense to you. I don't give a damn right now."

Brigsby's eyebrows rose. His mouth pursed. He disappeared as quickly as he had arrived, his steps going down the stairs to the kitchen far below. Almost at once his steps came back up, hurriedly. He passed the library door smoothing his hair and straightened his cravat. A moment later the sounds of a visitor broke the silence of the house.

"Sir, Miss Hepplewhite has called." Brigsby handed over a card, as if Chase needed proof.

"For the sake of—bring her in. Get on with it, man," he hissed.

Again those eyebrows rose. A minute later Brigsby ushered Minerva into the library and closed the door.

She looked especially lovely. For some reason tonight her face appeared even more luminous and her eyes dark like mink. He looked at her too long before he welcomed her and invited her to sit.

"I thought I should respond to your rude letter in person, lest you misunderstand my explanation in some way if I wrote."

"Did you find it rude? I thought it was direct."

"Directly rude. However, I understand why you were displeased. You thought I would tell you everything, like a good employee. Only I was never one of those."

"I thought you would tell me what you learned because we were sharing information equally."

"I see." She raised her chin and lowered her eyelids. "So you have told me everything?"

An awkward, damning silence ensued.

"I didn't think so. Well, here I am. Ask what you want and I will answer as I can."

"I know that you went to the packet offices to look at the manifests of passengers. Yet you did not tell me that."

"You did not ask. We spoke of other things."

Other things. Important things. More important than this damnable inquiry that would probably shred his soul before it was done. He wished they were back on that day, enjoying that afternoon tight in a new intimacy stronger than any wrought by passion.

He forced himself back to the topic at hand. "I have gone, and also looked. The clerk remembered a woman requesting the same week's manifests recently. You."

"So you know that your cousin Kevin was not out of

the country when your uncle died. That he came back from France for a few days, and then returned there."

He gritted his teeth, and went to stand at the fireplace. "I want to know what led you to even look for his name on those passenger lists."

"It was something Mr. Edkins said in passing."

"The valet?"

"He was talking about his master's habit of wandering at night, in the city after dark and on that roof at his estate. He mentioned that usually it relaxed him. Calmed him. But not always. At times he would return angry, talking to Edkins but really to himself. And he said that the night before the duke died he came down from the roof muttering about how they acted like he was a bank they never had to repay, how after everything he had given the boy, more was expected for that damned invention. Well, the invention part made it obvious of whom he spoke. It sounded like he met with Kevin, either that evening or that night. Only Kevin was supposed to be out of the country."

"Of course you checked if perhaps he really wasn't." He slammed his fist on the mantel. "Damnation, Minerva, *why didn't you tell me this*?"

An invisible veil fell over her face. Her expression dulled into utter blandness. She looked at a spot on the wall, not him.

She had retreated, totally. From the conversation, and him. She was withdrawing from anger, the way she had learned to with Finley.

He strode over and knelt beside her. He took her hands. "I apologize. Forgive me. I should not let my reaction to this news fall on you."

She did not pull her hands away. Eventually she looked down at them, then at him. Something of her spirit reentered her eyes. "I knew it would trouble you. I thought to spare you that for a while longer. Eventually it would come out, of course. You yourself would have checked each story regarding where they were, now that you know it was not an accident. I did not need to be the bearer of bad news."

He kissed her hands, not thinking whether he should. It touched him that she thought to spare him, for a while longer.

"Also," she said. "I do not think he did it."

"Don't you now?"

She shook her head. "He is not the sort to."

"There is no sort, Minerva."

"I disagree." She leaned forward, close enough to be kissed if he chose to. Which he didn't, much as he would like to. "Now, as long as I have you on your knees and feeling bad, you can tell me what *you* did not share with *me*."

He would have laughed, except that she was very serious. "A small detail."

"How small?"

"A spot of information, nothing more."

"I will decide if it was a spot or a large blotch."

He rested back on his heels. Not that he expected a blow to come, of course. "Whether Kevin visited him is yet to be confirmed. However, he did have a visitor."

"He did? Who?"

"A woman. That is all I know, and all that was seen. Not her face, or even much of the rest of her."

"Who told you?"

"Edkins."

She frowned. "He didn't tell me that."

"Did you bluntly ask? Sometimes that works best."

"My way worked quite well. However, perhaps in the future we should plan it so that I chat with them and get unintended droppings, and you bluntly ask and get your kind of answers."

He slid onto the divan beside her, still holding her hand. "That is a good plan."

Their proximity, their clasped hands, caused a change in the air. He did not much care about Mr. Edkins's revelations anymore.

She turned to look at him right in the eyes. "You did not tell me because the woman could have been me."

"I knew it was not. I did, however, worry that you would believe I thought it was you."

"How did you know it wasn't me, if no one saw her face?"

He raised her hand and kissed it. "I just knew."

Minerva had no illusions that Chase expected the night to end as it began. If the exquisite anticipation tightening her core was any indication, she had better make her decision soon. A nervous jumpiness descended on her. It seemed to spread from her blood out to the chamber they occupied. She felt it in him too, although nothing in his body or face revealed it. He appeared companionable and friendly, not lusting.

He would not seduce her. He would probably sit here for hours if she preferred that. From the looks of him, he didn't even care if they talked while they did so.

His manservant arrived with a big tray. Wordlessly he poured warm negus into two small glasses. She sipped the spiced port punch, glad for something to do. Once the servant left, however, she set her glass down.

"I cannot decide." She assumed he would know what she spoke of. "I weigh it and—" She shrugged.

"I do not think weighing it will resolve anything. I don't think the answer you seek will present itself that way. Nor do you need to decide now, or next week, or ever."

She did not want to remain undecided forever. How sad that would be. If she lived the rest of her life the way she had lived the last years, it should be a choice. If she denied herself that part of being a woman, after experiencing that fulfillment once, she did not want it to be because she lacked the courage to choose another way.

He spoke not at all, just sat beside her, his warm palm cradling hers. The nervousness she experienced hung thick between them, like a palpable excitement waiting to burst forth.

She looked at him, hard. Beth said not to trust him. She should sever their ties for his sake as well as hers. Only she didn't want to. She had done nothing wrong, and was tired of being a slave to the fear that no one would believe that.

She swallowed hard. "I think you should kiss me now."

He pressed his lips to hers so fast that the last words came out muffled. And with that connection the dam that had been barely holding back her want of him sank out of sight.

He turned to her and took her face in his hands and showered her mouth and face with kisses, some careful, others less so. His quick passion said he had not been nearly as blasé the last half hour as he had appeared.

He embraced her and kissed her neck, her shoulder, the bit of skin visible above her pelisse. She knew these pleasures and relinquished herself to them. She enjoyed the sly titillations perking in her blood, and the joyous freedom the sensations gave her.

Even while they kissed he managed to shake off his

coats. She felt his body then, strong and hard beneath his shirt. His cravat disappeared and she ventured a small kiss on his neck. He held her there, asking for more, while his hand went to the buttons on her pelisse.

She looked down at that hand, then around the chamber. "Do you think to do this here?"

Calmer kisses. Soothing ones. "Not unless you want to."

The carpet, while expensive and thick, did not appear very comfortable. "I do not think it wise."

One deep look in her eyes, and he lifted her by the hand. "Come with me."

He did not lead her far. His chambers spread over one floor of a house, so his bedchamber could be found nearby. They passed a back stairs and went a little farther. He opened a door, then released her hand while he turned and worked the latch.

It was a nice chamber. Masculine. Large enough but not excessive. Just right for one person, she thought. A little old in style, with dark wood panels coming up half the walls and also forming the bed. Shadows tried to rise in her memory when she looked at that bed, but she filled her gaze and thoughts with other things.

Simple white drapes framed the windows and bedposts. None of it surprised her. It looked like him. He would not concern himself much with fashion. His garments were current, but his haberdasher probably claimed credit.

He closed another door. She saw beyond it enough to know it was his dressing room.

"Do you want me to undress?" she asked.

"Just stay there." He took a key off his writing table and locked the dressing room. Then he stripped off his cravat.

They faced each other across the chamber. The bed loomed. The one lamp's glow turned the white drapes golden.

Her heart rose to her throat. He appeared so handsome there, with the low light flattering his face and form. Strong and deliciously masculine.

"Now you can undress."

While he watched, apparently.

She had worn a pelisse dress with little buttons down the front. She worked at them, wondering if buried desire had made her choose such a convenient garment. It took a long time to finish with the closures, due to her fingers trembling. Finally she let the dress slip off her shoulders and down her body. His gaze followed its descent, then slowly rose back up.

She went to work on her undergarments. The longer it took, the more nervous she became and the more clumsy her actions. He enjoyed it, she realized. That made her slow enough that her disrobing might appear more elegant. She also discovered a pleasant sensuality in revealing herself like this, layer by layer.

Down to her chemise and hose, she bent to untie the latter.

"I would prefer if you saved those for last."

That meant becoming naked before she was done. Blatantly so, and not while in bed or even being embraced. She steeled her courage and let the chemise drop.

She looked at him, so he might think her braver than she felt. Desire had tightened his expression and fired his eyes. His gaze captured hers and a thrill spun down her body. Then another. Like rockets, each one created an explosion of arousal that sent exciting sensations raining down.

He glanced down, reminding her of the hose. She stepped over to a chair to prop up her foot, untied one, and rolled it down. The implications of her pose, of her raised leg, stirred her deeply. While she set her foot down and raised the other one she noticed he had moved slightly to where he could view her exposure better.

So aroused that she could barely stand, she untied the other stocking and began removing it. Suddenly he was there, on one knee, right in front of her. He moved her foot to his other bent knee, and his hands to the roll of the stocking.

She looked down at his strong hands slowly moving the stocking down to her knee. His head dipped and he kissed her inner thigh. High up. Then another, higher yet. So high she felt his breath on her mound like a feathering tease.

She dared not close her eyes because she feared she might stagger or fall. So she watched his crown and his hands, and felt his kisses and came close to forgetting how to breathe herself. The kisses did not stop, but somehow the stocking was gone. Still he knelt there, caressing her leg too. Then he stroked high, and slid his hand between her thighs, into the dampness and heat he had caused. One deep, secret touch and the chamber spun. She had to hold his shoulders to keep her balance while he pushed her arousal higher and higher.

Kisses on her stomach, her hips. Caresses on her bottom, then sliding deeply forward. Maddened now, she fumbled with his shirt until she could push it down his shoulders and feel his skin. He removed it somehow, never pausing in what he was doing to her.

He turned her into the chair. "Sit here." He pressed her hips until she sat, then moved her forward to the edge. He kissed her thighs again, and touched the center of her tortuous pleasure. "I want to kiss you here. Will you allow it?"

She nodded without understanding what he meant.

She only knew she wanted whatever pleasure he could conjure, and was long past shock. Or at least she thought so until his head went low and she felt that kiss and an arrow of pleasure speared right into the throbs down there and every other sense ceased to exist except the one experiencing that.

It got worse and worse, better and better. She knew she moaned but did not hear herself. She knew he moved her legs so her feet rested on his shoulders, but did not see it. He lifted her hips and had better purchase, and devastated her with his tongue. The pleasure turned excruciating in the best way, compelling and climbing and growing ever intense. She thought she would die if she did not stop it, did not retreat. Instead, somehow the tight painful pleasure broke, snapped, and sent successive waves of astonishing sensation flowing out, creating a place where she lost herself completely.

He heard her fretful moans when she got close. His mind and tongue urged her on. When her scream sounded and her release flexed her body, he knew an exultant sense of victory.

He stood and watched her face while he undressed. She looked ethereal in her bliss. Almost girlish in her total contentment. He gathered her into his arms and carried her to the bed. She murmured something he could not hear or understand.

Once on the bed her eyes opened a slit. She scrambled atop him, straddling him like the last time. Sultry and still astonished, she looked down at him. She bent low and kissed him deeply, then sat up again.

He took her breasts in his hands and caressed lightly, lest she be too sensitive still. She smiled and threw back her head and leaned into it, so he might use his mouth. She moaned freely as he pleasured her, and soon squirmed on his hips.

Again she sat back, a little wild-eyed now, magnificently erotic. She looked down at his swollen cock and ran one finger up its length. He had to fight to maintain control. Proud of herself, she did it again and again, then experimented with a firm caress.

Having jumped off the mountain once, she could enjoy a leisurely second climb. He, however, could not take much more of this. Another time he would let her play as much as she wanted.

He lifted her hips. She understood and took him inside herself. He gritted his teeth as her tight warmth encased him. She began her slow rises and falls. He leashed his need and took what she gave for a good while, but his hunger finally turned savage. He pressed one hand on the headboard behind his head for leverage and took over.

Not so careful this time. He had no choice. His body howled with the need to thrust hard and deep and possess completely. His mind saw future takings in other ways, and those images only drove him on. The release, when he finally accepted it, proved cataclysmic.

She fell on top of him, into his arms, kissing his chest and neck, gripping his shoulders. Within his senseless ecstasy, he thought he heard her scream again.

They lay in silence for a long time. He was glad she did not need a lot of chatting. The quiet held an intimacy that words might destroy. Finally, however, she rose up on her elbows and looked at him.

"Thank you." Such depth in her eyes when she said that.

"I think you were heroic again, in a different way. Not so careful."

"Did I hurt you?"

She shook her head. "I liked it. Next time I don't think you will have to be careful either."

He had avoided thinking about a next time, since he had no standing to expect one. A new contentment settled on him with her words. She sat up, unconcerned with her nakedness this time, glorious in it, her breasts soft now that passion's firmness had passed. He looked at her, and felt himself stirring again.

"It is time I left," she said.

"Leave if you want, but you answer to no one."

"Beth—"

"She knows where you are."

"Yes, but—"

"She knew why you came, even if you did not."

She just looked at him, then swung her leg and slid off his body and the bed.

"Before you dress completely, Minerva, go look out the front window at the place directly across the way where the two buildings meet."

She pulled the chemise on and padded away. He heard her steps growing fainter as she entered the sitting room. Several minutes later the steps came back.

"When did you see him?"

"Early. Soon after you came."

"He must have grabbed on to the back of my carriage when it left."

"That or he jumped across roofs to stay ahead of you. He is fast and knows this town well. If he were not a partner in your inquiries, I might seek to make him one in mine."

She picked up her dress and shook it out. "I did not tell him to do this. I hope you believe that."

"It was his own initiative. He also knew why you were coming here, even if you didn't. So he waits out there, listening, in case you changed your mind and I was not a gentleman about it."

Her expression fell, as if she pictured the altercation that might have created. "I really should go, so he does not stand there until dawn."

"You could just open the window and call down and tell him to go home."

"As if I could do that on a street in this neighborhood." She laughed and carried her stays over to the bed. "Help me with these, please."

He sat on the side of the bed and aided her with the lacing. When she reached for her dress he did the same with his trousers and shirt. Together they became civilized again.

He drew her into his arms and embraced her closely. He kissed her, regretting that he would have to let her go. "You should settle this with him and his mother, Minerva. They do not have to trust me or like me. The decision is yours, though, and they do have to honor that."

She nodded. A troubled little frown marred her loveliness. "What I told you earlier. I don't really know anything. You have my word that I will not speak of it, or pursue it."

Her promise touched him, especially since it might come at some cost to herself. She might claim she really did not know anything about Kevin, but in fact she did. So did he, but she had just offered him the choice of pretending he didn't.

He brought her to the front door. "Stay here." He

went outside and walked right up to Jeremy, who all but blended into the shadows. He handed him some coins. "Go hire a carriage and bring her home."

Jeremy just looked at him a moment, his expression unfathomable. Then he ran down the street.

Chapter Eighteen

Minerva found herself useless the whole day. She wandered around the house in a sated daze, her head full of memories of the night.

She had always known there were women who said they enjoyed physical intimacy. She had thought those claims hollow and more than passing strange. Now they made sense. *Really* made sense. Who wouldn't enjoy that pinnacle of sensation? Presumably those women had married men who knew what they were about in bed. If there were shared affection, or even love, how much better just because of that.

That led her to asking herself if she and Chase had shared affection, at least while they kissed and embraced. She had to admit she felt some for him now, but she could not remember if she had before that night at Melton Park. If not, then such experiences perhaps could engender affection. She found that fascinating.

So engrossed was she in her thoughts that after their midday meal, one at which Jeremy had talked a lot but she had heard little, she dallied in the kitchen, barely noticing Beth cleaning the plates. She was still there when Beth sat down beside her.

"Now," Beth said. "How did your call on Mr. Radnor go?"

She looked at Beth and saw that her old friend knew everything. Jeremy must have told her how long he stood outside, and how Chase had come out in dishabille and sent him for a carriage. How she had floated down to the conveyance still besotted, feeling like a metamorphosis had occurred.

"Our discussion went very well," she said. "He was a little angry I had not confided in him, but he understood when I explained why."

"Very sensible of him."

"Wasn't it? So I would describe our conversation as successful."

"Would you now?"

"Yes. The whole visit was very successful." She met Beth's gaze squarely. "Actually, one part of it was nothing short of wonderful."

Beth pushed herself up. "I'm glad to hear it. I'm happier than you will ever know. I'll not speak a word against him from now on, unless he gives me fresh cause to do so."

Brigsby being Brigsby said not a word about the night visitor. He merely set about adapting to the requirements she had created. He drew a bath in the morning, and plucked up the remnants of Chase's clothing as if he found them strewn around the bedchamber all the time. He got Chase dressed for town, then served breakfast for one, not the two that Chase suspected he had initially arranged. He delivered the mail and the ironed newspaper.

Afterward, when Chase returned to his chamber and sat to write some letters, Brigsby arrived with a high stack of linens, and proceeded to change the bedclothes. Except for the unusual discarding of his own frockcoat in order to attend to the chore, one would think from his demeanor that his master had women in his bed on a regular basis.

Chase turned back to his letters. One had been easy to write. The second and third ones proved more difficult. There was little to be gained from putting them off, however, so he got through them just in time to hand the stack to Brigsby to be posted at once. No sooner had his valet left than he decided to write again. It promised to be a hellish day, but with luck it might end well.

At one o'clock he sent for his horse and rode to Gilbert Street, where Aunt Agnes lived. The butler escorted him to a small drawing room upstairs. In it he found both aunts sitting on opposite ends of a large divan. One looked to the wall and the other looked to the floor. The point, he gathered, was not to look at each other.

Dolores had remained in town after the infamous solicitor meeting, to campaign for her views on the matter. Twice she had written to him, demanding that he cajole Nicholas to see reason. Both times his response had been polite but firm. Nicholas already saw reason, and it was for Dolores to alter her opinion.

Now, however, he had requested this meeting and called on both aunts. Although similar in height, dark hair, and the tendency to be harpies, they differed in significant ways. Agnes's face showed a softness that might lead one to conclude erroneously that the rest of her was soft too. Dolores's possessed a sharpness in features and gaze that gave fair warning of what one had in her. Their figures followed similar forms. Agnes's thickness made her height twice as formidable. Dolores's extreme thinness gave her a frail appearance, even if the woman was anything but that.

It was Dolores who greeted him. "Sit, Chase. It is so rare to have you alone."

That sounded ominous.

"Have you been enjoying town?" he asked her.

"Not much. I prefer the country, as you know. I miss my little cottage in Kent."

"Little cottage, ha!" Agnes muttered.

Dolores's little cottage had at least fifteen chambers.

"Do you intend to remain much longer?"

"Yes, Dolores, do you intend to remain much longer?" Agnes roused herself to snap.

Dolores's eyes narrowed. "Until the matter at hand is settled."

"If you handle it the way you want, that will be years. Decades. You will die here," Agnes said. "As I said before Chase arrived, nothing that you do here can't be done by post. If your presence is needed, your *little cottage* is barely a day away by coach."

He had interrupted a row, it seemed, and asked the one question sure to have it continue.

"As I explained, I will not impose much longer." Dolores's throaty tone carried an edge of steel. "I will avail myself of my nephew's hospitality, if you prefer. I am sure Nicholas will not mind if I visit for a few days."

Chase heard that with alarm. Nicholas would have his head if he allowed this notion to stand. "Aunt Dolores, I am sure he would not mind, but I fear that you would. The household is still disrupted. New servants only slowly are being engaged. I hear a new housekeeper just took up her duties, so it will get worse before it gets better. It would embarrass Nicholas to offer you such poor attendance."

Dolores just stared at him. Agnes looked at her with smug satisfaction.

"If you want to remain in town for a few weeks or more, why not let a house? There are many available this time of year," Chase said.

"Why not indeed," Agnes said. "My thought exactly." She gave Chase an ally-to-ally look.

"*As I explained*, it is too costly. Under the circumstances that my brother left me in, I must count my pennies."

"So you stay here and eat my pennies instead. How convenient. A few days is one thing. Several weeks is another. Now it sounds as if you intend to live here permanently."

"*Only until matters are settled*."

"Heaven give me patience." Agnes turned to Chase for help, pleading with her gaze. "She met with a solicitor about challenging the will's provisions. Don't feign shock with me, Sister. Yes, I know about it and, yes, I am telling Chase so maybe he can talk sense into you."

"I had hoped Nicholas had done that already," Chase said.

"At her age, what does the threat of being cut out of *his* will matter?"

The two of them continued bickering. Chase suffered it for five minutes, then stood. "I am inclined to take my leave and return another day, so this meeting can start on a different topic. I asked to see you, Dolores, for a reason other than your living arrangements."

"I thought it was a social call," Agnes said, looking perplexed.

"Not exactly."

They both looked at him, then at each other. "Please sit, Chase. We will keep our sisterly arguments to ourselves," Agnes said.

"Then with your permission I will get to it. I have been conducting inquiries into Uncle Frederick's death. I went down to Melton Park, and learned some things there. I would like to ask you some questions."

"Her or me?" Agnes said.

"Both of you at first. Then only her."

Dolores stiffened. "Bold of you."

"You don't even know what the questions are yet," Agnes said.

Chase decided to ignore all asides and commentary. "Were either one of you at Melton Park the day that the duke died?"

Agnes looked aghast. Dolores's color drained.

Dolores recovered first. "What kind of a question is that?"

"A very simple one. I can find out other ways, but it is easier to ask you."

"Then have my simple answer. I. Was. Not."

"Nor I," Agnes added. "Did someone say we were there? Is someone impugning us and trying to say—"

"No one has impugned or accused or in any way named either of you. I had to ask this question in order to eliminate possibilities. Thank you for your honest answers."

They both relaxed but their alarm had subdued them.

"My other questions are for you, Aunt Dolores. They are less simple. You may want to hear them privately."

"I will go." Agnes began rising.

"Don't," Dolores blurted. She reached out her hand. "Please don't."

Agnes looked at her sister, whose worry dragged at her face. She glanced at Chase, then sat again.

"Aunt Dolores, did you have an old, long-held resentment against your brother? A slight that had not been forgotten?"

Dolores tried to appear surprised, but it didn't work. Rather her attempt dissolved into cold anger. "This is of no concern or interest to you, Chase. Whoever told you about this was disloyal and cruel. As you said, it was an old slight, from very long ago."

"But not forgotten."

She licked her lips. "I never forgave him."

Agnes reached over and took her sister's hand. "Tell him, Dolores, lest someone make more of it than it is."

"I will not speak of it. I cannot. But . . . I give you leave to do so, Agnes."

Agnes kept her hand on her sister's, her arm stretched in connection. "There was a man in her life, Chase. She was twenty-four, so not a child. She was very much in love."

Dolores closed her eyes.

"Unfortunately, he was a scoundrel," Agnes continued.

"He wasn't," Dolores said.

"Oh, Sister, he was. Believe what you want, but he was a rogue." She turned her attention to Chase. "A fortune hunter of the first order. An assumed name and heritage. A charlatan. Frederick saw the truth of it on first meeting him. Dolores was not to be dissuaded. So Frederick put the fellow to the test."

"He betrayed me horribly," Dolores said.

"He saved you."

"He condemned me to a loveless life."

Agnes ignored her. "He offered this worthless man a great deal of money if he left Dolores alone, and indeed if he left the realm. South America for a year, that was the requirement. What a quandary that must have been for the blackguard. Dolores in theory might be worth much more, eventually. This was immediate, however. Instant wealth that he could carry out the door." Agnes patted Dolores hand. "He was gone from town by morning.

Frederick then sent Dolores and me on a grand tour. We had a wonderful time."

"I hated it."

"You danced at balls at every court in Europe and flirted with princes."

"He shouldn't have done it. He shouldn't have tempted him like that, with so much—what man would turn down all that—like a devil my brother showed him the money. Gold, all of it. He always kept gold at hand but this was a huge amount. A mountain of gold."

"Did you and he ever speak of it?" Chase asked.

Dolores shook her head. "Other than the row when he first told me what had happened, we did not. He knew what I thought. I had said I would never forgive him, and he accepted that I never did."

"He was generous to both of us, nevertheless," Agnes said. "Only at the end, with this will, did he fail us."

"It was his idea of punishment," Dolores said. "His way of showing his disappointment in me."

"Oh, Sister, stop talking nonsense. He did not single you out, did he? Surely we weren't all disappointments."

"Who told you about this?" Dolores had reclaimed her composure. "I want to know."

"No one in the family, I assure you. It was someone I don't think you have ever met." *A brilliant woman who overheard one sentence and guessed the rest.*

Dolores sighed. "People talked, of course. I suppose some still do."

Chase stood. "Thank you both. When doing such inquiries, it is always good to cross something off the list of duties, without it taking days of investigating."

"Then we are crossed off the list?" Agnes asked.

He bowed and took his leave.

* * *

Gentleman Jim's was busy in late afternoon. Among the men boxing, Chase spotted Nicholas and Kevin near the far wall. He made his way over and watched from the corner.

Nicholas had an inch and several pounds on Kevin, but Kevin's lean strength and agility evened the contest. Both men's shirts clung to their bodies with sweat. Since Chase was late, they probably had been at it for some time.

Nicholas saw him and signaled an end. They both walked over.

"You are looking too tidy, considering we are here by your invitation," Nicholas said, taking a towel from an attendant and wiping his face and neck. "Off with those coats and Kevin here will go a round with you. He still has plenty of boyish excess in him even after two bouts with me."

"I had to call on the aunts, and it took twice as long as planned because I had to learn all about their grievances against each other."

"I'm surprised Agnes has not killed Dolores by now," Nicholas said.

"She has come close, but has decided that throwing her out will work just as well."

"Tell your father to lock the doors, Kevin. He is the only brother in town," Nicholas said.

"She thought Whiteford House would suit her better," Chase said.

Nicholas froze with the towel in the middle of a wipe of his face. He looked over its edge like a man just sentenced to the hulls. "I will go rusticate and leave the whole house to her if she invites herself to stay."

"I may have convinced her that the house is still too uncomfortable for visitors and not up to her standards."

"As it will remain for a very long time, if it spares me finding relatives on the doorstep." He cast aside the towel. "Since you are still fully dressed, I assume you are too afraid of Kevin here to go at it with him. Make yourself comfortable while we wash."

They aimed for the dressing rooms while Chase strolled around the perimeter of the room, watching fists fly and bruises rise. He regretted he had arrived too late to participate. He felt out of sorts when he did not regularly exercise. Last night with Minerva had removed the worst of that edge, but he still would have liked a round or two.

When his cousins returned both had been scrubbed and dressed and looked none the worse for their bouts. Kevin had a big smile on his face.

"A splendid idea, Chase, even if you missed it yourself," he said.

Chase had arranged it as a way to get them both together without being too obvious. That it had distracted Kevin from his preoccupation with the will was an unexpected boon.

"A tavern or a club?" Nicholas asked while they left the building.

"A tavern," Kevin said. "The White Swan, if you don't mind. There is a horse being offered through them that my father asked me to see."

They all mounted and rode east, then south toward the river until they reached the White Swan. Kevin asked about the horse at once, so they all went to inspect it.

Kevin proceeded to inspect it closely, from nose to tail. Nicholas and Chase did too. It was a horse, after all.

"How much?" Nicholas asked.

"Forty."

"Expensive."

"White ones usually are." Kevin gestured for the groom to walk the animal around the yard. "My father favors them, as many do. They look so nice as a pair. Unfortunately, half of his white pair has taken ill, so he requires another."

Nicholas began speaking, then shut his mouth. Chase could imagine what had almost emerged. *Why is he asking you to look at the horse when he can do it himself?* Apparently, Chase was not the only one arranging matters so Kevin did something other than brood.

"I'll tell him to offer thirty and settle at thirty-five."

They chose a table in the tavern and sent for ale. "We should make a day of it," Nicholas said. "We'll have a meal and drink too much, then go out looking for women this evening."

"There is Lady Trenholm's party tonight," Kevin said. "Unfortunately, I cannot go with you since I declined."

"Not those kinds of women," Nicholas said. "Chase here has told me to find an *inappropriate* woman."

"I am sure there will be some of those at her party too," Kevin said. "I have some names. Father does talk a lot over his port."

"If I attend a party, if any of us do so soon, people will consider it disrespectful of Uncle even if his will ordered us not to mourn. Furthermore, I would never get within ten feet of any of your father's inappropriate ladies, because a pack of baying mamas would block me."

Kevin laughed. "I suppose you have become the prize fox for their hunt this year. Once the Season starts—"

"I beg you not to speak of it. The mere idea of the Season throws me into deep melancholy."

"You could just visit a brothel," Kevin said. "Inappropriate, and uncomplicated. There are several that would celebrate your arrival as Uncle Frederick's heir."

Nicholas turned to Chase. "What do you say? We can show young Kevin here how it is done."

Kevin smiled slowly. "I am always grateful for your concerns about my education."

Chase smiled too, but his mind did not. He did not want to go to a brothel with Nicholas. A month ago, maybe. But not now. "I regret that I have a late appointment and can't join you."

Nicholas's eyes lit. "Damnation, look at that smirk. He has already found his inappropriate woman."

"Well, he does get around town a lot."

"I do," Chase said. "Both of you should try it. It is better than brooding."

"I do not brood," Nicholas said. "I worry. There is a marked difference. Yesterday I spent the day reading letters from men offering to be my head land steward for all the properties. I require a new one."

"Any who seemed worthy?" Chase asked.

"Hell if I know." Nicholas laughed. "How does a man who has never farmed know if another man is good at farming? I will have to rely on references, from other men who have never farmed."

They were back to the will. Chase didn't mind, although the hour respite had been welcomed.

"Will you be returning to France soon?" he asked Kevin.

Kevin shook his head. "The reason for being there has disappeared under current circumstances."

"How so?" Nicholas asked, truly interested.

"It will bore you."

"Not at all."

Kevin leaned in. "You know that I have been developing a small piece of machinery that increases the pressure and velocity of steam put out by a steam engine."

"I know it, but I've never understood it."

"I found a man in France who has another piece of machinery that if matched with mine will refine the process. If you put them together it will be a device that every engine will have to have. It allows a far wider application of the engines. I was in France trying to convince this fellow to sell it to me, or at least sell me the right to use it. I spent weeks there, working on him, earning his trust. He finally named his price, but of course I can't pay it."

Kevin's sharpness and tenacity impressed Chase. He had always been thorough in whatever he took on. Six years younger than Nicholas and four years younger than himself, at twenty-seven Kevin had long ago left his youthful friends to their pursuit of pleasure and embarked on a quest of sorts.

"How much does he want?" Chase asked.

"Eight thousand. It is worth far more. Especially to me, or anyone else who devises what I have. I came and asked Uncle Frederick, but—"

His expression suddenly lost its intensity. He swallowed the slip along with some ale.

When did you come back? Chase hoped he would not have to ask.

Silence slowly beat out time. Finally, Nicholas made a display of stretching and yawning and raking his hair. "Now, about those inappropriate women," he began.

"No." Kevin held up his hand. "You may as well know. It is bound to come out. Once I had that calibrator in my sights I hopped on a packet and came back. I met with Uncle Frederick. He was not convinced. He said I could have it created again here, for a fraction of the cost. That may be true, but what was saved in money would be lost in time. I had also made promises not to steal the design. Still, he would not agree. It was a disappointment to me, of course."

"So you returned to France."

Kevin nodded. "I hoped to salvage something of the arrangement. However, the price remains the same. It is just a matter of time before someone else finds him. He knows he has something of value."

"When did you return from France that first time, to speak with Uncle?" Nicholas asked, sparing Chase the question.

"Three days before he died. I went to Melton Park when I learned he was not in town. I sent a note when I arrived and asked to meet him in the park." He blinked hard. "We had a bit of a row out there among the naked trees. I started back to town that evening."

"It is understandable that you did not share this widely," Chase said. "It would be best if you continue not doing so."

"I did not harm him. I sure as hell did not go up on that damned roof that night. I was gone by then. We had met the evening before."

"True, but you were there and not where it is thought you were. Do not speak of this with anyone else."

Kevin looked him in the eyes.

"As for the money, can't you find another source? Another partner?" Nicholas asked.

"Who? You know my father dislikes my involvement in such things. He was furious with his brother for encouraging me. His stupid automatons are all fine and good, but heaven forbid a machine has a purpose other than amusement.

Nor do I have the right to take another partner now. The company is in limbo until my current partner is found and her agreement is required for *everything*. If she isn't found, all of you will be my new partners and I will require *all of you* to agree to every step I take. I'll be explaining machines to Aunt Dolores and, God forbid, Walter."

"Now, that is a special hell that no man deserves," Nicholas said.

"You would know, wouldn't you?"

"I do indeed." Nicholas looked around the tavern. "I am hungry. I remember they have acceptable meat pies here." He gestured to the proprietor and sent for three pies.

"They are very good," Chase said a while later, taking his third bite. "Sometimes simple food is needed."

"I agree. That cook at the house makes fine meals in the French style, but too big for me alone. It is a wonder Uncle Frederick did not get as stout as Prinny."

"He only ate one meal a day," Chase said. "He made do with bread and cheese otherwise."

"That sounds dull," Nicholas said. "You know the oddest details about him."

"It did keep him from getting stout, that is all I am saying." Chase glanced at Nicholas's middle section.

Nicholas noticed. He looked down. "Are you implying I need to follow Uncle in this eccentricity? How dare you. I am *not* stout."

"Not *quite* yet," Kevin muttered. He caught Chase's eye and they both laughed.

"This *not at all stout* duke still wants to return to the subject of women," Nicholas said. "I don't want to sound callous, Kevin, but the whole time you explained your inopportune visit to Uncle, I was occupied thinking about them in scandalous detail. My interest in the entire subject has, shall we say, grown."

"Not so much that you can't ride a horse, I trust."

"He has become damned impertinent, Chase."

"Which brothel do you want to visit?" Kevin asked.

"I will let you choose. I daresay that any of them will suit me." He stopped, and looked hard at Kevin. "Unless you frequent the ones that are favored by men with peculiar tastes."

Kevin looked innocent as a lamb. "No French cuisine for dessert, you mean. More simple pie. We will visit one that will accommodate you."

Chase stayed while they finished the last of their ale. He sent them off to their evening adventures, and turned his own horse toward home.

I need to see you tonight. I will send a carriage at nine o'clock. The letter had come in the early afternoon post. Minerva had debated what to do for at least two minutes before relinquishing any pretense that she did not intend to go.

No scolds came from Beth while she prepared after dinner. Rather the opposite. Beth insisted on redoing her hair. She laid out an almost fashionable dress, a deep green one with a tiny ruffle around the neckline. She kept watch at the window when they went below.

"It's here," she announced. "Does he not have his own carriage?"

"I don't think so. He doesn't have much use for one."

"He'll be needing one now, I should think. How else will he take you to the theater and such?"

"He has not said he wants to go to the theater, Beth. Perhaps he doesn't even care for it."

"Everyone likes the theater. If he doesn't suggest it, you

should. It isn't fitting for you to only see him for—" She snapped her mouth shut.

Minerva went to the reception hall to find Jeremy waiting. "What are you doing here? Don't you dare follow again."

"I'm only here to be your footman. Someone needs to escort you down and hand you in like a lady."

She muttered her annoyance, but actually was touched by their interest and concern. Under Beth's watchful eye, Jeremy helped her into the carriage.

To her surprise, the carriage was not empty. Chase sat within.

"Prompt as always," he said while he ensured she was comfortable. "Do you enjoy music? There is a concert at the Argyll Rooms tonight. It is sponsored by the London Philharmonic Society. I thought we would go if you want."

"I would enjoy that very much."

He gave the coachman the direction, then slid from his seat over to hers. He gave her a kiss. He then looked around the compartment they shared. He brushed at the slightly worn upholstery on the seat across. "My apologies. This was the best Brigsby could procure. I have been negligent in not buying my own and must attend to that."

She had not noticed anything amiss with the carriage. "Has Beth been interfering again?"

"I have not spoken to her. What makes you think she is meddling?"

"The concert. The carriage."

He looked perplexed.

She gave him a little kiss. "Ignore me. I am so used to inquiries that my mind makes them even when unnecessary."

"Let us forget about them this evening. I spent the day on them and need a respite from all of that."

"I think that is a splendid idea. Of course, that leaves us with little conversation. I can't learn about your life without touching on your family, for example."

"My family did not involve itself in my whole life. Ask away if you are curious about something."

She decided which of her many questions to pose first. "Was your father in the army? Did you follow him in choosing that life?"

"My father was a scholar. A very good one. He translated ancient Greek literature. He wrote books about it too. I'll show them to you someday. I was not a scholar. Far from it. Least of all in those topics. All young gentlemen are taught Latin, so I stood for that. He, however, wanted me to learn Greek too, as he had, and that was going too far."

"Did you join the army to avoid learning ancient Greek?"

"Of course not. I did make it a point to fail miserably at the task, though. Given the chance he would have had me sitting for hours in a library with him, poring over those old texts. I much preferred running and riding and fighting and sport."

"Fighting?"

"When you dine with Nicholas I will have him tell you about the fights we had, either with each other or as comrades in arms. You will receive an invitation in the morning, by the way. He has not forgotten."

"I suppose if you enjoyed fighting and riding and sport like fencing, entering the army seemed very natural to you."

"Not natural so much as inevitable. For the grandson of a duke the acceptable choices are limited. Of them only the army suited me."

The carriage plunged into a tangle of conveyances when they turned onto Regent Street and approached the Argyll Rooms. Chase pointed out the building. "Nash redesigned it when he altered the path and size of Regent Street here," he said. "Both the inside and the exterior bear his mark now."

"Isn't this where the Cyprian Ball is held?"

"You know about that?"

"Everyone knows about it. Did you ever attend?"

"Most gentlemen about town do at least once. It wasn't nearly as scandalous as I had hoped."

"What a disappointment for you."

The coachman maneuvered their carriage very close to the entrance before he stopped. Chase hopped out and offered his hand to her. Once she alighted he spoke to the coachman, palmed him some coins, and they entered the building.

"I have subscriptions, but we will use the duke's box," he said, guiding her up to the salon, then to a door.

"Will he be attending too?"

"He is otherwise occupied tonight."

The Duke of Hollinburgh possessed a very fine box. One of the best. Below the musicians had already been seated and they plucked at their instruments. A beautiful harpsicord stood to one side on the stage. She took a seat in the second row of chairs, hoping to avoid being on display the way the women in the other boxes were.

He sat beside her without comment on her choice. When an attendant arrived and began lighting the lamps, he told the man to leave them as they were.

"Thank you," she said. "I am not dressed for the occasion, let alone to sit in a box such as this."

"I should have been more thoughtful, and given you warning, so you were not uncomfortable. The truth is you look beautiful tonight, Minerva, and the equal to any of the ladies glittering across the way. You always look beautiful."

The musicians poised themselves to play. The music started. In the dark of that box, feeling very beautiful indeed, she allowed the music to enter her while she nestled against the shoulder at her side.

As arranged, the carriage was waiting for them when they left the building. Chase guided Minerva through the crush to its door.

Her expression in the lamplight reminded him of the one yesterday when she was leaving. Astonished. Transformed.

"Have you never heard music like that before?" he asked when he sat beside her and the carriage began nudging away from the other conveyances.

"Not quite. Not like the last piece. The first ones—I have heard something similar in church."

The first had been Bach. The second Beethoven. The first a fugue on harpsicord. The second a symphony that thundered through the theater. Uncle Frederick had not liked Beethoven's music. *Dionysiac*, he had called it. *The structure is there but buried in storms that rouse the emotions, not the mind,* he had said. *On the other hand, when you want to seduce a woman, it is useful to have her listen to Beethoven first.*

"Did your church in Dorset have such sophisticated music?"

"No, but when in London I would attend St. George's near Hanover Square. I never missed Sunday service. Beth and her son would come too, and we would walk both ways, even in bad weather, to make the outing last a long time."

There would be no way Finley could object to his wife attending church. That must have annoyed him. Not enough that he accompanied her, though. Such a man knows his soul has no business in such a place. "How far was it?"

"We normally let a house west of Portman Square, so not too far. I would have to leave quite early, though, because we would walk very, very slowly." She kissed his cheek. "Thank you for tonight. It was a special treat. I feel as though the music is still inside me."

He turned and gave her a full kiss, such as he had been wanting to do since she left her house. "I will return you to your home now if you want."

"Don't you dare."

He needed no more encouragement than that. The music was still inside him too, and he released some of the passion in kissing her. Things were more equal this time. She parted her lips, inviting the deep exploration of her mouth. She nipped his lip, testing her own power a little.

It was hell releasing her when the carriage stopped. They both pretended they were normal while he settled with the coachman and they walked calmly to the door. Up the stairs they trod, when in truth he wanted to sling her over his shoulder and run.

Once the door closed on his apartment he grabbed her and swung her into his arms. There was no sight or sound of Brigsby, who must have taken shelter in his chamber. He held her head with one hand and shrugged off coats and cravat. She dropped her reticule. Amidst kisses and bites and grasping embraces they inched through the apartment with garments flying.

Only when they dropped onto the bed naked did he seek some restraint. He might not have to be heroic, but he could not ravish her either. Yet he craved to be in her, thrusting deeply, feeling her tremors and hearing her sighs and—he forced himself to find the final tether to sanity that still existed.

He took his time after that, to make sure she knew pleasure. The rhythm of her sighs and gentle moans, slow at first then rising in speed and sound, found union with the hard beat of his heart. She abandoned control fast, like a woman more than ready. He put his hand to her mound while he used his mouth on her breasts, to push her further into delirium.

He gently pushed at one thigh. "Open, darling." He slid a finger down her cleft while he spoke. Her mouth fell open and her back arched. He almost pulled her atop him then, but instead again resisted. He touched her more purposefully. The intensity had her cry out.

She moved against his hand, seeking more. Her cries turned loud and desperate. A series of small tremors shook her and with each one she stopped breathing. He circled his touch around the edge of her passage, then brought it forward to the nub. A series of frantic cries rang through the chamber. Then she screamed, and even as she did she scrambled atop him, and took him inside herself. She came down hard, absorbing him.

She looked glorious and perfect and he wanted her only more now. He gritted his teeth and restrained himself yet again, so whatever she experienced would not be interrupted.

It seemed like forever they remained like that, with him throbbing inside her, hot and demanding, with his whole body tight as a bowstring. He was about to give up on heroics when she opened her eyes and looked down. She leaned forward, kissed him, and began moving.

She soon joined him again in frenzied passion. The coil of pleasure tightened, increasing his hunger and pushing for more. He thrust hard again and again. His release came in an explosion of pleasure that buried him.

She sank down on him, her fingers gripping his shoulders and her breathing hard and short. He wrapped his arms around her back and bottom so they stayed together a while longer in every way. She remained with him as sensations slowly gave way to thought. Even then he kept her there, because most of those thoughts wandered around her.

He finally loosened his hold. She rolled off him and onto her back beside him. He figured out how to cover them both with the tangle of bedclothes they had created. He embraced her with one arm so she came closer.

"I am speechless," she said lowly into his ear. "I have no way to know for sure, but I think you are probably a very good lover."

He enjoyed her flattery to a ridiculous extent.

She nestled down closer and deeper. "You spent the day on inquiries, didn't you?"

"I did. You were correct about Dolores. There was an old resentment, over a man that my uncle warned off most effectively. He paid the fellow to disappear. She is still angry." He was going to let it rest, but found himself adding. "And Kevin admitted to me that he indeed returned from France earlier, and met with Uncle Frederick. They had a row."

She didn't move or speak for a long time.

"Not on the roof," he felt obligated to add. "And not that night, but the evening before."

"Well, that's different, isn't it?"

It is if he is telling the truth. Damnation. For hours he had not been turning that over in his head. Inevitable that it would all start again, though.

"It is difficult to investigate one's own family. Perhaps

you should wait for an official inquiry. If there isn't one, you can take it up again if you think you should."

He watched her profile and the way the low light limned it. The tangle of her hair spread out over the pillow, its silken strands feathering his face. He had not told her, or anyone, that his inquiry *was* the official one. It had crossed his mind to tell Peel to find someone else to do it, though. Only then he would have no control over it. No ability to turn that blind eye, or avoid ferreting out information on people he did not think required investigation. Like Kevin. Or Minerva.

He had wondered when she would go to this topic. Right now had been a good choice. Their intimacy allowed more honest talk than daylight ever required.

"If it is someone in the family, I would want to know first," he said.

"So you could tell that person to purchase packet tickets?"

"Something like that."

She turned her head to look at him. "Have you ever done that?"

"There was one time when I might have. I was too trusting of the person's innocence, however, until it was too late."

"I hope you did not blame yourself for trusting, no matter what it meant to the direction of events."

"It was a mistake that I paid for dearly, that is all."

She peered at him, as if trying to see his thoughts. When he said no more, she looked away. There was no hurt in her, from what he could tell. She merely accepted that he chose not to share the story with her.

He looked away too, at the ceiling. She turned into his arm and rested her head on his chest.

Did you kill him? Only twice had he answered that question, and even then not told everything. He did not speak of it. He did not explain.

"I was in the army and at times conducted investigations. That was where I started and learned. After Waterloo, I was with my regiment in France, part of the army that remained there while matters were sorted out. A Frenchman was found dead in the town. Knife wounds. Someone said one of our men had been seen nearby. I was told to look into it."

She did not move or react. She only listened.

"I learned this man had a lover. A woman of renowned beauty. And he had a rival. One of our officers. A friend of mine. A good friend."

Only briefly did he consider not finishing. Yet it felt good to speak of it, finally. With her.

"I knew it could not possibly have been him. I *knew* him. I had for years. I would have sworn to his character. So I kept searching for another, and yet—there was no one else. I did not accept the truth until they arrested him. One of her servants came forward and admitted she had seen it all. An argument over the woman. A crime of passion, the French called it. The British army claimed jurisdiction, however, and we have no provisions for such an excuse. He was sure to hang."

"How terrible for him. And for you if he was a friend."

"It meant an ignoble death, and the loss of his good name. An embarrassment to his family and all who claimed him as a friend." He was there again, hearing the damning evidence, and knowing all that it meant, even beyond death. He could see the fear in his friend's eyes, worse than any seen in battle. *Did you do it? Did you kill him?*

"On the second morning of the trial he was found dead in his cell. A single pistol wound, well placed. A suicide wound, it appeared, but no pistol was found."

She turned her body so she looked up at him.

"Did you kill him?"

Brave woman. Braver than he was. He had never asked her that question, after all.

"He admitted his guilt to me, then asked me to. Begged me to. I refused. I gave him my pistol, however, and stood aside, outside the cell while he used it. Then I took the pistol, so he would not in fact be a suicide." He only got it out by speaking without pause, by forcing down the emotions of that dank donjon of a gaol and the friendship that led him to such a choice. "No one could prove a thing, but they guessed. Few thought the less of me for it. 'I would have done the same,' one senior officer confided, even though I had admitted nothing. When asked if I killed him, I said I had not."

"You hadn't."

"Not officially. But in a way I had."

"Is that why you left the army?"

He smiled into the dark, ruefully. "You *are* good at inquiries, aren't you? It was recommended that I sell out my commission. It was the kind of story that follows a man throughout his career. As for now, and the rumors even in my own family—there is no good way to explain it, is there?"

She kissed his chest, gently. "There is no blame for you in this sad story. I hope you don't tell yourself there is."

"If I were not so trusting of my knowledge of him, I would have known sooner. I might have had better choices then."

"Such as telling him to run?"

He stroked her crown. She stretched up and kissed him. "So now you only trust evidence and proof that you can list on paper, because when it mattered your deeper knowledge of a man got it all wrong. Yet, I think you did know back then. Your heart and your loyalty and your youth would not accept it, but deep inside you, even before the evidence and proof, I think you knew."

The argument that rose in his head died on his lips. She sighed deeply, and began to doze off. He held her, glad she had not reached for her garments instead of falling asleep in his arms.

Sleep crept up on him as well. Thoughts and fragments of memories floated in what remained of his consciousness. Bits of Dolores's story, and of conversations with Kevin and Minerva, and of events from that old inquiry. Oblivion pulled at him, making him drift down. With his last awareness he felt her body against his, and his hand and arm around her nakedness.

Yes, damn it. I knew.

Chapter Nineteen

"I have been thinking. You said in passing that you could use someone like Jeremy at times. If you meant that, you have my permission to offer him a situation, as long as I don't lose his services."

They were in a carriage, riding to her home in the gray light of dawn. Not that anyone at her house would be unaware she had been gone all night. Still, she thought it best to maintain the normal standards of deception.

"In other words, if you have no use for him, I can make use of him."

"If he agrees. He might like earning some coin. I think he grows restless when I don't keep him busy."

"I will see what his thoughts are on it, and if his view of his value is as high as yours. I hope not. Will you loan me Miss Turner too?"

"She is still a little green, but holds much potential. In a few months, perhaps."

He went back to kissing her, which her comment about Jeremy had interrupted. He didn't stop when they arrived at her house until she gave him a gentle push.

"He will be awake by now, if you want to speak to him," she said. "He has lived in the little carriage house in back the last two years."

"At his age I expect he was getting underfoot here with you two ladies."

"It was all his idea to move out there. Beth was too aware of his movements when he lived in the house." There had been some rows about that, with Jeremy letting his mother know that it was time for her to mind her own affairs. At first the house seemed empty without him, and less safe, but he was close by in that carriage house, and by nature watchful.

"What will you do today?" he asked, dallying at the door, his hand resting on her arm as if he did not want to stop touching her.

"First, I will sleep."

He smiled wickedly at the meaningful look she gave him. Among the other things she had learned in that bed to her amazement was that people on occasion did that more than once in a night. The pleasure had been quieter the second time, even languid, but no less moving. After his revelations, their closeness seemed even deeper, as if they had absorbed parts of each other.

"Then I will start on my new inquiry."

"An interesting one?"

"I am to find a relative who has gone missing. There was an estrangement, and now one party wants a reconciliation, but has no idea where to find the relative in question. I think I will start with advertisements."

She worked the latch and opened the door. "I would love to stand out here with you and kiss and embrace and shock the neighbors, but I do have to send you home."

A charming smile. An elaborate bow. He turned away and she shut the door. She went up to her chamber, hoping Beth would pepper her with questions and force her into confidences. If she did not tell someone about last night, she would burst.

* * *

Chase untethered his horse and sent the carriage on its way. He definitely would have to purchase one, and arrange for the services of a coachman and groom.

He tied the horse to a post, then strolled to the side garden portal. If Jeremy was awake and about, he might as well see if Jeremy had the same view of being shared as Minerva had of it.

The narrow house had a narrow garden with old walls separating it from the neighbors' property. The carriage house way in back looked to have a new roof, but Chase doubted a carriage had lived there in many years.

He walked around to the front and rapped on the door.

"In here," Jeremy called.

Chase entered. It was a small place, but had been made comfortable. A wooden floor made it into a house if anything did. The gates for the carriage were firmly locked and bolted, becoming a wall. Simple furniture, probably borrowed from the main house, created a little sitting room.

Another door gave off from this one, and he walked to it. On its threshold he saw that it was the bedchamber. Inside Jeremy washed, stripped to the waist, his youthful body bent over the basin while he rinsed his face. He heard Chase, and glanced over. Smiling, he stood and faced the door while he pulled on a shirt. Then he opened the door fully and came out. "I thought it was my mum. I didn't expect callers. I don't have any."

Chase looked around the chamber. "You have made a pleasant home for yourself here."

"I like it. Mum doesn't." He smiled again. "'We'll be killed by intruders and you'll be none the wiser out here,' she said. As if any intruder would stand a chance with those two, as you learned to your pain. Also, they can shoot better than I can."

"Is that who taught Miss Hepplewhite? Your mother?"

"It was. Mum was a farmer's daughter. Tenant on some estate somewhere. But she married an army fellow. Not like you. Just a soldier. He got killed in the war early on, and she went into service to be able to keep me." He pulled on his coat. "Come and sit down. If you are here, there is a reason I expect."

Chase and he returned to the sitting room. Jeremy built up the fire a bit and soon the flames broke through the night chill still hanging in the house.

"I would offer you something, but I take meals at the house and there's not even coffee here."

"I have no need of anything, but thank you for the good intentions. Miss Hepplewhite suggested something to me. I thought I would talk about it with you, since you may not think it as good an idea as she did."

"Could be, although she usually has good ideas."

"She said that there are times when she does not have much use of your services, and that if I do have need of such services then, perhaps you would like to make yourself available to my inquiries."

Jeremy absorbed that. He frowned vaguely while he thought. "There'd be wages for this?"

"I will match whatever she pays you."

Jeremy smiled at the floor and scratched his head. "I'll be wanting a bit more than that, because she doesn't pay me anything. Not yet. She feeds me and I live here, and she is like my family."

"Then let us settle on wages that are suitable, since I am not like family."

It did not take long to do so. Jeremy seemed pleased. "It could be complicated, what with you sending for me and I'm maybe not even here to know it because I'm somewhere for her."

"We will see if we can keep it from being too complicated."

Jeremy just looked at him with a half smile on his face. Something amused him, and Chase suspected it was he himself. "What?" he asked, when that gaze continued.

"I'm just thinking how Minerva is the smartest person I know, and you seem to have your wits about you too, but neither of you can see it."

"See what?"

"Hell, if you are going to share workers and you are going to share a bed, why don't you just share a business?"

The notion had never entered his mind. Yet it made some sense, especially because their methods complemented each other.

Ridiculous, of course. He could name five reasons why it would never work, and might well ruin too much. Still, he had to give Jeremy some credit for his own wits.

"I will go now. Oh, I had a question on another matter. When you would visit London with the Finleys, where was the house they let?"

"Old Quebec Street. Up a ways off Oxford. It is near Portman Square."

Chase left Jeremy to go get his breakfast, and let himself out the side portal. The image he had seen when entering the bedchamber held steady in his memory while he mounted his horse. Before Jeremy had pulled on the shirt, while he bent to the basin, marks had been visible as raised lines on his shoulders. He had been beaten at some point. Chase had seen marks like that often enough in the army, only deeper and wider, on men who had been whipped.

These scars had healed better than most. Time had gone far to fade them. That meant they were quite old, and the back on which they were laid had been young. The mere act of growing up had changed them.

Finley had been a brute with more people than his wife, it seemed.

The caller came two afternoons later. Chase was not expecting anyone, least of all this man.

Mr. Martin Monroe, the card said. *Private Inquiries*.

Monroe entered the sitting room and looked around, as if taking its measure and assessing its worth. Chase waited for him to do the same thing with the apartment's owner.

A big smile beamed on Monroe's florid face. In his early middle years, he had thickened around the middle and a few gray hairs salted his dark hair. The smile made balls form on his cheeks. The blue eyes, however, showed more shrewdness than his bonhomie manner suggested.

"I've come on a professional matter," he said once they had greeted each other and he had sat. "Professional courtesy, actually. I'm told you and I share a calling."

"You have been conducting inquiries into me, I see."

"Well, I saw you at the concert and asked my friend who was that there and he told me. He's not a friend of yours, but he knows that box and the family that uses it."

It all sounded innocent, but Chase heard the architecture behind the façade. "Why did you ask about me?"

"Ah, that is the whole of it, isn't it? I've some information that may be of use to the man in that box and needed to know his name. Imagine my surprise to learn it was a duke's relative, and one whose days are spent much like mine."

"Of course if what you know is of some use, I will be grateful to hear it. Perhaps you should inform me of your fees before you share the information itself."

Monroe was not insulted. He was in the business of information, after all. Still, his smile demurred before his words did. "No fees as such. My thinking is that if I do you a good turn, professionally speaking, that someday you will return the favor. Our sort needs to stick together, right?"

Apparently, Mr. Monroe had sought him out with the best of intentions. "I have been remiss as a host. Let us share some brandy while you visit." Chase went to the decanter, poured two glasses, and brought them back.

Monroe sipped his, expressed delight, then set it down. "So, here it is. That woman you were with at the concert. I know her. And, to be honest, I'm wondering if you really do."

"I think so."

"She uses the name Hepplewhite now. But she was not six years ago Margaret Finley. That's her real name. Married she was, to one Algernon Finley."

"I am aware of that."

"Are you now? Do you also know she killed the man? Came within an inch of hanging for it."

Chase kept his reaction in check, but astonishment slowed time for a solid ten count.

Monroe saw his surprise despite his efforts to hide it. "I know of what I speak. This is not idle gossip."

"How do you know?"

"I was in Dorset on another matter. When it finished, I stayed on a spell and did a spot of work for her husband. An inquiry. Into her."

"Algernon Finley wanted your services regarding his wife?"

"He did indeed. She'd left him, and he was sure there was a lover behind it all. Had me looking into that. Not the sort of work I much care for, but there I was and I thought it would be an easy assignment. I was wrong. The woman was sly. She guessed I was watching and that lover never came to her house. Sometimes she would get out somehow without my seeing, and she probably met him then. I was working my way into a friendship with a neighbor who might know something, when Finley turns up dead. He went riding in nearby hunting lands on occasion, and one day he got shot there."

Hell. Finley had not merely died. He'd been *shot*.

"A hunting accident, most likely."

"So the coroner eventually said, but no man who dies by an accident ends up with a lead ball directly to the heart, does he?"

Hell. "Pistol ball, mind you. Not a musket. Who hunts with a pistol?"

Almost no one.

"She carried one, tucked into this shawl she wrapped around herself back then. I saw it once. She said she was in the market at the time it happened, but the market people didn't know just when she was there seeing as how it was so busy. Could have been then, or earlier. I had learned about how she left, and knew her husband assumed the only way she got the money to live was from another man. I saw how that lover could have helped her or done it for her. I swore down that information."

Minerva had told him most of this. Not about the pistol wound to the heart. Not about Monroe looking for a lover. She had to know she was being watched by Monroe, though. She was too good at inquiries to miss when one had her as the object.

"Why was she not accused and tried?"

Monroe took another sip of his brandy. "Evidence too thin, the coroner said. No proof he was murdered at all, and none that she was in that forest. Then it turned out he left nothing, was in debt, so any motive fell apart, since I had never found that lover. But I'm telling you that she did it, as sure as I'm sitting here drinking your very fine brandy. Telling you unofficially, of course, and only due to our common profession. I know all about criminal libel and am making no actual accusations."

"I thank you for all of this. I know it was imparted with the best intentions. Tell me, do you often work out of London?" Chase managed to keep an even tone, despite his silent cursing.

"Never do. I'm here on a family problem. For all the good it will do. Normally I am in the Midlands and such, and the northern cities. Liverpool at times. Manchester. Business inquiries. Financiers and industrial men. It's more interesting than domestic matters, and for all their ruthlessness, cleaner. They aren't gentlemen for all their money, but at least you don't feel like you are pawing through someone's underclothes." He began to sip again, then stopped as if a thought had dawned. "One inquiry touched on your family, now that I remember. The last duke."

"How interesting. You must tell me about it, if it would not be an indiscretion." Chase rose and retrieved the decanter while he spoke. He refilled Mr. Monroe's glass, to the man's surprise and delight.

"I can tell you a bit, since we are colleagues of a sort, I suppose." He enjoyed the brandy a moment before continuing. "Was up near Manchester. There's a canal up there and them that own it were thinking of widening it. Only one of the partners would not agree. He said doing so would only benefit factories owned by two other partners, and not bring in enough to pay for the work or show a profit. Well, those two were angry, and one of them had me doing a few inquiries into the partner who stood in the way. Looking for secrets or such. Something that would be embarrassing if it came out. Was the late duke I was trying to learn about. He was the stubborn partner."

The rogues had wanted to blackmail Uncle Frederick. "Did you learn anything of use?"

"Nah. First, it is hard to do inquiries on a duke. Then, I learned that he didn't much care what was said about him, so what little I did find would not embarrass him. A taste for whores, for example. Common enough, but there's those who would be mortified if the whole world knew. Was clear he didn't hide it at all. I guess being a duke makes it all different."

"Mostly."

"I did learn that he would show up wearing costumes. Like he had attended a masquerade. Only he hadn't. Took me a week to learn that. Wormed it out of a housemaid in his London home that he had a whole wardrobe of such things, and at times wore them in his house too, for no good reason. Even when he was alone." Flush-faced now, he leaned in confidentially. "I confess I wondered if maybe he was a little mad, when I heard that."

"Not mad. Only unusual."

Those balls had taken permanent residence on Monroe's cheeks above his big smile. He chortled, and firmly put down his glass. "Enough of that, and I thank you. Now I should return to my sister's house and have some dinner. I am glad you received me, sir. I hope I have done you a good turn, as was my intention."

"You have. I look forward to returning the favor." Chase still expected a request for payment of some sort. When it did not come, he felt very cynical.

He accompanied his guest to the door. As the man started down the stairs, Chase asked a final question. "Who had you investigate the last duke?"

Monroe paused. "Well, now, I shouldn't say."

"I understand."

Monroe stood there a minute, then came back to the door. "Excuse me. I've remembered that I need to write a quick letter to post when I leave. Do you mind?"

"Not at all. Make use of the writing desk."

Monroe entered the sitting room, went to a writing desk, and used the pen on a piece of paper that he blotted, folded, and slipped into his frock coat. As he returned to the door, the paper fluttered to the floor.

With an innocent farewell, he went down to the street.

Chase picked up the paper that had "accidentally" been dropped. He read it, then tucked it away in the writing desk.

He looked out the window and watched Monroe walk down the street. Jaw tight, he barely managed to contain his anger with himself.

He had been negligent. With his mission, with his duty—hell, with his honor. He should have made hard inquiries into this mystery woman who inherited so much of the duke's money. Instead he had engaged in a flirtation with her, and become entangled. He had allowed desire to interfere with learning even the most basic information about her past in a timely manner.

Small wonder Minerva was so cautious with him, and so interested in the duke's death. Not only her inheritance put her high on the list, but so did her past. If anyone learned she was once suspected of murder—

I know you did not kill him. Hell, right now he didn't know anything at all.

Minerva gazed in her looking glass one last time. Huge dark eyes gazed back.

The duke's invitation to dinner had arrived last week,

and she had swallowed any trepidation until this evening. The only solace she found now was knowing Chase would be there, and she would not face this alone. She looked forward to seeing him too. They had been four days apart, as his inquiries kept him busy.

She pretended not to be nervous, but by the time she picked up her reticule she was in a state. Beth stood back and examined her. "That dress is very flattering, and the equal of anything worn by the other ladies that will be there, I'm sure."

Minerva wore the primrose silk dinner dress that had mysteriously arrived at her house. Upon her writing to Madame Tissot saying there had been a mistake, the modiste had merely written back that her shop did not make mistakes.

Other ladies. Of course there would be some. She had not thought about that, however. Now she wondered how many and who they would be.

Beth pinched her cheeks. "You need a bit of color, that's all. Get your wits about you now. You are the ladies' equal too. More than their equal. I doubt a one of them will have done as much as you have in life, or enjoy the freedom you do every day. Who knows, maybe if they learn of your inquiries, we will get clients we can charge very high fees to."

"Beth, you know just what to say. I will find a way to make sure they do learn of my inquiries. This is a wonderful opportunity, and I intend to do more than eat an incredibly fine meal."

"Don't be slighting the eating part. It will probably be the best food you swallow in your entire life. I'll be wanting all the particulars tomorrow. Every sauce, every savory, every joint—" She sighed. "I can taste it now."

Minerva went below to wait for the carriage. It would not do to keep a duke waiting. When she heard it in front of her door, she collected herself and stepped out.

Jeremy waited to play footman. So did Elise, to gawk. Her arrival interrupted their conversation and laughter. Jeremy snapped to attention to perform his duties. Elise watched with wide eyes.

She was so distracted by them that she was at the carriage door before she realized how nice a conveyance it was. Not as large as a typical hired coach, it sported green paint and polished brass and the coachman wore a very neat coat and hat. Inside plump cushions in deep red waited.

Jeremy closed the door and peered inside. "You will roll up Park Lane in style."

Chase had done this. It touched her that he wanted her to feel "equal to those ladies" when she arrived at his cousin's home. She opened the curtains and peered out at the way the town glowed from streetlamps and windows while they rolled along.

Formality greeted her arrival. Two liveried footmen tended the door and carriages. One handed her down and escorted her inside, delivering her to the butler. He in turn handed her to another footman who brought her up to the drawing room.

At least a dozen people moved within, chatting. The duke came over to greet her. A bow and curtsy and off they went, winding through the little group that included some very fine ladies indeed.

She spied Chase across the chamber, chatting with a lovely woman in red who flirted with him boldly. He didn't seem to be minding. That cleared the dazed befuddlement out of her head at once. She turned her full attention to the introductions, memorizing every name she heard.

"That is the Countess von Kirchen. She is visiting from Vienna," the duke said, noticing where her attention kept returning.

"She is very . . . lovely." She almost said voluptuous. Due to her ample endowments, the countess's bodice revealed more bosom than it covered. Minerva glanced down at her own décolleté. Upon donning the dress she had thought it daring. Suddenly it appeared sedate enough for a church.

Eventually the duke brought her to Chase, and pointedly eased the lady in red away. The chance to flirt with a duke proved an effective lure. Minerva watched the red stroll into the group.

"She is beautiful," she said.

"I suppose so."

"Of course she is. You have eyes."

"My, you are snappish. Are you jealous?"

"Of course not."

He tipped his head closer. "Not at all? I am wounded. As for my eyes, I saw only you once you appeared. It was all I could do not to be rude, and to these eyes no woman here is as beautiful as you are."

Now she felt foolish. She *had* been snappish. "Perhaps I was *a little* jealous. I suppose lovely women flirt with you shamelessly all the time. I should not make too much of it."

"Still snapping a bit, I see." He stepped back and looked at her from head to toe. "The dress makes you look seductive."

It was not a word she would have used. Certainly no one else ever had. Yet his calling her that made her *feel* seductive. "Perhaps I should flirt shamelessly too."

"Only with me, darling. Now we will walk over and join Kevin and that woman who has been pursuing him for months. She is a viscount's wife—the viscount is that man over there—and apparently she finds Kevin's preoccupation with his invention attractive."

"Perhaps she only finds him attractive. He is a very handsome man in a somewhat dramatic way. All the Radnor cousins were blessed by nature. Even that one whose wife talks for him."

They made their way toward Kevin and the eager viscountess. "Thank you for the carriage. It was a treat. I felt like a queen."

"I'm glad. I bought it yesterday."

She fingered the raw silk of her skirt. "Thank you for this too. I assume you were my mystery benefactor."

"I make no claims or denials."

Kevin greeted them with what looked like relief. The viscountess appeared less than pleased. Her expression cleared when she learned that Minerva aided Chase on some of his inquiries. With a long look she regarded them both. Minerva all but heard the woman's head drawing conclusions. After that, the viscountess was very friendly.

"I am too full," Minerva said. "I feel as portly as your cousin's butler."

Chase patted her stomach. "You did enjoy yourself heartily."

"Blame Beth. She said she wanted all the particulars and I could hardly give them if I didn't taste it all."

They sat together in the new carriage. Chase thought the dinner had been successful for Nicholas, his first as the new duke. A small affair, he had invited people not given to hard criticisms. If any were there, Minerva at least did not notice them. She was bright-eyed and vivacious throughout it all, behaving as if of course she should be sitting with those lords. She had perhaps overindulged herself at the table, though. She had only taken the tiniest taste of most of it, but even that was enough to put her in her current state.

"You probably should take me home," she said. "I am not fit for anything else."

"If you want, I will do so. I would like to hold you for a while, though. I don't need anything else." Except conversation. He needed to talk to her about her husband's death. Finally.

It had been a bad three days for his conscience. He had engaged in more self-reflection than he normally embraced. The conclusions he had drawn, about her, and himself, and their liaison had surprised him. Nor could he ignore that once his anger subsided, the strongest reaction became an urge to protect her, not investigate her.

"You can visit at my house, if you want," she said. "I would feel better there, in case I—"

He told the coachman where to go. "You will feel much better in an hour or so. You drank a fair amount of wine, and that is only making it worse."

At her house, she went above for a while. When she returned she wore the new undressing gown. Her expression suggested that just removing her stays and dress had helped.

"Won't Beth mind?" he asked, embracing her shoulders when she sat beside him.

"It is *my* house."

"Of course."

She lolled her head on his arm. "It was a wonderful

dinner party. I'm sure in the morning I will relive every magical moment. The flickering lights, the silver and gold, the food—oh, my, the food. Your cousin's friends were very gracious. A few of the ladies asked about my inquiries with interest. I think one or two will be asking for my help in the future."

Good for Minerva. Probably good for the ladies. Not so good for him. A day ago, should they want an inquiry, they would have called on *him*. Rather suddenly, with one dinner party, she had become a competitor thriving in his own garden.

He had competitors already. Some good ones. One other who moved in the same circles. Minerva, however, presented a special appeal, one which he could not match. She was a woman. If an inquiry touched on any matter that could be called *delicate*, another woman would be most likely to seek out Hepplewhite's.

"I spoke with Jeremy," he said. "He was agreeable with your idea."

"I'm glad. He could use the work. It suits him far better than some of the things he does to earn some coin."

"He said you do not pay him."

"I don't pay Beth either. Or myself. He lives here. He eats here. However, if the inquiries keep coming as I anticipate, I intend to give him wages soon. And, of course, in due time I will have some of the trust's income too."

He did not mind that those wages would derive from inquiries he should have had instead. Not at all. He did not really need the income. And yet—he looked at her. Head back, eyes half closed, hair mussed—she looked ravishing in her dishabille. Now that she had one toe in society, he did not doubt she would build Hepplewhite's quickly.

He was happy for her. Truly. Someday, however, he would probably give Nicholas hell for inviting her to that dinner.

"When we were talking, Jeremy said something provocative."

That got her attention enough that she raised her head. "An odd word, provocative. Are you saying he made you angry?"

"Not at all. He said he didn't understand why we don't share a business, if we are going to share workers."

She turned her body so she faced him. "How was that provocative?"

"It provoked thought."

"Are you saying you would want to do this?"

"I am only saying that it makes some sense. You have abilities I don't have. I have some you don't have."

"I can hire a man with your abilities. You can hire a woman with mine. We could even hire each other."

"True. Clumsy, but true."

Her eyes narrowed. "You are not suggesting that I become a regular employee, are you? With wages and such?"

It was a topic he had not considered much. While being provoked to thought, he had not really done much thinking.

"You tried that at Melton Park, calling me your employee even though I wasn't one. I found the deception useful there, but I don't care for the notion."

"I had no intention of suggesting such a thing." The look in her eyes made that the right thing to say, no matter what he might one day think, when he thought.

That mollified her. "Whose business would this be then?"

Mine, of course. There was no alternative that would pass muster in the world. Men would never engage them if she were the owner. Women *would* engage him if he owned a service in which a woman supplied some of the services.

It certainly couldn't be *hers*. That would make *him* the employee. A gentleman who conducts inquiries was one thing, a man who works for wages was another.

Her mind must have been traveling the same paths, because she shook her head. "I don't think it would be a good idea."

"Probably not." He eased her back into his arms. He could not avoid the next topic any longer. "I need to tell you something. A Mr. Monroe called on me."

Her eyes opened, wide. She sat up and turned to him. "What did he want?"

"He saw you at the concert. He came to tell me about you. He thought I should know about your history."

"That nuisance of a man. He was always there, following me, poking his nose into my life, watching my home."

"He was hired to find evidence of a lover."

She lowered her eyelids. "How like Algernon. First he accuses me of being cold and less than a woman, then he decides I am engaging in orgies with another man. There was no lover, of course. Monroe was wasting his time and, as I said, being a nuisance."

"He said Finley was shot while out riding. That it was not a normal death. He said the magistrate speculated on your involvement." *He said you carried a pistol. He said it was a pistol ball to the heart, which is an unlikely accident.* He swallowed the new revelations while he looked at her. Did the army officer doubt her? Did the man who conducted private inquiries? If not, there was no reason to insult her with questions about those details.

He wished he could say he did not think she could ever

kill. There were those who couldn't. Even the army had some, and they died on the field fast. Minerva was not such a person. Given the right circumstances, to protect herself or her own, he could see her doing it. Was her danger from that husband of hers reason enough?

She was eyeing him sharply now, watching him while his mind worked. "I was wondering why you had not found a way to see me the last few days. I think you have decided to end this liaison."

"I have decided nothing of the sort."

"I would decide it for you, if I were brave enough. If this becomes known—when it becomes known—any friendship with me would compromise you in several ways. Mr. Monroe told you that I was suspected in Algernon's death. That alone would make me suspected again in the duke's. You know I am right."

"I will only tell the solicitor what is necessary to establish your history as Margaret Finley. The rest does not signify to his duties as executor. With any luck, no one will learn the rest of it."

She caressed his jaw, then his mouth. "I had no reason to kill him, if you are wondering. I had my freedom. The separation probably saved his life, until someone else did the deed, that is."

Damnation, she had just admitted she might well have killed her husband but for the separation.

"You may not be able to protect me, if you are thinking that way," she said.

"That remains to be seen." He thought he could, though. These revelations had altered his view of many things. Like seeing a battlefield from high ground suddenly, he had realigned certain evidence like so many troops.

The path to victory would require some inquiries she would not like, however, and a retreat of sorts, for now.

She leaned closer, and gazed right into his eyes. "Chase, you once told me that you knew I had not killed your uncle. You just knew. Are you that sure that I did not harm Algernon?"

He took her hand in his. "Minerva, I don't think you did this, but I do not know it the way you speak of a better sense knowing. The devil of the truth is this—I have realized that I don't care if you killed that rogue. In fact, a part of me hopes that you did."

Chapter Twenty

Chase left Minerva's house at dawn and rode to Park Lane. He went up the stairs of Whiteford House and entered the duke's apartment. He strode over to the sitting room windows and drew the drapes.

A silvery mist hung over London, obscuring most of the rooftops. A few lamps still glowed, not yet extinguished. Down below the gardens and mews showed as little more than blotches of grays. While he watched, however, the sun's slow rise began defining the forms more, etching trees and houses. The mist slowly thinned.

He gazed to the northeast. The broad swath of Oxford Street ran nearby. A few streets beyond it an opening in the buildings' rooftops showed Portman Square's location. A little to the southeast the much larger opening of Grosvenor Square loomed, and beyond it Berkeley Square.

"What in hell are you doing here?"

He turned his head to see Nicholas squinting at him while he tied a banyan around his body.

"I am thinking about Uncle Frederick."

Nicholas came over and looked out while he yawned. "Town looks peaceful at this hour. Almost beautiful."

Chase opened the window. "It is coming alive, but the

sounds are still distinct. At night there are moments of silence. He liked that silence. He liked the world at night."

"It might have been better if he had not."

Chase was not thinking about the duke's death now, but about his life. "He walked at night here. Did you know that? Just as he walked along that parapet at Melton Park. His valet made a comment about it, and he had mentioned those walks to me himself."

"I can see him haunting the shadows."

"At night, if lamps are lit inside houses, you can see inside when you pass. Even those with drapes drawn, often you can see. One wonders what he saw, or if he even noticed."

Nicholas raked his hair. "Listen, I said nothing last night because it was not the time, but since you are waxing nostalgic about Uncle now—I am concerned about Kevin."

"As am I. It might be best if he left England for a few months. A man has a better chance at justice here than anywhere else, but this is a duke's death and if it is called other than an accident, there will be those looking for a resolution." It soured his mood to think about that development, and how if it occurred it would be on his conscience that it had. He wrestled every hour with the weight of duty versus family. Versus love.

"If it becomes necessary, he can hop a packet."

Nicholas crossed his arms. "Do you think there is any chance that he—I refuse to believe that."

"Someday I will tell you about the dangers of refusing to believe that which the facts support. You asked if I think there is any chance. I do. However, I don't *believe* there is any chance. Kevin will be at the mercy of what others believe and think, however."

"This is a damnable business. I hope that you don't hold it against me that I dragged you into it."

"You did not drag me in. I was already there."

Nicholas walked away, as if from the topic itself. "Miss Hepplewhite looked quite lovely last night. Very spirited."

"I believe she had an enjoyable time."

"Lord Jennings commented on her healthy appetite."

"She paid dearly for the self-indulgence. It would embarrass her to learn others noticed."

"Jennings was impressed, not critical. As for me, it was a compliment to the new chef. He just started a few days ago. Mrs. Fowler said all her old friends were gone, and she didn't want to continue because it was not the same." He wandered aimlessly around the sitting room before landing in an armchair. "Kevin asked about Miss Hepplewhite. Twice. I could not put him off the second time. I think he sees her as an eligible inappropriate woman."

"What did you tell him?"

"You had warned me off when she was called Mrs. Rupert, but I did not know if you still guarded her. I would say protected, but I don't want to imply anything."

"Tell Kevin to turn his attention to the viscountess. She would love to devour him one bite at a time."

Nicholas raised his eyebrows. "You are easily vexed when it comes to Miss Hepplewhite. I will assume that means that whatever had her fleeing Melton Park has been resolved. You appeared good friends last night."

"I am not keeping her, if that is what you are trying to ask."

"I am not asking that, although that dinner dress was far nicer than what the woman who visited Melton Park might wear and I don't think she as yet has access to her new fortune. I am asking if I should directly warn Kevin off if he inquires about her a third time."

"Tell him to stay away from her. Hell, tell him to go to the devil."

He *was* vexed, and he did not know why. This was not a simple jealousy darkening his mind. The temporary nature of their affair ate at him.

They shared pleasure and a deep familiarity. They shared confidences and, he liked to think, a mutual affection that touched on the profound at moments. She was his lover, but not his mistress, and he had no rights where she was concerned. None. He did not even have the right to warn off his cousins. Or to protect her in other ways.

Nicholas headed to his dressing room. "I'll have the valet send down word that you will be at breakfast."

"I have a question before you start your dressing."

Nicholas turned, waiting.

"Did you find any gold in the house? Coins."

Nicholas looked surprised, then grinned. "Damn, you *are* good. I discovered a large stash at Melton Park the day after you left. I opened a drawer in an unused wardrobe off his dressing room, and there it was, behind a false back. Guineas half filled it. I enjoyed an hour of exultant relief before I started to wonder if I had to inform the solicitor and turn it over to the estate."

"You inherited the ducal houses and their contents. That was part of the contents."

"So I concluded. It was enough to balance the accounts for at least a year. How did you know about this?"

"Dolores mentioned something about it while telling me an old family story." *A fortune that he could carry out the door*. On hand. At the ready. Uncle might have brought gold in, just for the bribe, but Chase did not think so. "I will be in the morning room when you are ready." He gestured to the chamber. "There is probably more here, somewhere. It shouldn't be hard to find."

* * *

Minerva's advertisement on behalf of Mrs. Jeffers produced results immediately. A letter came that very afternoon. An anonymous one. It said the man she sought, Douglas Marin, lived on Litchfield Street.

Grateful for something to distract her from her worry over what Chase had learned, the next morning she dressed in her serviceable gray, tied on her bonnet, slid her reticule over her arm, and set off on foot. Litchfield Street was not very far from her home, although as she walked east the neighborhood quickly changed for the worse, reflecting that she neared the Seven Dials.

Mrs. Jeffers's cousin must have been down on his luck if he lived here. He would be glad to learn that his cousin sought him out and wanted them to make amends. There were times when conducting inquiries could result in good things for people, and it raised her spirits that this would probably be one of them.

Finding Mr. Marin's building did not take long. A boy playing in the street pointed it out before running after his friend. She approached the front steps while a woman came down them.

"Pardon me, but are you Mrs. Marin?"

The woman burst out laughing. "As if I would marry such a man. There's enough worthless drunkards in the world without going and marrying one of them."

The man drank. She would have to get him sober before he met his cousin. "He does live here, though. Am I correct?"

The woman pointed over her shoulder. "Right there. First door to the right after you enter. Have your hand-kerchief at the ready. The place stinks." She walked down the street.

When a woman who lived in this neighborhood said a chamber stunk, Minerva did not argue the point. She loosened the drawstring on her reticule so she could reach her handkerchief quickly. Then she mounted the steps, opened the front door, and found the first one on the right.

She hoped Mr. Marin had risen by now. If he drank perhaps he hadn't. But then if he drank who knew when he would be awake or asleep. She rapped on the door.

Sounds came from within. Scrapes and thuds and at least one curse. The door opened a crack and red-rimmed eyes peered at her.

Mr. Marin looked younger than she had expected, even if bad living had aged him before his time. Blond hair hung around his head in tangles, long and ungroomed. He stood a little taller than she did. Mrs. Jeffers said they had played together as children, but she must have had at least a dozen years on him.

"Who are you? Some reformer lady?"

"No. Do I look like one?"

"A bit. No need for you here. You go above. There's a man there with two women who need saving. They make too much noise all night."

"Mr. Marin, I am not here to save anyone. I have come—"

"How'd you know my name?" He eyed her suspiciously.

"I have conducted inquiries in order to find Mr. Douglas Marin and I have succeeded, I believe. If you open the door another few inches, I will gladly explain why. It is in your interest to hear me out."

He made a face, thought about it, opened the door wide, and walked back into the chamber. Minerva followed. The odor assaulted her so badly she almost reached for her handkerchief. Instead she braved it out and picked her way amidst the alarming trash covering the floor. She stopped ten feet into the chamber and noted with some relief that the door remained open, letting in better air.

"In my interest, you say." Mr. Marin faced her from the end of the chamber. "Unless you know of an inheritance, there's not much you can say in my interest."

"That is not true. You will perhaps be astonished to learn that your cousin Mrs. Jeffers is looking for you. She wants to reconcile." She smiled brightly, and waited for his joy to break forth.

His eyes narrowed. "She sent you?"

"She did. She engaged me to find you."

"Wasn't enough to ruin me, now she has to run me to ground, eh? What if I don't want to be found? Ever think of that?"

"There are times a person does not want that. However, this is family. Surely having family again is better than this." She gazed around the chamber in dismay.

"Suits me." He paced, agitated and angry. "You are a troublemaker, nothing more. Trouble for me, that's certain. My cousin is not looking to grasp me to the bosom of family, woman. She's hoping to finish what she started, and what brought me here."

He was not making sense, but clearly he did not welcome this intrusion. The drink had all but deranged him, and she would only make it worse. "I will leave you, since you are content as you are." She turned and walked toward the door.

"The hell you will. I'll not have you telling her where I am."

Her instincts screamed in warning. She turned to see a blur of movement. A blow landed on her head, one so hard that she staggered. Shock immobilized her. The door slammed, blocking her.

The next time, fight back. She held her balance, barely. She reached into her reticule. He came at her, crazed, with what looked like a chair leg raised above his shoulder.

She saw him through blood, and almost swooned. Finding some strength, she stepped forward and raked his face with her hatpins.

Her vision blurring, she left him howling and pulled open the door. She staggered out of the building before her legs turned to liquid. She landed on her rump in the middle of the street. Her last thought was that she would probably get trampled by a carriage.

Chase sat in the library that served as his office, plotting his thoughts on paper. He pretended he was writing a report in the army, and lined up the facts and evidence accordingly. Even as he did it he could see certain holes. He did not anticipate much trouble filling them. He knew how it had all happened. Knew in ways that facts would never prove.

A racket down below barely penetrated his concentration. When it moved up to his own door he gave it his attention. Brigsby hurried to the door, not pleased. Moments later Jeremy barged into the library.

"You must come at once. There can be no delay. I've a carriage outside waiting."

Jeremy looked as if the French army was at the closest tollgate. Ashen-faced, he stared, wide-eyed and fearful, and looked much like the boy he had recently been.

"It is Minerva. She has been hurt. She was—"

One moment of shock, then Chase moved fast. He sped past him. "Tell me on the way."

They jumped in the carriage and Chase told the coachman to use all possible speed. The carriage shook enough to prove his command had been heard.

"What in hell happened?"

Jeremy licked his lips. "They brought her to the house. Carried her in. She has a wound to the head. There is a lot of blood."

"Who brought her? Where did they find her?"

"I wasn't there. Mum said she had her cards in her reticule and they brought her to that address. A wagon, I think. Mum is tending to her and sent me for you when I returned. Said to tell you she was attacked while on an inquiry."

He opened the trapdoor and told the coachman to go faster. "She was on a dangerous inquiry alone? Why didn't you go with her?"

"*I wasn't there*. I was helping at the stables today. They asked me to come because one of their men—so I wasn't there. Mum said she received a letter in the post, and set out soon after breakfast. An easy end to it, she said to mum. She didn't think it would be dangerous. She wouldn't have gone alone if she did."

The worst danger was when you don't expect it. "Who did this? Is the letter still in the house?"

"I don't know." Jeremy steadied his voice and his gaze. "She isn't stupid, or careless. If you think to upbraid her, you can get out now."

Was this pup scolding him? He almost snarled back a curse, but caught himself. None of them, least of all Minerva, needed him with his blood up. That could wait for another time, and another person. "All that matters is that she has the best care, and recovers."

The coach careened down streets and around crossroads. He and Jeremy swayed. When it finally stopped on Rupert Street they both were out in an instant. "Wait here," Chase called to the coachman over his shoulder.

"Where is she?" Chase asked while they ran up to the door.

"Library."

He paused outside the library, calming himself so he would not look like a madman. He turned the latch and entered.

Beth sat by the divan, looking down on its cushions. He walked around its back to see Minerva lying there, pale and half undressed. A bloody bonnet had been thrown to the floor, and a ruined gray pelisse draped a nearby chair. A compress covered her forehead and a bowl of water rested in a little puddle on the floor.

"Head wound," Beth said. "They bleed a lot. I've stopped it, and put on a poultice. I expect there will be a scar. It was a bad wound, Mr. Radnor. Ugly. Like someone had taken a club to her."

He pulled over a wooden chair and sat beside Beth. Jeremy hovered behind the divan. "Where did they find her?" He touched Minerva's limp hand. It felt too cool.

"Out on the street. Smack in the middle of it. She was seen sitting there, then she fell over. They thought she was drunk, until someone noticed the blood. She still had these in her hand." She reached to the chair with the pelisse and lifted two long hatpins. "Must have used them on whoever did this to her, and gotten herself away."

He gazed at those tiny foils. *Good for you, Minerva.* "Has she opened her eyes?"

"A bit, a few times. I think she is sleeping, not unconscious. She recognized me. I take that to be a good sign. Them that brought her said she seemed unconscious at first, but stirred while in the wagon."

Head wounds could be dangerous, with the damage invisible. The blood on Minerva's face and clothing was the least of it. "I am going to send for an army surgeon,

Beth. They see more of such things than anyone else. I'll have a physician come too."

Beth removed the compress and dipped it in the water again. "I thought I was done with this. I thought I'd never see it again."

He grasped her shoulder by way of comfort, then went to the writing table. He jotted off a hurried note and called Jeremy over. "Take the carriage outside and bring this to the Duke of Hollinburgh on Park Lane. Make it clear to the servants that it is from me and that he must receive it at once. Wait to see if he needs you. If not, when you return tell the coachman to wait again." He plucked some coin from his pocket. "Use what you need with him."

Jeremy ran out. Chase returned to the divan. He raked his memories for images of men hurt this way in battle. What had the surgeons done? "Help me to raise her head a bit, Beth. Then draw the drapes. We will wait for the doctors before moving her to her chamber, lest it not be advised."

Together they made Minerva as comfortable as possible. She opened her eyes a slit while Beth added pillows under her head and shoulders. She looked down her body, then at Beth. "My dress is ruined," she murmured.

Beth almost wept. "That is of no account."

"How did it happen?" She grimaced and pressed her fingers on her forehead. "I have a headache."

Chase knelt beside the divan and looked in her eyes. "You were hurt, Minerva. Do you remember?"

She shook her head.

"Then don't try to. Not now. Close your eyes and rest."

Beth made up the compress and laid it on her head. Minerva sighed as if that felt good. Her hand went out, blindly. "Will you stay here a little while, Chase? It hurts badly, but if you are here I can be brave."

He folded her hand between his. "I will stay, and you do not have to be brave. Not for me, darling. Not for Beth."

Tears leaked out from under her lids. "Dear Beth. Poor Beth. Such a trial I am for her. She should have gone."

Beth stiffened. Her face went slack. "Like my daughter you are. No one else will tend you if I have a say."

Chase held up his hand, asking for Beth's silence. "She wants to take care of you."

Minerva vaguely nodded. "Not fair to her. To Jeremy. To live under the roof of such a man so as to take care of me."

She was not talking about now, and this hurt. "You got them away from that. What you feel now was done by another man," Chase said.

Minerva frowned. She opened her eyes a little, and looked at him. Her dazed mind seemed to be trying to sort it out.

"Rest now. Sleep if you can." He stood, leaned over, and kissed her.

She seemed to doze then. Beth went to work on the compress once more. "She'll come through fine," she said belligerently. "Been through worse, hasn't she? She'll be right soon, you'll see. Not some fool delicate woman."

"Do you have any soup made, Beth? There should be something for her if she will eat."

Beth set her hands on her knees. "I had only started cooking. I could make soup, though. Only I'm needed here."

"I think she will sleep for a while. I'll sit with her. I promise to call you if you are needed."

Beth's hesitation said she was of two minds. She finally stood. "The water is still cool, so you wet the cloth again every ten minutes or so. If she wakes you plump those pillows again. Call me and I'll help. Don't you go kissing her or anything either. Not the time or place for that."

He let her lecture him on a few more points before she plodded to the door.

He sat, and tried not to spend every second of the next half hour scrutinizing Minerva for proof he did not have to worry as badly as he did.

Chapter Twenty-One

Voices. Talking near her. Around her. Almost whispering. Even so the sounds of them made the headache scream.

She kept wanting to open her eyes, but dared not. Even looking very far hurt. Only lying here, not moving, not talking, seemed to make it better.

Another voice. Chase's.

There are doctors here, Minerva. They are going to examine you. Please let them.

Touches on her head where pain carved into her scalp. Then on her temples. A quiet command told her to open her eyes. She did, and looked into the round, florid face of a plump man wearing spectacles.

Another face appeared beside his. Gray hair. Thinner face. Peering closely, right into her eyes, but not really looking at her so much as through her.

She has mostly been sleeping, you say? Was only out a short while?

As I understand it, yes. I am almost certain she has not lost consciousness the last two hours.

Good. Good. More peering. *And she knew who you were? No confusion?*

Only a little regarding what happened.

That is common. In a few days she will remember more.

The two faces pulled away and became heads attached to two bodies. Those heads tipped to each other. More whispers. The bodies turned and the plump man addressed someone else who stood behind her head. Since no one seemed to care if she kept her eyes open, she closed them again.

She has been fortunate. A taller man, a stronger one, and the attack could have been fatal. Even so she must rest. A week at least. In bed. No reading. Low light. As little noise as possible. You can move her from here if you are very careful while carrying her. If she has not recovered in a week, we will have another conversation. The sounds of footsteps walking away.

It was wise to call for him. You did not need me with his experience at your disposal. He has seen the effects of artillery, swords, and musket butts.

I thank you for coming anyway.

When a duke sends for a royal physician, the physician normally complies. A pause. *His woman?*

No.

Ah. Lest it not be obvious, I need to say that there should be no sexual congress this week of rest.

They walked away and she heard no more. She remained a little aware even as dreams gathered. She knew when Beth returned just from her footfall, and thought she heard Jeremy whispering far way.

Two arms slid under her. Her body rose. She forced her eyes open and saw Chase's face near hers, and felt her head resting on his upper arm. "I feel much better when you hold me," she whispered.

He smiled down at her, but his brow remained furrowed and his eyes stern.

"I was careless, Chase. I did not inquire sharply enough about why Mrs. Jeffers sought her cousin. I assumed it was for a reconciliation he would welcome. Only he did not want to be found."

"Don't think about it now. Don't think about anything."

She really did feel better, in his arms like this. She closed her eyes again and floated in the strength of his support.

Chase waited in the library while Beth undressed Minerva and tried to feed her some soup. He fingered a small piece of paper and a card, impatient for Jeremy to return. He had sent him to Bury Street to fetch his own carriage. Once it arrived, he had something important to do.

Beth came down the stairs just as Chase heard the horses outside. From where he sat in the library, he saw Jeremy enter, then stand aside. Beth stopped in her tracks and stared.

"He insisted on coming," Jeremy said. "Refused to hear my explanation of what was wanted."

Beth crossed her arms. "Who might you be?"

"Brigsby. I am here to attend to my gentleman." With that Brigsby took the steps forward that brought him into Chase's view, and almost nose to nose with Beth.

Brigsby had donned his most supercilious manner. Beth looked like a woman who saw a man who needed taking down a few pegs.

"Did your gentleman tell you to come here? No, he did not. I heard clear as a ringing bell what he sent Jeremy to do, and it was not to fetch *you*."

"The request as given by this young man made no

sense. Send a valise with clean shirts. As if that is enough for a journey." He lifted a valise hanging from his right arm. "I will make sure this is sufficient, and if it is not I will return and—"

"He isn't going on a journey, you fool man. He just isn't going home. You give him that valise, then go back where you came from so you aren't underfoot." She walked away, shaking her head. "As if we need valets and such here."

"I am not a valet," Brigsby said to her back. "I am a manservant, and skilled in many responsibilities. If necessary I can perform your duties better than you can."

Beth stopped, straightened, and pivoted.

Brigsby looked down his nose even when not trying. Now he did try. "I am a cook, for example. I also attend to my gentleman's household. All that he requires, I do for him." He lifted the valise high and moved it up and down. "Please show me where his chambers are, so I can settle him in."

Beth walked back toward Brigsby with murder in her eyes.

Chase thought it a good moment to cough. They both turned their heads, startled. Brigsby recovered first. "Ah, there you are, sir. I have what you will need." He carried in the valise while Beth disappeared. Jeremy lingered at the doorway, caught Chase's eye, and gestured to the street. Chase let him know to bide his time.

He opened the valise. He had indeed sent an incomplete list with Jeremy, since his thoughts had been on little besides Minerva. Brigsby had packed the shirts, but also a stack of clean cravats, an extra waistcoat, small clothes, and grooming implements. It was enough for a journey of five or six days, not a night or so in a house right in town.

"Your pistol and some lead is under it all," Brigsby said quietly. "You usually take it with you when you travel, so I thought I should bring it too."

"I don't think I will need it, but you would not know that so your forethought was understandable." He closed the valise and set it aside.

"That woman appears to think I should leave, sir." Brigsby appeared as bland as ever. "If that is your request, I will now do so."

"That will have to wait until I return. I need the carriage for a few hours."

"If you tell me where your guest quarters are, I will unpack for you while I wait."

"I have no idea where they are. Perhaps right in this library. Ask Beth. She is the woman you just spoke with."

Brigsby's mouth pursed. "Am I to address her as Beth, sir?"

"It might be better, considering your first meeting, to call her Mrs. Shepherdson. She is down in the kitchen now. She would rather be above with Miss Hepplewhite, so you can offer to make some supper for the household in her stead. She may decide you are not a nuisance then."

Brigsby's eyebrows rose a fraction. Chase walked around him and strode to the door. "Come with me, Jeremy. We have a small errand to address."

Jeremy caught up at the carriage. "If we are going where I think, you might take that pistol."

Chase climbed in. "If I take it, I will probably use it on the rogue. Get up with the coachman and make sure he doesn't dally."

"—so the duke sent for a royal physician, who was the other man here, the one with the long, skinny face. Useful to have a relative who is a duke. I could use one." Beth chatted on, her spirits rising with each minute. Minerva watched from her bed in the room lit by only one lamp. Her headache was almost gone, but Beth insisted on laying damp compresses on her brow every few minutes. She could feel the pull of the poultice on her head, somewhere on her crown above her left eye. There had been no fresh blood, even when she demanded that Beth help her to sit more upright.

She finished the last of the soup and bread and lifted the tray. "It was delicious. Thank you. Tomorrow perhaps I will eat something more substantial. I am somewhat hungry."

"Soup wasn't all mine. That valet finished it. 'Where are your herbs,' he kept asking. 'Where is your cream? Where is your pepper?' I left him to figure it out himself, since he is so special."

"If Brigsby is here, where is Chase?"

Beth stood and took the tray and turned to set it on a table. She fussed with the dishes. "I expect he will be back soon. Maybe he went to talk to his cousin."

After a very long while facing that table, Beth returned to her chair beside the bed. She reached into the bowl for a newly dampened cloth.

"No more, please." Minerva removed the cloth still dripping water onto her nose. "I don't think I need these anymore. In fact, I don't think I need to be in this bed anymore."

"Since it is night, where else would you be?"

"Doing something other than this. I am not tired at all. I slept all day. I am not an invalid. I was well shocked and very shaken, but I am recovered now." She cast the bedclothes aside. "In the least I will sit in a chair, not this bed, and light more lamps so I can read."

"You are to remain in bed," Beth said, blocking her from rising with her body. "Two doctors said so. *Two*."

"Oh, what do they know."

"More than you do."

"I'll go mad if I have to stay here when I am not even tired. Now, stand aside so I can—"

"What do you think you are doing?"

She froze. Not Beth's voice. Chase's.

She looked up to see him at the doorway to her chamber, looking in. He appeared tired, disheveled, and not happy.

"Back in bed, Minerva." He stepped in. Beth gave her a self-satisfied look and left with the tray.

"It is not necessary."

"Bed rest. One week. The doctors were explicit." He held up the bedclothes and gestured. She swung her legs back on the bed and punched the coverlet.

He sat in the chair. "Your restlessness is a good sign, though."

It was not only restlessness that she experienced this moment, but also sharp annoyance. "*You* did not rest in bed after *you* were hit on the head, so why should I have to?"

"That was different."

"It wasn't. Not at all."

"You bled profusely."

"You bled enough. Head wound, you said. They always bleed a lot, you said."

He tried to appear sympathetic, but only looked stern. "You were unconscious. There could be damage inside your head."

"You were unconscious. Did you not worry about damage inside your head?"

"I could tell there was none. And I was only unconscious for a few moments."

"It was many moments. And if you could tell there was no damage, so can I. My headache is almost gone, and the light does not bother me. Watch, I'll stare right at the lamp." She did just that. He reached over and moved it so she no longer could.

"I am telling you it is not the same," he said firmly.

She punched the coverlet again. "It is not the same because I am a woman, is what you mean."

"Exactly. Also because if anything happened to you because you ignored the doctors' advice, I would never forgive myself. So indulge me, and do as you were told."

She didn't like it, but he had a look about him that did not encourage more rebellion. "I will stay resting in bed three days. However, if after that I am myself again, and have no pains or anything else, I will decide I am fully recovered and I want you to admit as much too."

He closed his eyes in forbearance, but nodded.

"Now please move the lamp back next to the bed so I am not in shadows."

A big sigh, but he did so.

She took his hand in hers. The knuckles looked red. "Where were you?"

"Out and about."

She ran her thumb over those knuckles. "Did you kill him?"

"No." He gave her hand a squeeze. "I brought Jeremy. His mission was to make sure I didn't, much as I wanted to. There were some fisticuffs, however, in order to subdue him."

She pictured him walking into that fetid chamber, hard and angry, with Jeremy at his side. Mr. Marin must have panicked at the sight of two men looking for vengeance. "What did you do with him?"

"I gave him a choice. He could enter one carriage that was waiting, that would take him to the establishment in the country where his cousin hoped he could be treated. Or he would enter another one, and be taken to the magistrate to answer for attempting to kill you."

"I trust he chose to go to the country."

"As I said, there were fisticuffs. I'm sure when it was over, he agreed with me that would be the better decision."

She looked him over again. "You had better not let Brigsby see you, if he is still here. He will insist on bathing and grooming you within an inch of your life if he has the chance."

"That is why I came right here. That and so I could make sure you were not being disobedient. Which you were."

"Was it your intention to stand watch all night to make sure I did not move from here?"

"My intention was to stay here all night and lay cool compresses on your head. I did not expect to find you so recovered."

She looked at her body making hills in the bedclothes. "You don't have to sit in that chair. I have been ordered to stay in bed. I have not been ordered to stay in bed alone."

He laughed a little. "Unfortunately, I was ordered not to impose on you. It was the last thing the physician said before going out the door."

"Sleeping beside me is not imposing. I am sure I will recover all the faster if you hold me." She moved over in the bed. "It isn't big, but you should fit."

"I'm sure I will." He stood and shed his frockcoat and waistcoat. He untied and pulled off his cravat. After removing his boots and turning out the lamp, he lay down next to her.

"You could get under the sheet with me."

"Beth is sure to arrive at dawn to take my place by your side. Better not to." He did turn and slide his arm under, so he could embrace her. That felt unbearably good, as if his hold made the whole day's ugliness go away.

"I realized something today," she said. "When it was happening, I remembered something I had forgotten. It was just there in my head."

He yawned, and turned on his stomach. "What was that?"

"That day when I was given that money, he said something to me. The boy who brought it. I forgot it almost at once. But when he handed that box over, he said something. 'I was told to tell you, next time, fight back.' I heard that in my head today. And I wonder—"

"Wonder what?"

"I wonder if whoever sent that money knew what was happening in our house."

"I think he did know. I even think I know how. He had to know."

"Because otherwise he would not have given me that money?"

"Because when he died he left you enough to take care of yourself."

She stared at the ceiling. The notion did not shock her as much as it should. "It was the duke, you think."

"I am almost sure of it. It is the only possible connection between the two of you that I have found."

"Why didn't you tell me this?"

"I was going to, but you got yourself hit on the head and it became something for another day." He yawned again. "It still is. Now go to sleep."

She pretended to, but she didn't. He soon slumbered beside her, however. She listened to his breaths, and hugged the arm draped over her, and dwelled on the poignant emotions his presence raised in her whenever he showed how he cared for her.

Chapter Twenty-Two

"I demand that I be allowed to leave this chamber."

Minerva spoke with determination. Her eyes blazed. Beth turned to Chase, holding out her hands like a woman beset by big troubles. "Called for you to talk some sense into her."

Chase faced Minerva across the chamber, the bed that they had shared for two nights now neatly and crisply made. She wore the undressing gown he had bought her, and had attempted to dress her own hair. One of her ensembles lay on the chair. He doubted Beth had put it there.

She looked much herself. Other than the bruise surrounding the poultice high on her forehead, nothing appeared amiss. Her whole manner spoke of her irritation at her confinement. At most they could hold her here one more day. After that, she might well tie the sheets together to make her escape out the window.

"You agreed that after three days if I felt recovered I could stop being an invalid," she said.

"I lied, to ensure you rested at least three days. However, if you promise to do it my way, perhaps you can leave this chamber for a short while."

Beth opened her mouth to object, but shut it just as

quickly. Minerva eyed him as if to see if he was trying to trick her.

"What is your way?"

"You will only go down the stairs with me. You can take some air in the garden if you dress warmly. And you can go for a carriage ride with me this afternoon, and a short walk, if you swear you will admit when you get tired or if at any time you are in distress of the slightest amount."

"Your way doesn't sound like much fun."

"The alternative is we lock you in."

"You wouldn't dare."

He said nothing to that. She assessed his mood with a long look. "Fine, but it is very unfair. You are allowed to get hit on the head and still go about your business, but if I get hit on the head I become an invalid. Beth, help me to dress. I intend to eat breakfast down below."

He stepped out while they took care of that, then escorted Minerva down the stairs, watching for any indications that her balance did not hold. In the little morning room, food awaited. She helped herself to a full plate, then sat to enjoy her freedom.

He joined her. As soon as he sat, Brigsby arrived and set down a high stack of mail and paper. Chase had already checked two letters when he realized what had just occurred. "How did you get these?"

"I sent the young man for them."

"Jeremy is not your lackey, Brigsby."

"He didn't mind going. I said he could take your carriage and gave him permission to allow the young lady to ride in it too."

"*You* gave *your* permission?"

"You were otherwise occupied, sir. I thought it unwise

to disturb you." A little cough punctuated his pride in his discretion.

"Young lady?" Minerva asked.

"Miss Turner. She visits on occasion. I saw them chatting in the garden yesterday. I thought she would like a ride in the carriage." He went to get the coffee and poured into both of their cups. "You needed a new frockcoat, after the disaster you made of the one we had here. I asked the young man to fetch your blue one, and to see about the mail while he was there. The newspaper I went out and procured on my own."

Pleased that his morning duties had been completed to his own satisfaction, Brigsby left the chamber.

"Jeremy and Elise?" Minerva said.

"They live near each other, and worked at Whiteford House together and also now for you. It is not surprising that they have formed a friendship. Surely you do not disapprove."

"If there is something more there, it could complicate my inquiries."

"How so?"

"Jeremy might become protective and worry about her. He might interfere with assignments I have for her if he thinks she will be in even the slightest danger."

He flipped through more mail, making his stacks. He saw one from Peel. Damnation. "I'm sure that won't happen. He is reasonable enough and you would never endanger her anyway."

He had almost finished with the mail when he noticed the silence coming across the table. He looked over to find Minerva regarding him with high skepticism. He quickly reviewed their brief conversation for whatever he had said to provoke that expression.

"I am happy that you are sure Jeremy will not become too protective. If you think that is the response of a reasonable man, I am reassured you will not now become too protective about me."

That is different. It really wasn't but, then again, it was. He had no intention of being careless regarding her safety, and fully planned to ensure she was not either. This, however, was not the best time to broach that topic, or the little list of changes in her habits regarding inquiries that would ensure she never was hurt again.

When he failed to react in any way other than to smile, Minerva raised the subject of her day's activities. "I do not want to sit in the garden all morning," she said. "I want you to explain what you said two nights ago, about being almost sure that the duke was my benefactor. You said it was a topic for another day. Well, here we are in another day."

He looked out the window and checked the weather. "We will take the carriage ride now, not this afternoon. It will be easier to show you what I mean than only explain it with words."

She finished her meal quickly. "I will fetch my bonnet and cape and return shortly."

He made it to the door before she did. "I will get them. You sit here and do not go near the stairs." He aimed for the stairway, hearing a long sigh behind him.

"I do like this carriage," Minerva said. "I am very snug here." Too snug. Not only was she encased in her cape, but Chase had tucked a carriage blanket all around her. He now sat across from her while they rode west.

"You are to tell me if the sway or jostling in any way—"

"Yes, yes, I promise. And the next time you are conked

on the head you are to tell me if in any way riding in carriages, or on horses, or walking, or reading, or anything at all gives you discomfort."

He did not like her repeated references to her unfair restrictions, and it now showed in his eyes. She only returned to the topic because she was sure that he was going to be a problem now, and attempt to issue edicts on her movements and decisions.

She could hardly conduct her inquiries if she had to answer to him about every move. She had no intention of explaining herself that way, to anyone. His concern and care touched her deeply, but she dared not allow either to turn her into a weakling.

She had been careless. She admitted that. Mrs. Jeffers had not been as forthcoming about her history with Mr. Marin as would have been wise. She could be excused for assuming this was a reconciliation that a man living in such a state would welcome. However, she knew that when she had seen him, in that first moment, she should have heeded her better sense which told her to retreat.

Had she been fully attentive to the matter at hand, she might have. A month ago, she most likely would have feigned finding the wrong door, or used some other excuse to turn and leave. Instead at least half of her mind had dwelled on Chase, and their affair, and on the way her heart weighed her love for him against the potential danger still hanging over her.

Love. She smiled to herself. She had not called it that before, but now it had simply emerged as part of her thoughts. She did love him, though. She marveled at that.

She looked across to find him watching her, his gaze warm and the smallest smile on his face. What did he think when he saw her? Did he still wonder about Algernon, and whether she had arranged that her estranged husband could never hurt her again? He had said that he hoped she had killed him, but that was a retort made after she questioned his belief in her. He had not said that he was sure she had not killed him, the way he was sure she had not harmed the duke.

The carriage rolled down Oxford Street. Since it was morning, it was fairly quiet. The afternoon would bring out many more people. She gazed out at the shops lining the street, their owners preparing for the customers who would arrive later in the day.

Chase opened the trapdoor and told the coachman to stop at the next crossroads. Minerva looked at the shops here, and across the way. She knew this crossroads very well.

Chase pointed out the window. "If you look at the rooftops over there, you can see that of Whiteford House. It faces Park Lane, but the back is very close to where we are. When my uncle went into town, to Oxford Street or most places in Mayfair, or even toward the City, he would not go down alongside the park. He would come out this way on one of the streets, east."

"I expect so."

He slid over to the other window and bid she do the same. She was so bundled that she could not slide. It was more a matter of waddling her rump. She knew what they would see from this side, though.

"I was told you lived up that street, Old Quebec," Chase said. "Not far from my uncle at all." He reached for the door latch. "If you are feeling up to it, let us take a turn."

She fought her way out of the blanket and let him hand her down. The fresh air felt wonderfully crisp and the sun shone brightly. Chase escorted her across the street until they stood at the bottom end of Old Quebec.

"He often went out at night, Minerva. In the country he spent time at that parapet. I think here in town he went into the squares and parks. Portman is actually the closest, but he probably wandered some distance at times. So I can see him going to Portman Square, or walking through it, gazing up at the stars that are so hard to see in much of London." He took her hand. "Let us walk to the square, if you can manage it."

"Of course I can manage it." She began striding off, to prove it, but halted in her tracks as if she had hit a wall.

"We can walk up the next street over, if you do not want to see that house," he said.

She could see the house, and a bit of its door.

"Come this way instead." He guided her back down Oxford, to the next crossroad. "Now, use your imagination. He leaves his home and walks. He aims for the square. Most likely, he walked past your house some nights. I think he passed it many times."

She stopped on the street, at about the spot of that house on Old Quebec. "You think he saw or heard something, don't you?"

"I do. This area is quiet at night. Sounds you might never hear during the day can be clear. Lamplight inside the houses reveals more than one ever sees in daylight."

It sickened her that others might have seen or heard what happened. "How would he learn who I was?"

"He would ask. Just as you and I ask when we want to learn who lives in a house or which house is the home of this person or that. A casual question at the shop on the corner would elicit the name."

She pictured the duke casually asking at the haberdashery

on the corner if they knew who had the house four doors up. She saw the haberdasher give the name, and perhaps also give a look that said all was not right there.

"How long have you wondered about this?" she asked.

"Almost two weeks. You said you did not know him, and I believed you even that first night. So how was it he made that legacy? He knew your old name, and your new one too. The money you received—it was almost bizarre that an anonymous gift like that was made, but he could be strange in his own way. However, I was only sure when you told me about what the messenger had said to you."

Next time, fight back. That money had allowed her to. Not with fists, but with her wits and Algernon's own weakness.

They strolled up the street, then over to the square. "I visited here so rarely even though I lived a few minutes' walk away," she said. "When Algernon left the house, sometimes Beth and I would come here if the day was fair, but only briefly. I dared not be gone when he returned. I was in London, but I had no freedom to leave the house, to have friends, to attend parties. I was in a different place, but still in prison."

He squeezed her hand.

"I still don't understand why the duke left me that fortune, Chase. He didn't know me."

"Perhaps he thought it would do more good for you than for any of us. He obviously knew about your husband's death, and that you were making your own way in London now."

"I tried so hard to make sure no one knew who I was."

"Dukes have their ways. I expect he had someone conduct a discreet inquiry to find where you went after you disappeared from Dorset."

"I wish he had sent a note with that money, so I could thank him."

"I think he preferred your not knowing. He often did things without claiming credit. I believe he interceded on my behalf when I was leaving the army, so there would be no questions or scandal. He never said a word about it, but I'm convinced he used his influence."

She looked at him. "So we both owe him much."

They retraced their steps until they reached the carriage. She let him settle her in and even wrap her again in the blanket.

"A short ride in the park is in order," he said.

"Please tell him to go past Whiteford House first. Slowly."

Five minutes later they rolled past the house. Minerva looked out at it, feeling very close to the man who once owned it, whom she had never known.

That night Chase had made a decision. He needed to make some kind of report to Peel in the next few days. He saw no alternative but to pursue one more thread in Minerva's history before he did. He might never need to use the truth about Finley's death, but he wanted it in his pocket just in case he had to reveal it to protect her.

He slipped into her bedchamber after the house was quiet. He had sent Brigsby home, explaining that he would return himself tomorrow. Beth's snoring hummed down the corridor as he closed the door.

He undressed, and slid under the bedclothes to hold Minerva's warmth against his skin. She turned on her side to face him.

"I thought you were asleep," he said.

"I was waiting for you. I sleep better when you are with me."

He pulled her close and pressed his lips to her crown.

She placed her palm against his chest, over his heart, then slid it down to his torso. "Your skin does not feel like mine. The surface is soft, but what it covers is not, so it is very different."

Her continued curiosity about the simplest things charmed him. She did a bit of pressing and exploring, to see just how different it could be.

"What are you doing now, Minerva?" Her hand had lowered considerably on his body.

"Seeing if I can seduce you."

"I promise you can. However, the doctors said—"

"—whatever they thought would convince your cousin that they took a duke's charge very seriously." One of her fingernails etched a line up his phallus. "I see that did not take long at all."

"I have sworn not to impose on you while you recover. Much as I would like—stop that!" An unexpected tweak on the tip of his phallus sent lightning through his blood.

"Didn't you like that? I'm sorry."

"I liked it. Very much. However, we cannot—"

"You cannot, seeing as you were so foolish as to swear not to. I swore nothing. You will not be doing any imposing. I will not need your help, so just lie there and be true to your word. No embraces. No caresses." She rose up on her knees and drew her nightdress off. "Only, don't fall asleep."

As if that were likely. A stronger man would leave the chamber at once. He didn't.

Still on her knees, she gazed down with hunger, as if

deciding where to feast first. His cock swelled more at the very thought of her feasting anywhere at all.

He looked perfect. Strong and hard and handsome. Not only his appearance made her stir so deeply. The ways he took care of her, and talked to her, and treated her moved her profoundly. She lowered herself to her hands and knees and kissed him to release the fullness in her heart. Then she moved her lips to his shoulder and his neck, to his arm and his chest, praising him, thanking him with her passion.

He accepted it, as if he knew she meant it when she said she did not want his participation. She wanted to express her own emotions this way. She needed him to just accept them. He did, not embracing her, not taking over. Just skimming his body with her breasts aroused her. She needed no direct caresses. Inhaling his scent made her heady. Licking his skin began driving her mad. She could tell he liked it all. His body showed her that, and his gaze, and finally his low sounds of pleasure.

She sat back on his thighs and caressed him fully, all along his chest, wondering in the feel of him, admiring his beauty. Lower then, following the taper of his body to the hardness of his hips. She circled her finger around his phallus, then caressed it more purposefully. He closed his eyes then. His hard jaw and tense expression made her feel wicked and powerful and seductive.

He looked down his body at her with a hooded gaze. "Are you feeling brave?"

"Invincible. Like a warrior."

"Then move up here, so I can use my mouth on you."

It took her a moment to sort out what he meant. She

moved forward on her hands and knees. He slid down enough to take her breast in his mouth. His kisses alone had her halfway to insanity, but the way he licked and sucked her breast made her tremble with need. The first tensions of her release started tightening, and he had not even really touched her. She started moving back, so she could take him into herself.

"Don't lose your courage now. Move forward. Keep coming up here."

She did come close to losing her courage. She wasn't sure she wanted to wait, for one thing. She sensed this was something he wanted, however. The pleasure would not really be hers alone.

She inched up, moving her knees forward. Eventually she had no choice but to kneel upright. She grabbed onto the headboard and looked down at how his head was positioned right below her body. He gently pushed her knees apart, then lifted his head.

His first kiss caused a sharp, deep pleasure to shriek through her. What he did after that left her grasping the headboard for support. The intensity of the sensations caused her mind to spin. She was sure it could not get more astonishing but it did, again and again, until she lost all sense. She heard herself begging for him to stop but also for more, in the same breath. Finally a release split through her violently.

Somehow she moved again. No, he moved her. She found herself bound to him, connected and deeply joined. He filled her like never before, stretching her so she felt his power inside her. She hovered over him while he thrust hard and long and even so she would have wanted more if he could give it. His finish came so forcefully that it took her breath away.

She collapsed on him, utterly spent. She lacked the strength to move. He wrapped her in an embrace and held her tightly while their deep breaths met in the night. "You are perfect, Minerva. Magnificent and beautiful."

She believed him. She felt magnificent and beautiful. With him. Because of him.

Chapter Twenty-Three

"I expect there was a good reason you told me to meet you here." Beth spoke before he even greeted her. She did not look at him, but at some tiny shoots of growth under a tree, heralding the coming spring. "Was a long ways for me to come just to chat."

Meet me at the same place, when you go out to shop. That was the note he had slipped her after breakfast. Her empty basket rested on the grass at her feet. Her face, round and wrinkled, appeared very sober.

"I didn't tell her you wanted to speak with me," she said. "No reason to."

"Just as well."

"She told me you've a man who has told you she killed that husband of hers. I suppose that means there is still some danger for her about that."

"Some. Not too much, I think."

He could barely see her face with the way she looked down and with her cap's long ruffle obscuring her profile.

"There was a decision about all of that. One that excused her of any blame," he added.

"I never trusted that. More a matter of maybe putting the pot to the back of the hearth, away from the flames, but close enough to grab if one had a need for it. Could that happen? If they decide this duke was killed, could they look back to that and not only think she might have done it, but even start digging into that worthless brute's death again?"

"They could. It wasn't like being found innocent in a trial. The matter can be reopened."

"I'll be counting on you to make sure that doesn't happen."

"I can make no promises, I'm afraid. She knew the risks, but decided to brave it out."

Beth did not move or look at him. She just stared at the ground, her thick body bent a little from her heavy thoughts.

He picked up the basket. "Walk with me."

They ambled along the perimeter of trees that surrounded Portman Square, both of them silent.

"I saw the marks on Jeremy's shoulders," he said. "He must have been very young when someone laid those down."

She walked a little taller at that, and gazed straight ahead. "Thirteen years. The first time."

"Finley?"

She nodded. "I should have known it would happen. Such a stupid, little man. He took pleasure in cruelty. His horse, his wife—I should have known eventually he would go after my boy too."

"If he tried again, after you left his house, if he came upon Jeremy anywhere, in the street or on his property— he wasn't a boy anymore. A few years older and he might have refused to take it. No one could blame him if he decided to allow no one to do that again."

A deep breath entered her, and a deep sigh left. "Is that what you think? That my son killed him? Are you thinking to swear that information in order to spare Minerva?"

"I don't intend to swear anything. I have nothing to swear. I only have a sum I added up in my head, with no facts to back it up."

She crossed her arms and looked him in the eyes. "You added wrong. Jeremy would never do that."

"In the right circumstances, any man might do it. That is how wars get fought, after all."

"I'm telling you he didn't do it. I know he didn't."

He did not say that she couldn't know. That even if we are sure of someone, we can't be totally sure. He did not say that as a mother, she of course would believe her son incapable of such a thing, no matter how justified the act might have been.

"I know for certain he didn't kill that poor excuse for a man," she said firmly, as if she heard his thoughts. "I know because I shot Finley myself."

"He took after him again. I never saw Jeremy so angry. There comes a time when a boy isn't a boy anymore, and won't stand for it. You had that right." Beth told her story while they continued their stroll in the park. "I figured it was only a matter of time before Jeremy did something about it. Then he'd end up either hanged or transported, even though he was provoked to it."

Chase knew better than to ask questions or demand information. He had considered Beth, but had rejected the idea. Beth was the person who healed and helped. Not a person who killed.

"Then there was that man poking around," she added. "One like you. Mr. Finley had hired him to look for evidence about Minerva, that she had a lover or whatnot. I didn't like that. I feared he would either find enough to convince a court, or he would make it up. If he didn't,

Mr. Finley was likely to just steal her. Who would care or know, except me? She weren't really safe, even if she had left him, was she?"

"No." With no family to rely on or run to, Minerva was vulnerable as long as she remained married to Finley.

"What did it, though, was seeing him again. He came right to our door on his horse. Minerva saw him and she looked like death itself. Jeremy went out there and told him to go, that he had no rights there. The man's response was to use that crop on Jeremy again, slashing down from on high on that horse, again and again. Jeremy finally grabbed the crop and threw it aside, but his face was cut and his neck—it was like the old nightmare come alive again. So I took the pistol we kept in the house, and waited for him while he was on his ride in the forest. He liked going there, even if the land weren't his. Liked pretending he was lord of some manor, when he was lord of none."

"Did he think it not odd that you were there?"

"At first he thought I had brought a message from Minerva. He actually looked pleased. When I told him not to go near her or my son again, that I would not stand for it, he tried to use that crop on *me*. I will admit my mind turned black then. I had the pistol in my hand under my wrap, and I just—" She blinked hard. "I tried to feel bad about it, what with being a God-fearing woman, but I couldn't believe any God would blame me too much. A mother doesn't sit by while her child is hurt. He was only seventeen then. Still young. And Minerva—I couldn't watch her go through that again. I don't think she would have taken it either. She had grown a lot, in her mind and self. She would have fought him if he got her back. And he would have killed her for sure, eventually. He had it in him."

She stopped walking and folded her arms and looked

out over the park. He folded his too and looked with her. What to do now? That question hung heavily between them.

"I would have gone forward and admitted it, if Minerva were ever taken to gaol. I want you to know that. I would never have let her hang. I was preparing myself for it, settling matters as best I could, when they said it was an accident. It was a gift, really."

"I believe you would have come forward if you had to. I don't doubt that."

She turned to look at him, her eyes filmy with tears and memories, but not repentance. "Are you going to tell Minerva about this?"

He doubted he had to. Minerva was good at inquiries. She knew she had not used that pistol, so who had? There were only two likely possibilities. "I don't see any reason to tell her. You may want to eventually, in case she has wondered about Jeremy."

"I'll still come forward if need be. If all of this comes alive again, and there's those trying to harm her."

"It was ruled an accident, and may just lie there as that. If anyone starts asking questions, I will try to turn their eyes on the poachers known to frequent private hunting grounds like those woods. It would be like Finley to confront one of them. It is my hope it doesn't even get that far. But if necessary—it is good to know you would do the right thing."

She nodded. "I'll be hoping it goes the way you say."

"Come. I will take you home so you don't have to walk or hire a carriage. I have mine here."

She brightened. "I've been wanting to ride in it."

"We will have to make a stop first, if you don't mind. Minerva will be wondering where you have been all this time. We'll tell her I took you to buy a new dress. That means a dress must arrive, so we will stop to have one made."

She walked faster. "I tell you I killed a man and you buy me a dress? Doesn't seem right somehow, but I'll not complain about it."

He would buy her a whole wardrobe for easing his worry about Minerva.

"I have been thinking," she said, to divert them both.

"That is often dangerous."

"My thoughts were about this legacy, and the others."

That captured his attention.

"If he knew me in such a slight way, perhaps that was how he knew the other two women whom you now must find. Perhaps like me they are not even aware that he previously touched on their lives."

"Our minds are much alike when conducting inquiries. I trod my path and you walk yours, but we tend to arrive at the same destination. If we are right, they will be harder to find."

"One of his habits brought him into contact with me. Perhaps that same one, or a different one, made him aware of them."

"I have been pondering what I know of him, and what his habits were, to find new directions to investigate."

"Are you going to tell me those habits?"

"No."

"I may be able to help, walking my way."

"Soon you are going to be a wealthy heiress. You will no longer need to conduct inquiries, Minerva."

Not conduct inquiries? She wasn't sure she wanted to stop. She enjoyed it.

"What do you plan to do with it?" he asked.

"Some I'll put aside to help the new enterprise. Then, I will buy new wardrobes for all of us. Jeremy should have private chambers, such as you have." She warmed to the topic. "A carriage, perhaps. A modest one. I might also have inquiries conducted in America, to see if I can find my cousins. It would be nice to know what became of them and my uncle. Mostly I would like to find a way to help women who need to find sanctuary from their situations, who need a place of safety."

"If there is no charity doing that, you can start one. Do not deny yourself the wardrobe and carriage, though. Indulging yourself a bit will only use a tiny amount of what you will receive, and you should celebrate your good fortune." He opened the carriage door. "We are here."

She looked at the door of the Bank of England. Minerva Hepplewhite would withdraw fifty pounds today, from the account that held the income from her trust.

Wealth waited. A new life would start.

He cocked his head, his hand still holding hers, waiting for her to step down. She wished they did not wear gloves so she could feel his warmth on her palm. She gazed in his blue eyes, so warm and kind within that harshly handsome face.

"Will you stay with me through this?"

He coaxed her out with a gentle tug. "I will come in with you. And I will stay with you as long as you want me to."

It sounded as if he did not understand what she had meant. Then again, maybe he had.

Together they entered that door. Side by side they found the man Mr. Sanders had referred her to.

A half hour later, she walked out an heiress.

Chase welcomed Nicholas's message when it arrived. *Call at one o'clock, if you can.*

He had spent a restless evening and night. He had left Minerva with her "family" to celebrate that money she had taken home. He had not told her to come to him when she wanted to. She would know she was welcomed. However, he also did not make arrangements to see her on his own initiative.

In one half hour, much had changed. He could not pretend it had not. He had known it would, but experiencing the implications soured his mood. Beneath his rumbling frustration, nostalgia put down roots.

She had taken the first step to enjoying the fruits of her good fortune. She had no need of inquiries, or his protection. That inheritance, now in hand, would change things. Change her. He pictured her receiving calls from ladies, and attending parties and balls. He saw her in silks that would make that dinner dress pale in comparison.

He imagined men flirting with her. Not only fortune hunters. She would spot those immediately. Other men, however, would be drawn to her flame. Lords and industrialists and men of greater wealth than she possessed. The day would come, perhaps quickly, when he was only one of her friends, and not a special one at that.

He couldn't stop any of it. He didn't want to, yet he did. He did not want to see other men considering her as a prospective wife of good fortune, or as an inappropriate woman with whom to dally for a while. Even if she rejected them all, it would drive him mad.

He arrived at Whiteford House a quarter hour before one o'clock. He had rehearsed the words with which he would inform Nicholas that he had been conducting an inquiry for the Home Office even while he conducted one for Nicholas. It was time to do that, since Peel's request for a report could not be put off any longer. He did not expect his cousin to take the revelation calmly.

Nicholas waited in the library. "There you are. Come in, and prepare yourself," Nicholas said.

"Prepare myself for what?"

"Family doings. Walter and his wife are coming soon."

"To ask for money?"

"Undoubtedly. However, from Walter's note, I think there is more to it than that. He referred to information of the utmost importance."

"Before they come, I need to tell you something, also of the utmost importance."

Nicholas made a waving gesture with his hand. "We will talk after they have left. I can only take one utmost importance at a time."

At exactly one o'clock, the butler delivered Walter's card. "Of course he is promptly on time. One would expect nothing less," Nicolas said.

Walter entered with Felicity at his side. After greetings, Nicholas invited them to make themselves comfortable.

Walter glanced at Chase, then addressed Nicholas. "I was hoping to do this with you alone. The matter is very delicate."

"Chase is here at my request. If you intend to tell me that the Countess von Kirchen is not the widow she claims, I already know that."

Walter colored. "I have no interest in your mistresses.

This, as I wrote, is a matter of *utmost importance*." He leaned in, very sober-faced. "It has to do with Uncle's death."

"Then Chase most certainly should be here. Perhaps you will share what you have come to tell me."

"My wife was in town a few days before Uncle died. She had some shopping to do. She was on Bond Street and—"

"Perhaps you will allow her to tell it, since it is her story," Chase said.

Walter frowned at him. He turned to Felicity. "Are you up to it?"

"I am sure she is, aren't you, Felicity?" Nicholas said.

She nodded. "I was in town, shopping. I saw Kevin while I was on Bond Street. Riding down, as plain as could be. Later, when everyone said he was in France, I didn't know what to do. On that day, at least, he was not."

Chase glanced at Nicholas just as Nicholas glanced at him. *Hell and damnation*.

"You are very sure?" Chase asked.

"I would recognize one of my husband's cousins, wouldn't I?"

"Not if it were foggy, or you did not see him head-on."

"I am sure it was Kevin."

"It is rather late to be remembering this," Nicholas said.

She colored. Walter looked ready to huff on her behalf. "I remembered at once. I did not say anything, even to Walter, because I did not want to cause trouble for Kevin."

"And now you do?"

Chase had never seen Felicity show anger, or even much emotion other than wifely adoration. Now her expression sharpened. "I thought, since the matter remains unresolved, that I should tell my husband. He thought you should know."

"How good of you both," Nicholas said. He stood. "I will speak with Kevin about this, and if necessary, when necessary, inform the Home Office."

Walter looked up in dismay, then rose to his feet too. "Come, dear. It appears the duke has a busy day planned and we should not impose on his time."

Nicholas did not say one word to disagree with that.

"It may be time to tell Kevin to hop that packet," Nicholas said after they were gone.

Chase had already decided last night to do just that. "You could have been more gracious. You all but threw them out."

"I can't abide Walter. He *enjoyed* telling me this. He is probably doing the calculations to see how much more he might get if Kevin is hanged."

"He left feeling insulted. By tomorrow he will be a hot air balloon of self-righteousness."

Nicholas slammed his fist on the back of a divan, cursed again, then calmed. "I will apologize. Now, what was *your* news of utmost importance?"

It would be better to give Nicholas some time to recover from Walter and his wife. "Call for your horse. Let us ride along the river."

Nicholas went to the door. "I'm not going to like your news any more than I liked Walter's, am I?"

"Walter seemed to believe the Countess von Kirchen is your mistress. Is she?" Chase threw out the question after they slowed their horses and walked them along the riverbank west of town. Nicholas had not accused him of betrayal outright when he revealed the Home Office inquiry, but the wait for his horse had been very silent.

"I suppose she is."

"You don't know?"

"'Mistress' implies an arrangement. There isn't one. At least I have not willingly agreed to one."

"Might you have, in a weak moment, agreed to one unwillingly?"

Nicholas laughed, more to himself than at Chase. "Possibly. There were a few weak moments in the last few days."

Chase remembered how the countess had shown an aggressive side at Nicholas's dinner party. When he foisted her off on Nicholas himself, he had not anticipated an entanglement. If he had been thinking about anyone other than Minerva, and how beautiful she looked when Nicholas brought her over, he might have guessed that the countess would make her own arrangement with the new duke, and quickly.

That was the problem with inappropriate women of a certain class. They had expectations, even if those did not include marriage.

"Speaking of mistresses, how is Miss Hepplewhite?" Nicholas asked.

"She is not my mistress."

"Forgive me. Speaking of lovers, how is she?"

"Doing quite well. Sanders informed her that some of the funds were being released, and she availed herself of a few pounds. Also the valuation of that business came in handsomely high."

"That complicates matters for you, I expect," Nicholas said.

It was not a turn in the conversation that Chase had expected. "Somewhat."

"In the least you do not have a clear field anymore. Word will spread fast. Every lord with more privilege than money will consider her a catch. If not for your interest in her, I would myself."

"They will be wasting their time. She has no interest in marrying."

"And here I thought I might be hosting a wedding breakfast soon. She doesn't seem fitting for the inappropriate woman category either. I assumed she was your lover, but that things were moving to a more formal arrangement."

"It is complicated, as you said."

"Perhaps not as much as you think. It isn't like you are a fortune hunter. She probably knows that your vocation is by choice, not necessity." Nicholas turned a big smile on him. "Why not propose, and see just how uncomplicated it might be?"

Because she has said, bluntly, that she will never marry again. In light of her first marriage, he understood that. He would like to think she knew she could trust him to never be like Finley, ever, no matter how provoked or how drunk or how angry, but he wondered if she could believe that about any man.

He had not weighed marriage in a specific way because of that, but he did not want to lose her either. He certainly did not want to watch other men pursuing her, even if he did not think she would change her mind about marriage.

"My thinking on finding some semblance of a formal alliance has taken other directions," he said.

"You had better finish that thinking soon. I give you a fortnight at best before the calls start. She met enough people at my dinner for a few families to have a foot in the door."

"I was expecting to annoy you today, not have you annoy me."

"You annoyed me plenty. I'm just getting revenge,"

Nicholas said. "I am actually enjoying myself. Say, are you going to tell me why uncle gave her that legacy?"

"No."

Nicholas shrugged. "I suppose it was another example of his eccentric generosity. I have received letters from some other recipients. They are hoping, I think, that I am just as peculiar as he was and will continue the tradition of passing out gold coins on impulse."

Chase stopped his horse and grabbed at the harness on Nicholas's. "Now I am truly annoyed. You might have told me about this."

"I assumed you knew. You asked about the gold. You were correct, by the way. There was another hoard in Whiteford House."

"Not about the gold, about his eccentric generosity of giving out those coins."

"He had to be doing something with them. What did you think? That he sat in his study making stacks and counting them?" Nicholas jerked his horse free of Chase's hold. "I think that he never left his house without some of them in his purse or pocket. One here, ten there—one letter said he would show up at an orphanage at night and hand a little sack of them to the servant at the door. He never told them who he was, but they made it a point to find out. Now they are hoping the visits continue despite his death."

"Have they?"

Nicholas rode on a ways before answering. "Once. I doubt I can continue. The pile in Whiteford House won't last long. But better that orphanage get it than Walter, the greedy scoundrel."

Which was exactly what Uncle Frederick had concluded, Chase thought.

* * *

Chase wrote out his case, the one he would make to Minerva. It was his best chance, he decided, to line up the reasons she might agree to his ideas about their future alliance.

He examined his final paper, the one without all the cross-outs and comments to himself about being an ass to include this or that. The list of benefits to her appeared sadly small. That his own list also appeared small hardly helped his mood.

He had never before seen in ink on paper how little a permanent alliance between a man and a woman had credence, once you removed practical things like financial support, heirs, and social demands. There was damned little left to encourage a woman like Minerva to give up one whit of independence and freedom.

Fortunately, he had no intentions of asking her to do that.

He checked his pocket watch, and realized he had to leave or he would arrive late to her house. His horse would already be waiting. He gathered his wits but left the lists.

As he crossed the apartment to his door, he saw Brigsby there, receiving a letter. Brigsby turned with the missive in his hand. He brought it over ceremoniously. "Hand-delivered. From the Home Office."

Two thoughts rushed into Chase's mind. The first was a curse that Peel had been so impatient. The second was a prayer that Kevin had heeded his advice and hopped a packet to France. He opened the letter. Peel required him to call this afternoon at two o'clock. Not a request this time.

"Brigsby, send word to Miss Hepplewhite that I will be

delayed. Better yet, to be sure she receives the message immediately, carry it to her yourself."

"May I ask, sir, if this has to do with one of your inquiries?"

"It does."

"So you are not expecting me to be a messenger, which is not part of my responsibilities. You are instead asking me to serve as one of your—I believe they are called agents." Brigsby considered that. "How novel. It might be interesting."

"Call it what you want, just make sure she gets the message."

At two o'clock, Chase tied his horse outside the building that housed the Home Office. Peel did not wait outside this time. The meeting would be more official than that.

Very official, it turned out. Peel waited in his office. Chase sat down and set a portfolio on the desk. "I have the preliminary report that you requested."

"I requested it some time ago."

"I had a few details that I needed to check for accuracy first."

Peel set his arms on the desk and leaned forward. "How did he die? That is the detail that matters most."

"He was killed."

Peel sat back and closed his eyes. Chase imagined the man was picturing the problems and complications awaiting his office now.

"Who?" Peel asked after a deep sigh.

"I have not determined that yet. There are currently several possibilities." He handed over his portfolio. "Each page is one of them, with the evidence for and against such a suspicion."

Peel removed the sheets and began to look through them.

"You have not yet identified this woman who visited him that day?"

"No."

"It could have been one of these two who have not yet been found."

"Possibly."

He flipped again. "Ah. The one who has been found. Miss Hepplewhite." He read down the sheet. "Her husband's death was ruled accidental, you write, but also that it might not have been." More reading. "Good heavens, poor woman. Did she do it? She certainly had provocation."

"I was engaged to make inquiries into my uncle's death, not her husband's. However, she did not."

"How can you be sure? Once murder is done, it is easier to do again."

That was exactly the reaction that Minerva had feared. "I know she did not because I know who did."

He looked up, surprised. "You should inform the magistrate down there."

"I have a verbal confession, but no evidence. Nor, as I said, was I engaged to make inquiries into the husband's death."

He accepted it, but with a frown. He turned the page and looked up again. "You are more honest than I expected, if you have included your own cousin in this stack of suspects."

It sounded like a criticism, not a compliment. "It is the sort of evidence that is easily found, should you take this further. There was no point of trying to hide it. He was in England, and he visited Melton Park. The day before, he said, but since he was not seen at all, I can't prove it either way."

"He seems to have had motive, if he was denied funds

for furthering their partnership. Business can bring out the worst in men sometimes."

Chase just let that comment lie there.

Peel turned that sheet, revealing the last. He read it, expressionless. For a very long time.

He looked up, right into Chase's eyes. Scrutinizing. Weighing.

"What led you to include my father in your inquiries?"

"Evidence presented itself to me that there had been a falling-out when the duke refused to agree to widening that canal that would benefit only two of the partners. Your father was one of them. He did not take it well, and sought to find information that might persuade the duke to change his mind."

"They were friends."

"Not recently, if such persuasion was being considered."

"Who gave you this evidence of attempted persuasion?"

"Someone I believe and trust." He had not included Mr. Monroe's name. "I verified the information about the canal independently, however."

Peel turned that last sheet, rested back in his chair, and closed his eyes again. Chase just waited.

Alert again, Peel leaned forward and patted the pages. "Inconclusive. All of it."

"I think so. Preliminary findings. Enough for your office to continue, however, if you choose." *Or not, if you choose.*

Peel pursed his lips, still looking at the papers. "Even your determination of the manner of death is inconclusive and not sufficiently supported by facts."

Not really. "If you say so."

"I do. If you had brought that alone to me a month ago,

I would have saved you much time." He stuffed the papers back into the portfolio. "Short of direct proof of a crime, it was an accident. I hope that you will accept that. It would not do to have agents spending months making further inquiries if a man of your abilities found so little to establish the death was a murder."

"Then my assignment is over." Chase stood. "Do you want to keep the notes, or should I remove them."

"I will hold them for a while if you don't mind."

"I don't mind. I make copies of all of my notes. Good day to you." He turned to make his escape.

"Radnor."

He turned.

"You are very clever."

Since that did not sound like a compliment either, Chase just left.

Minerva paced. Chase was now three hours late. He had warned her, but she still experienced an agony of impatience.

They had planned a full afternoon that with each passing minute became less likely to be realized. First, they were going to look at carriages she might purchase. Then, she intended to return to Madame Tissot and order some new garments. Visions of fine wood and brass, of soft wool and silks had danced in her head all morning, only to be dashed when Brigsby arrived with the news Chase would be delayed.

"Look who is here," Beth had announced, bringing the manservant to the library without ceremony. "Mr. Radnor's valet."

"As I have explained, I am not a valet, even if those

are among the duties I execute. Nor am I here as the manservant I am."

"No? Then why do we have this rare honor?" Beth asked.

"I am here as one of Mr. Radnor's agents."

Beth burst out laughing. "Minerva, he is one of Mr. Radnor's *agents* now. Aid him in his inquiries, do you? I'll believe that when I see it."

Brigsby ignored her. "Miss Hepplewhite, I have come with a message. Mr. Radnor will be delayed some hours. An important matter, an urgent one, claimed him just moments before he was to leave his chambers to come here."

"Don't sound like an associate to me," Beth said. "You sound like a messenger."

"Messengers are not entrusted with such as this, that pertain to important inquiries. Only agents are."

"Call it what you like, I know a donkey when I see one."

Brigsby did not miss that Beth had come close to calling him an ass. Minerva thanked him and sent him home.

Now she waited. Something was happening. Something important. She would go mad if Chase did not come soon to tell her what it was.

He did not arrive until close to six o'clock. He let himself in before she reached the door. He took one look at her and raised both hands in a calming gesture. "All is well. I was called to the Home Office. The official finding will be an accidental death."

"That is not possible. We both know—"

"That will be the official finding, Minerva. I am not inclined to argue the point. Are you?"

The owner of Hepplewhite's Office of Discreet Inquiries most definitely wanted to challenge this finding.

The woman who was once suspected of murder realized it was a gift. With no one looking for the person responsible for the duke's death, no one would decide she was an excellent suspect.

"Do we simply pretend it was indeed an accident?"

"For now. Should other information present itself, however, I am duty-bound to pursue it."

"For now might last forever, I suppose."

"It won't, trust me." He fell onto the divan and pulled her down into his lap. "For now, however, I am setting it aside. I have other things occupying my mind, and distracting me from inquiries."

"You will save all your lists and notes and such, I hope. Just in case they are needed."

"Only if you save yours."

She laughed, because they both knew she had no notes. She pecked his nose with a kiss. "What has been distracting you?"

"You have. My entire performance on this inquiry has not been up to my own standards because of you. I think about you all the time. I desire you constantly. Had that not been happening, you would have never bested me when it came to learning Kevin was not in France, for example."

"So you say. I wonder if you are not using me as an excuse to salve your pride that I did best you."

He kissed her, but his mouth smiled in the middle of it. "Perhaps."

The kiss lingered long enough that her blood sparkled. "It is too late to purchase a carriage or wardrobe."

"We will do it tomorrow."

"That leaves us with nothing much to do now." She kissed him again. "How ever will we fill the time?"

"With a necessary conversation."

"That sounds serious."

"It is, but hopefully not in a bad way. I have been thinking about us, and our inquiries, and our different methods. You do not want a formal partnership, but we can form an alliance that is not formal. There will be times when you will want a man to speak with someone, for example."

"Such as another man?"

"There will be some who will never take your questions seriously, and there will be others who won't even hear them. You know I am right about this."

"You would do that for me? As my employee?"

"I do not take employment. My thinking is we would share any inquiry that requires us both. We would consult on strategy and tactics, and divide up what to do. That will be more efficient, and also be twice as fast."

"It sounds a lot like a partnership, no matter what you call it."

"I am sure there will be inquiries in which I will not be useful, so you would conduct those on your own."

She could not think of any kind of inquiry in which he would not be at least somewhat useful. The idea of a partnership had not set well with her when he proposed it, but now . . . She was sure it did not hold appeal only because it would ensure she would see him with continued frequency, although that played a role in her reconsideration.

"It sounds complicated," she said. "Perhaps in the days ahead we should talk about whether we should forge a more formal alliance. If you promise not to become the officer commanding the troops, I might agree to that."

He turned very serious. His embracing arm tightened. "If I had my way, I would be proposing the most formal alliance possible, Minerva, even knowing that with your new situation you have no use for it. I have accepted you will never agree to that, however, and understand why."

He looked at her warmly. Wistfully. Her own emotions turned poignant. "I have thought about it," she said quietly. "You are not the only one who has been distracted."

"If I tell you that I treasure you, that I love you to the point of not only distraction but madness, would it make a difference? Because I do, darling. I will swear to anything you want, if it will encourage you to continue thinking about it."

His declaration caused tears to well up in her. She had made a terrible mistake once when facing this choice, but she was no girl now, and this man was no enigma. This would not be a practical marriage, or one she needed for security. It would be a love match, with a man she already trusted with her body and her heart.

And yet—that old shadow had not completely faded. She could not deny she would lose much if she did this. She gazed deeply into his eyes, while her mind weighed it all.

"Would you swear to never play the army officer, in any way, with me or mine?"

He smiled. "You have my word as a gentleman. Should I ever forget, I am sure you will remind me of this moment."

"You can be sure of that. I also never again want to worry about making my own way should I need to."

"Part of your inheritance is in trust, and I cannot touch it. If you sell the partnership, that money can be added to it. A husband has certain rights to the use of his wife's property, but not the capital that is in trust. Sanders will explain all of that when you meet with him, should you decide to marry anyone. As to the income, we will declare it yours to use as you wish in our settlement."

"Would you allow me to continue my inquiries? I truly enjoy them, and do not want to stop."

"We will be together in that, as in everything."

Did she trust him to keep that promise, or would he try to force her to stop if she ever was hurt again? Sending him to speak with the men did not mean it would never happen. Women can hit someone over the head too. She had proven that, hadn't she?

He said nothing to press her for a decision. He had the good sense to remain quiet. That was another thing she liked about him. He did not demand she share her thinking. He did not argue against her emotions.

"There is much to recommend this," she said. "I might well get with child, for example. I would rather not be making such a decision due to that happening."

"That is an excellent point."

"One you neglected to make."

"I was sure you have been aware of that possibility already."

She rested her head on his shoulder. "I suppose I will have repeated contact with that family of yours, no matter what I do. Your aunts will want to inspect me, in the least, since they think I all but stole from them. It would be useful if you were standing between them and me, to take the heavy fire."

"I promise to protect you from them. Heroically."

"I will admit I am of more than half a mind to be brave again," she said. "Love has me thinking that way. I only see one serious problem."

"What is that?"

"I'm not sure that I can live with someone who makes lists all the time."

He laughed. "I promise you will never see me write one."

"Then take me to bed, and while we are together propose to me if you want to, and let us see what I say."

Not long after, as one last test, she rolled so that he covered her with his body for the first time while they were joined. She waited for the old emotions to rise, prepared to battle them, fully aware of her vulnerability beneath his strength and size. She discovered her heart was too full to allow anything to dull her love and joy.

She held him to her heart while he moved in her. His words of love entered her head and touched her essence. At the height of their abandon he paused, heroically, and looked down with love and passion in his eyes. "Will you honor me by being my wife, Minerva?"

Of course, my love. "Yes."

Don't miss the next Duke's Heiress romance
from the *New York Times* bestselling author
Madeline Hunter . . .

HEIRESS IN RED SILK

Kevin Radnor is angry that his late uncle,
the Duke of Hollinburgh, bequeathed half of Kevin's
invention and company to a total stranger—a woman no
one in the family knows. When he meets his new partner
he is surprised to find she is an attractive, bright-eyed,
desirable young woman. A milliner, of all things.
What was the late duke thinking? Kevin swallows his ire
and befriends Miss Jameson, hoping to convince her
to accept the role of a very silent partner. If she resists
his arguments that she should accede to whatever he
wants to do with his enterprise, perhaps kisses and
caresses can convince her to see reason . . .

Rosamund Jameson is shocked to discover she is an
heiress, but fully intends to make good use of her new
fortune. Her plans are to establish her sister's future,
to expand her millinery business, to better herself so
maybe an old lover will marry her, and—oh, yes—to
involve herself fully in this business she now owns with
Kevin Radnor. She wants to make sure this handsome,
charismatic man who has more vision than practicality
does not ruin her. She intends to keep it all business
with Kevin, too, which proves much more difficult when
she discovers that his many areas of brilliance and
expertise include sensuality and seduction.

On sale in May 2020!

Connect with Us

Visit us online at
KensingtonBooks.com
to read more from your favorite authors, see books
by series, view reading group guides, and more.

Join us on social media

for sneak peeks, chances to win books and prize packs,
and to share your thoughts with other readers.

**facebook.com/kensingtonpublishing
twitter.com/kensingtonbooks**

Tell us what you think!

To share your thoughts, submit a review,
or sign up for our eNewsletters, please visit:
KensingtonBooks.com/TellUs.